THE BLAZING OCEAN

THE BLAZING OCEAN

Cyril Abraham

NEW ENGLISH LIBRARY/TIMES MIRROR

A New English Library Original Publication, 1979

First NEL paperback edition February 1979

NEL Books are published by
New English Library from
Barnard's Inn, Holborn,
London EC1N 2JR.
Made and printed in Great Britain by
C. Nicholls & Company Ltd.,
The Philips Park Press, Manchester

45004080 1

To All *Conways*
Wherever they may be

CHAPTER ONE

THE FLEET opened fire with the sun setting in the west and turning giant plumes of water into blood-red fountains.

Mr Dean, the ship's baby-faced third officer, remembered the day as long as he lived.

Slowly pacing the bridge on his lonely vigil he had boredly watched a small rusted coaster, flying a tattered tricolour and manned by an indolent Arab crew, round the breakwater to thread her way between the sleek grey shapes of a flotilla of French destroyers lying sleepily at anchor.

The harbour was crammed with craft of all shapes and sizes. Sloops, patrol vessels and fleet auxiliaries lifted to the gentle swell rolling in from the Mediterranean. Gaily painted feluccas and polaccas nestled against the quay, the smoke from their cooking pots curling high into the washed-blue sky. A pair of hump-backed submarines hugged the breakwater, gulls skirling above scavenging for scraps.

It was a scene with which he had become over familiar. Ever since, homeward bound from Australia with fifteen thousand bales of wool stowed below, they had heard the shattering news that France had surrendered. With the Italians entering the war, to pick at the remains like vultures, the Mediterranean could no longer be considered a British lake.

Proceed Oran and await escort, the message had read. So for eight days they had lain alongside the breakwater, condemned to this plague spot for what promised to be the duration of the war.

At first the French authorities had shown surprise and not a little embarrassment at the unexpected appearance of their visitor. Then, as the terms of the Armistice filtered through and Goebbels' propaganda machine turned its invective against their former ally, the French attitude had hardened. A couple of gendarmes now patrolled the foot of the gangway and the ship's radio room had been sealed.

Dean yawned and idly watched the snail-track of the coaster until the vessel crunched alongside the quay to lie panting with exhaustion as though the effort had been too much for its ancient bones.

Overhead the July sun beat down upon the bridge awning, bleaching it white and baking the air to oven heat.

On the foredeck the bosun and half a dozen of the hands were lethargically washing down the ship. The water from the hose sparkled in the sunlight and a faint haze of steam rose from the green tarpaulins covering the holds as pools of water spread and dried beneath the fierce blaze of the sun.

A trickle of perspiration ran between his shoulder blades, his white uniform shirt stuck to his back and the tapes of his epaulettes with their single gold stripes scratched uncomfortably against his skin.

Dean stretched his arms, yawning again, and turned his bored gaze toward the harbour entrance.

His mouth remained agape. Across the ten-mile-wide mouth of the Bay of Oran the gigantic grey shape of a battleship slid through the sea mist, the turrets of her huge 15-inch guns trained fore-and-aft. She was followed by two more 30,000 ton battleships in line ahead. Then came a flat-topped aircraft carrier flanked by a pair of cruisers. A screen of destroyers covered the sea as far as the eye could see.

Dean, forgetting to close his mouth, ran from the bridge, clattered down the companionway and rushed breathlessly into the saloon to impart his news.

'Our escort!' he blurted out to the assembled diners. 'My God, you should see them! I think the whole bloody Navy is here!'

Captain Sloppy Joe Turner, the Master of the *Kentucky Minstrel,* swabbed a slice of Yorkshire pudding in gravy before turning mournful eyes upon the young man.

'You got a report to make, son?' he asked kindly.

'Aye, sir,' replied Dean, suddenly remembering protocol.

'Then keep calm, take a deep breath and spit it out.'

Dean looked at the row of inquiring faces. Mr Furlong, the ship's dyspeptic Chief Officer, even now stifling a belch from a rebellious stomach. Second Officer Potter, as cold as a fish and a stickler for routine. Paddy Phelan, ship's Radio Officer, a phlegmatic roly-poly who carried more secrets in his head than a confessional. Mr Turnbull, the Chief Engineer, a dapper man of unflappable temperament and with the drawling accents of a minor public school. And the Old Man himself, seated as of right at the head of the table. Captain Turner was a large untidy man of thinning sandy hair, shaggy eyebrows and heavy jowls. He wore a grubby white patrol jacket with one of the tarnished buttons missing. He had a habit of wandering about the ship like an amiable hippopotamus; but there was little that escaped his attention, and his soubriquet – as many a shore-based panjandrum had learned to his cost – masked a fearsome reputation as a slayer of giants. It was said that one of Sloppy Joe's *bons mots* – delivered with an air of sublime innocence – could scald the hide from a man's back.

So young Mr Dean gulped and slowly repeated his information. 'They are approaching Cape Falcon, sir,' he finished lamely.

Turner savoured his mouthful of Yorkshire pudding, swallowed and smacked his lips appreciatively. 'Mixes a lovely batter, does Albert. The best ship's cook in the business. I've always held so.' He sighed. 'Well, son, let us into your little secret. Are they ours? Or theirs?'

Dean thought hard for a moment. He felt sure, quite sure, that he had seen the great white battle ensigns with their scarlet crosses fluttering in the breeze.

'Ours, sir. I – I am sure of it.'

'You'd better be, son. Because if it's the Ice-creamers they've caught the Frogs on the hop and we're going to be in the thick of it.' Turner gazed sorrowfully at the remains of his meal, picked up a uniform cap green with age and clamped it on his head. 'I am sorry to spoil your lunch, gentlemen, but I think we'd best cast an eye over things.' He lumbered to his feet, hitched up a pair of elephantine trousers, and beckoned the steward. 'Clear up, but don't tell Albert. He'd be mortally offended.'

On the bridge even Turner was taken by surprise. He expelled a long whistling breath. 'Our escort? You have quite a talent for understatement, young man. That is a British battle squadron, cleared for action.' He picked up the ship's binoculars and subjected the squadron to a prolonged inspection: 'The *Hood*,' he pronounced. 'No mistaking her. Then *Resolution* – she's an old war-horse – and *Valiant*. The carrier will be *Ark Royal* unless I'm much mistaken. The cruisers look like *Arethusa* and *Enterprise* and I count around a dozen destroyers.' He swung the binoculars around to cover the harbour. 'They certainly seem to have stirred the Frogs out of their usual torpor.'

It was true. The once quiet harbour was now seething with activity. Ships' boats and pinnaces scurried between docks and anchorages. Bugles shrilled their imperatives, while aboard the destroyers seamen raced along the decks to the sharp piping of bosuns' whistles and gun turrets began to swing ominously seaward.

Turner lowered his binoculars and out of habit began absently to slap at his pockets.

'Have one of mine, sir,' Paddy Phelan suggested, proffering his cigarette case.

Turner helped himself. 'Very civil of yer, Sparky. Now what the devil is this feller up to?'

One of the British destroyers had detached herself from the defensive screen and, signal light winking and blinking furiously, come to nose about the net stretched across the entrance channel like a dog sniffing out a bone.

'Can you sort out her dots and dashes?' asked Turner.

Paddy concentrated, scratching a grizzled head as round as a cannon ball. 'She's asking permission to enter harbour.'

He turned his eyes upon the shore signal station. In a few moments its light snapped out a short sharp reply.

'Permission refused,' said Paddy laconically.

The destroyer tossed its head and returned to its former station in a welter of foam.

'Rum set of allies we got,' grunted Turner. 'Won't let her in, or us out.' He rubbed reflectively at the stubble on his chin. 'One of them bowler-hats sitting in an office in Whitehall got taken with a fit of the jitters, ordered us here, then went home for his dinner and forgot all about us. You can't trust a bowler-hat. I have often remarked upon it.'

Ash from his cigarette dribbled unnoticed down his patrol jacket. 'Gentlemen,' he announced at length, 'I think it high time we took matters into our own hands. Take advantage of the maximum confusion and make a run for it. Chief – light your boilers and raise steam. But remember – softly, softly, catchee monkey.'

Mr Turnbull cocked a lazy eyebrow. 'No problem. We'll be as quiet as church mice,' he promised and loped away to roust out his engineers.

The Mate burped and nodded toward the anti-submarine net. 'I doubt they'll oblige us by lowering the boom.'

'We shan't trouble to ask,' said Turner. 'It's not designed to take the strain of a seven thousand tonner loaded to the scuppers, so we'll take it with us.'

Mr Potter cleared his throat. 'There are the two gendarmes, both armed, and we shall require a couple of hands on the quay to cast off.'

Turner nodded approvingly. 'I'm glad to see that you fellers are entering into the spirit of the thing, so I think we'd best be off to me quarters for a conference. Bring your fags, Sparks, I'm trying to give 'em up.'

He led the way below, leaving Dean to resume his solitary pacing.

He watched the battle fleet steam steadily westward until it disappeared from view behind the out-thrusting finger of the Murdjadjo headland with the ancient Spanish fort of Santa Cruz perched atop. Gleaming bone-white in the sun it overlooked the wide sweep of the fortified naval base of Mers-el-Kebir.

Here, sandy, treeless and arid, bare dun-coloured foothills rolled back from the water's edge to the salt flats of the Sebkha and then south to the vast emptiness of the Sahara.

The base was protected by a mile-long mole and the coastal batteries of forts Santon and Mers-el-Kebir. Moored with their sterns to the mole lay the pride of the French Atlantic Fleet the 26,000-ton battleships *Strasbourg* and *Dunkerque*; the battleships *Provence* and *Bretagne*. Lying at anchor were six heavy destroyers. The whole a formidable fighting force which, if it fell into the hands of the Axis, could decisively affect the balance of naval power.

The mingled scents of musk, incense and spices heralded the approach of the scorching wind of the sirocco. The awning fluttered over Dean's head and the waters of the harbour ruffled into lines of molten gold.

A persistent bee-like buzzing attracted his attention and he raised his eyes to see a Fleet Air Arm Swordfish lumbering in from the sea. It dipped its wings and circled lazily on a tour of inspection, roared low over the breakwater, then droned away to the west.

Dean jumped as a voice breathed down his ear. 'He's a devious man, is our Sloppy. Very devious.'

'I wish you wouldn't pussy-foot around like that, Sparks, he snapped testily. 'I almost jumped out of my skin.'

Paddy Phelan grinned. 'Thank your lucky stars I wasn't Sloppy, he don't take kindly to day-dreaming watch-keepers.' He wandered into the wheelhouse and peered into the compass binnacle. 'Just checking the ship's head. We have work to do, my boy.'

'We?'

'Us. You are to sneak me into the radio shack while the French bobbies are looking the other way. Then I'm to take bearings of the squadron and listen in to their chatter.'

'But how . . . ?'

'Fetch a couple of thumb-tacks and don't worry, Third Mate. Sloppy's thought of everything.'

The sound of a trio of voices chanting *left right, left right,* floated through the air.

'That will be the comedians,' said Paddy. 'I told you our Sloppy was a devious man.'

They walked to the wing of the bridge and looked down.

An ungainly, six-legged, hump-backed camel marched down the gangway. Three seamen with a heavy cargo net slung over their shoulders were making their way down to the quay. Harry Jason, a stocky, broad-shouldered A.B., led the way, easily carrying one end of the rolled net. In the centre, shouldering almost the entire burden, came the obscenely swearing Lowrie, a lean sinewy seaman of notoriously short temper. In the rear pranced the ebullient figure of Cloud, a tall flaxen-haired young man who had long taken upon himself the mantle of ship's wit and humorist.

On reaching the foot of the gangway Cloud released his end of the net, stuck out a long leg and deliberately tripped Lowrie.

Paddy tapped Dean on the shoulder. 'Look lively, Third Mate. The show's not for our benefit.'

While the gendarmes watched grinning as a furious Lowrie emerged red-faced from beneath the swathe of cargo net to launch himself murderously at a laughing Cloud, Dean and Paddy hastened round to the radio shack.

The radio room was housed immediately abaft the chart-room with the door facing aft. A pair of wax seals with a tricolour ribbon suspended between spanned the door opening.

Paddy prised off one of the seals and unlocked the door. 'Sharp's the word, Third Mate, unless you want to finish the war in a French pokey.' He disappeared inside while Dean hastily closed the door and drove home a thumb tack through the wax wafer.

He was surveying his handiwork with mingled relief and pride when the flip-flop of slippered feet heralded the approach of his captain.

Turner leered evilly. 'Waiting for the coconuts to fall, are we?'

'No, sir. Everything in order, sir.'

Turner sniffed. 'On the *Conway*, weren't you, son?'

Dean blinked. 'Aye, sir.'

'Then they should have taught you something of the art of command. Exercise it, young man, and put a stop to that tumult on the quay.'

'Aye, sir.'

'And tell 'em it's fish and chip time.'

Dean couldn't believe his ears. 'Fish and chip . . . ?'

Turner gazed at him sorrowfully. 'Didn't the *Conway* also teach you to carry out the lawful commands of the Master without question?'

'Aye, sir.'

'Then jump to it, son.'

Dean, wishing he were back on the schoolship safely moored in the Mersey, hurried away, leaned out of the cab window and called down to the struggling figures rolling in the dust below.

'Ahoy! Below there! Belay that horseplay! Fish and chip time,' he added weakly.

To his surprise they seemed to fully comprehend this gibberish for Lowrie and Cloud stopped pummelling each other and scrambled expectantly to their feet.

Jason raised a hand in acknowledgement. 'Aye, aye, sir,'

he called and turned to the nearest grinning gendarme. 'Fish and chip time,' he told him.

The man shrugged, smiled, and nodded uncomprehendingly.

Turner joined Dean. He seemed in high good humour. 'I daresay me subtlety has you baffled, eh, young man? The fact is we got to prepare to put to sea without the Frogs being aware of it. We also need to know just how much of a civilised language those two Herberts understand. Not much from the look of 'em. Fish and chips,' he continued, 'is also by way of being a code word. Now it's the Mate's turn.'

Dean looked forrard to see Mr Furlong leaning over the fo'c'sle rail and bawling down at the loiterers below.

'You three! Come for'ard and check the headlines! The breast rope is fouling the eye.'

Dean could see nothing wrong with the headlines leading from the fairleads to the bollard but the three seemed to understand for they broke into a shambling run, Cloud's voice raised complainingly: 'You near stove me ribs in, Lowrie. You come it too heavy. It's not on.'

'Ye tripped me, ye domned loon an' a' but broke me ankle. So it's ti' for ta',' responded Lowrie with equal ire.

'Singling up,' Turner explained. 'Right under their noses.'

The hands on the fo'c'sle head, who normally worked with the monosyllabic discipline of professionals, now raised a pandemonium of bawling and shouting as they slacked off the hawser from the bitts.

On the quay Jason beckoned to one of the gendarmes sauntering toward them. The man grasped what was needed and bent to lend a willing hand as Cloud and Lowrie made hard work of hauling the heavy eye-splice over the bollard. Once cleared they cast off and the hawser splashed into the oily surface of the harbour to be hauled inboard by the shouting crew.

The gendarme, evidently pleased with his efforts, stepped back, smirked at his colleague, and wiped his hands down his sand-coloured uniform trousers.

'Smart young feller, that Jason. Smart as a whip,' commented Turner approvingly. 'Get the Froggies involved and they're less likely to interfere.' He went through the routine of flapping at his pockets until Dean resignedly offered his packet of cigarettes. 'Thank you, son. I doubt I'll ever give 'em up when you fellers have such generous natures.'

Turner accepted a light and sucked in a satisfying lungful of smoke. 'You'd best go below, son, and enjoy your lunch. I think it's going to be a long day.'

Dean thankfully left Captain Turner in charge of the bridge and took himself off to eat his solitary lunch. He fended off the steward's pointed inquiries, enjoyed a peaceful cigarette with his coffee, and returned to find Captain Turner stretched out on the chartroom settee.

'I am having a thinks, Mr Dean,' he pronounced grumpily. 'Close the door as you leave.'

Dean did as he was bid and in a few moments the Master's snores punctuated the silence.

A soporific stillness seemed to have once more settled over ship and harbour during his absence. The hot breath of the sirocco funnelled through the open charthouse doors, drying the perspiration and tormenting the skin. The sun had passed its zenith and commenced its long slow journey to the west. Heat layers turned the harbour into a shimmering mirage of ships and houses. Nothing moved. The war seemed far away, remote and as unreal as half-remembered battles fought on the pages of history books.

Dean wandered out on to the bridge. The gendarmes were taking advantage of the shade of the transit shed and leaning against the peeling stucco of the wall, across which someone, either in irony or defiance, had scrawled: *France est blessée. Mais France n'est pas morte!* Beside the legend another hand had painted a large black swastika.

He ran his gaze over the length of the ship. She was now singled up fore and aft and both fore and back springs had been slackened off sufficiently to allow of their being cast off quickly.

He sauntered across to the starboard wing of the bridge and looked out at the sinister shapes of the French destroyers. He counted seventeen, and with their gun turrets still pointed seaward they looked lethally businesslike and efficient. He wondered queasily what it felt like to be under fire. The only knowledge he had had been culled from the cinema, where model ships erupted into spectacular showers of smoke and sparks, and heroic officers wiped away blood from minor cuts and abrasions, firmly jutted their chins and exchanged a few pleasantries before finally defeating the enemy. The real thing, he imagined, would be vastly different and he wondered how he would behave when the time came. *I shall be sick,* he decided, *as sick as a dog,* and became aware of a high-pitched whine growing in intensity. Shading his eyes against the glare he saw a flight of three single-winged Skuas whistling across the harbour. They climbed steeply, changed formation and began to circle like predatory birds of prey.

The reason for the manoeuvre soon became apparent as a deeper drone heralded the approach of a pair of the more vulnerable slow-moving Swordfish. The leader headed for the harbour entrance, swooped low, and a pot-bellied object tumbled lazily from beneath its fuselage to splash into the centre of the main channel.

Dean, pale-faced, hurried to the chartroom and threw open the door.

'Sir,' he babbled. 'Our aircraft are bombing the harbour!'

Turner was awake instantly. 'Mr Dean,' he said severely, 'you really must learn to control your impetuosity.' He heaved himself to his feet, lumbered out on to the bridge and picked up the ship's binoculars as the second Swordfish, flying at a height of about 150 feet, dropped a second object into the seaward side of the entrance.

Turner lowered the binoculars. 'Not bombs, son – mines. They've blocked the channel. It looks like they mean business.'

On the quay the two gendarmes had detached themselves from the wall and were staring open-mouthed at the departing planes. One of them shook a fist at the sky. His colleague turned his head, hawked and spat malevolently at the ship.

'Bang goes the intent cordial,' grumbled Turner. 'Just as I'd got those two eating out of our hands. Lend us one of your fags, son, I seem to have left mine below.'

He accepted a cigarette and thoughtfully began to pace the bridge.

The headland slowly became bathed in a halo of light and the washed-blue of the sky gave way to a deeper hue.

Turner threw away his cigarette. 'Mines or no mines,' he pronounced, 'we put to sea before dark, even if we have to fend 'em off with boathooks. Does the thought curdle your stomach, son?'

Dean nodded dumbly.

Turner grinned. 'I thought it might. I know it plays havoc with mine.'

The bridge phone suddenly pealed shrilly. 'That'll be Sparks,' he announced. 'I was beginning to think he'd gone into hibernation.' He rolled away to the phone, listened intently, and drew a scribbling pad towards him. 'It's a heathen language, Sparks, so you'd best spell it out.'

Turner licked at a stub of pencil and began to write slowly and laboriously. Then he replaced the phone and stared irritably at the slip of paper. 'Did they teach you Frog on the *Conway*, Mr Dean?'

Dean shook his head. 'No, sir. But I did take French for two years at school.'

Turner pushed the pad across. 'Then bend your mind to that, young man, and pray that your father's money was well spent.'

Dean's heart sank and his confidence evaporated as he struggled to remember long-forgotten grammar and dredge from the depths of memory rusted fragments of vocabulary. His hands trembled and he began to sweat as the import of the message became clear.

Turner watched understandingly. 'Take your time, son,' he advised gently. 'Just make sure you get the sense right.'

Dean swallowed. 'It's from Admiral Somerville aboard the *Hood*. He says: "Unless one of our propositions is accepted by 4.30 I shall sink your ships."'

Turner glanced at the ship's chronometer and whistled softly. 'Don't leave us much time, do they? According to Sparks they are patrolling 'way out to the west. So we can't expect much in the way of help when we run for it.'

The air seemed perceptibly cooler as the bulk of the headland threw long shadows across the quay and darkened the water of the harbour.

Dean shivered, stole a glance at the menacing array of destroyers, and wiped clammy hands down his trousers.

Turner followed the direction of his gaze. 'Don't worry, son. We'll bluff our way out.' He rang the engine room. 'Stand by, Chief. We should be under way in a few minutes.' Replacing the phone he straightened his shoulders, clasped his hands behind his back and pushed out his chin. 'Look a bit like Churchill, don't I, son? People have often remarked upon it. We have the same gift of the gab – I expect you've noticed?' He winked ponderously and then with a chameleon-like change of character put the snap of authority into his voice. 'Stand by fore and aft, if you please, Mr Dean. Not the docking telegraph,' he warned as Dean took a pace forward. 'We don't want to alert those two bobbies, do we? Just lean over the bridge and give the bosun a hail. He knows what to do.'

Dean obediently walked out to the starboard wing of the bridge, called down to the bosun and was rewarded with an answering hail.

'Man to the wheel and hands to stations,' he instructed.

'Right, Mr Dean. Now take yourself off to the port side and keep an eye on the quay in case we have to call out the reserves.'

Dean quickly crossed the bridge in obedience to Turner's command and looked down at the quay.

The two gendarmes were standing at the foot of the gangway flexing their legs, but there was an angry set to their shoulders and one looked up at Dean and spat contemptuously into the dust.

Dean glanced for'ard and noticed the fo'c'sle head gang sauntering unconcernedly along the port side of the foredeck. On the starboard side the Mate and the carpenter were strolling unobtrusively in the same direction.

Looking aft he saw a similar picture. A group of seamen were lounging around the after housing, smoking and chatting, while above their heads the stiff-faced second mate leaned against the rail of the docking bridge.

A faint tremor ran through the ship as the engineers opened the main steam valves. Puffs of oily black smoke rose from the funnel and a wisp of vapour writhed and twisted about the organ-pipe mouth of the siren. To Dean's heightened consciousness they seemed to be shouting their intent to the world, but the guards, now absorbed in a hissing expostulatory discussion, were obviously quite oblivious to the stealthy preparations taking place behind them.

He stole a glance toward Turner who was standing, legs braced apart, and slightly teetering on his toes, in his habitual attitude of command. Dean thought he detected a twinkle in his eye. *The old bastard's enjoying it,* he thought and returned his attention to the quayside.

Matt Honest, the bosun, was leading Cloud and Lowrie down the gangway. The swarthier of the two gendarmes raised a hand and imperiously waved them back.

The bosun twisted his features into an ingratiating smile, pointed to the cargo net and gestured that he wanted it aboard.

The gendarme considered for a moment then stepped back nodding surly agreement.

Cloud and Lowrie trotted down the gangway and picked up opposite ends of the net.

'All right, lads,' said the bosun easily. 'Parcel 'em up.'

The two A.B.s raised the net high in the air and with one quick throw enmeshed the gendarmes in its enveloping folds. The bosun grabbed the pair by their collars and, jerking them off balance, bundled them into a cocoon of thick manilla netting.

'Cast off!' he roared. 'You two – jump to it!'

This latter order was to the two Ordinary Seamen who had been waiting at the head of the gangway. While Cloud and Lowrie raced to cast off head and sternlines, the others hauled the heavy wire springs clear of the bollards.

The bosun, bending over the two struggling figures, was dexterously reeving lengths of rope yarn through the interstices of the net and drawing them together. He eyed the venomously spitting bundle with an air of satisfaction then, as an afterthought, removed their holstered pistols and threw them into the dock. 'Hard luck,' he told them cheerfully. 'It's just not your day.'

The windlass on the fo'c'sle head yammered as the headline snaked in. The steam winch aft stammered its reply as the eye of the sternline rose clear of the propellers.

The docking telegraph jangled. Dean glanced at the telltale. 'All clear aft, sir,' he reported.

On the fo'c'sle head the Mate was making passing motions with his arms above his head.

'All clear, for'ard,' Dean reported.

'Thank you, Mr Dean,' said Turner. 'Let me know the moment the shore party is aboard.' He picked up the radio room phone. 'Come out of your hidey-hole, Sparks. I want you on the bridge.'

Jason was already standing at the wheel, his big hands gripping the spokes, and fractionally turning it from port to starboard to test the pressure of the telemotor valves. He checked the heading of the compass card against the figures shown on the steadily ticking gyro-repeater.

'Helm in order, sir,' he reported.

Dean looked over the side. The running figures were scrambling up the narrow gangway. The bosun came last. 'All clear,' he called to Dean, and kicked the gangway ashore.

'Gangway clear, sir.' Dean's voice sounded hoarse and his heart began to knock against his ribs.

'Thank you, Mr Dean. Stand by the telegraphs, if you please.' Turner glanced at the chronometer, screwed to the bulkhead behind Jason's head. It showed 4.43. Turner sniffed: 'The Navy's late. Unless they've changed their minds. Wouldn't put it past them. Bowler-hats with gold braid, most of 'em. Slow astern starboard, Mr Dean.'

Dean swung the telegraph handle and the engines responded immediately with the explosive hiss of the compressor and a deeper throbbing as the screw bit into the water.

The stern edged out from the quay. The docking telegraph rang.

'All clear, aft,' said Dean.

Turner nodded. 'Stop engines. Port easy.'

'Port easy it is,' said Jason, spinning the wheel.

With the engines stopped the only sound was the rapid tick-ticking of the gyro as the ship swung and the bows cleared the quay.

'Midships the helm,' said Turner, and the ship slid stern first into the deeper water of the harbour.

The harbour now lay in a hollow of darkness. Ashore, a few lights twinkled, flickering like fireflies. The sky above was a bowl of blue streaked with pale yellows and deeper gold. A sombre stillness hung over all.

'Starboard easy. Slow ahead both,' ordered Turner as Paddy Phelan puffed on to the bridge. 'Call up the signal station, Sparky. Send: "To Admiral Jarry. Compliments of Captain Turner and many thanks for your good offices in expediting our departure." That should keep 'em busy and those fellers on the destroyers should pick it up if they have their wits about 'em. By the time they've translated it, passed it from hand to hand, and rousted out the old boy, we should be well on our way. Steady as she goes, Jason. Half ahead both, Mr Dean, and perhaps you'll oblige me with one of your cigarettes?'

Paddy began to tap out the message on the small brass key while Dean swung the telegraph handles and the ship pointed her head toward the harbour entrance and the waiting mines.

Turner took one of the proffered cigarettes then, as an afterthought, pocketed the packet.

'There's nothing like the solace of tobacco in moments of stress,' he commented. 'On the other hand it's a filthy habit and not to be encouraged in one so young.' He struck a match and blew out a satisfying lungful of smoke.

He did, thought Dean, have a certain Churchillian look about him. A sort of lop-sided Churchill as though his Maker, in an errant moment, had changed his mind and altered the features from bulldog to bullfrog. Otherwise the only characteristics they seemed to have in common were a mordant wit and an eccentricity of dress.

On the monkey island above the signal light winked and blinked its message. Paddy signed off and watched the signal station. Its light flickered briefly.

'Acknowledged,' he told Turner.

Turner grunted, his gaze concentrated on the main channel, searching for the first of the mines.

'So far, so good,' he said, then the western sky suddenly erupted into a sea of flame.

There was a tremendous concussion of sound followed by a tumult of tearing shrieks like the onrush of a dozen express trains. The sound changed to a mournful howl increasing in crescendo as the shells reached their apogee and began their descent.

The first salvo fell short, straddled the harbour of Mers-el-Kebir, and raised giant columns of water towering 500 feet into the air.

The sky flamed again and again as the Devil's tattoo repeated itself. Again the onrushing roar, the throaty whistle.

Then a new note added itself to the uproar, a deep thudding and pounding as the French gunners took up the challenge.

The succeeding salvoes scored direct hits. Dean, in the grip of paralysing fear, saw, beyond the headland, a vast black cloud of debris twisting and turning and floating in the air. Geysers of oil and smoke rose and fell. There was the thunderclap of an explosion and a sheet of yellow flame as a French warship blew up and sank. Lit from below as though by the fires of Hell a heavy pall of smoke, reeking with the stench of cordite and the raw smell of fuel oil, rolled across the headland and enveloped the *Kentucky Minstrel* in its choking fumes.

Turner's voice aroused Dean from his stupor.

'Mr Dean,' he snapped. 'Pay attention to your duty, young man. Keep your eyes peeled for those mines.'

Dean tore his gaze away from the distant inferno of flame and sound and found himself shaking uncontrollably from head to foot. *My God,* he thought. *It's worse, far worse than anything I ever imagined.*

Turner, without altering his position, held out Dean's packet of cigarettes. 'Here you are, son. Try one of your coffin nails.'

Dean dazedly took the cigarette. The tobacco had no effect whatever, but the succession of tiny habits – putting it in his mouth, striking a match, inhaling – helped to re-establish a sense of normalcy. He peered through the swirl of smoke, now being rapidly dissipated by the evening breeze and the forward motion of the ship, and caught a glimpse of the wildly gesticulating figure of the Mate on the fo'c'sle head. Mr Furlong's mouth was opening and closing but against the thunderous roar of the bombardment no sound could be heard.

'The Mate. On the starboard bow!' said Dean urgently.

'I see him,' said Turner and hurried across to the starboard side of the bridge. Following Mr Furlong's pointing arm he looked out and down. A cable length ahead and fine on the bow a domed object, half submerged and bristling like a porcupine, bobbed on the surface.

'Stop engines. Hard aport,' he ordered.

The sky flared with light and the sea ran blood red. The bows began to swing away from the object rushing toward them. Caught in the diminishing bow wave it lurched and surged like a buoy in a tidal race. The ship, rapidly turning, was now broadside and swinging its stern across its path.

'Hard astarboard. Half ahead port.'

The wheel spun. Far aft the steering engine responded with its mad chatter. The twin propellers churned the water into a welter of foam. The ship began to turn, slowly at first, then with increasing momentum. Turner craned his neck and looked directly down at the mine. It was rotating and drifting inexorably toward the midship section – the slowly turning axis about which the ship revolved. The mine lurched closer, its horned prongs reaching for the thin plates of the shipside. It swung pedulum-like and a flurry of spray broke over its head, temporarily masking it from view.

Turner's mouth ran dry, his stomach-muscles tightened into knots and he found he had lost the power of breathing. Then the spray whirled away and the gap between shipside and mine began to widen as pressure waves from the ship's displacement pushed it aside. The stern came round in a wider arc and the mine, rising and falling in the rippling swell, drifted further and further away.

Turner found breath and voice at the same time. 'Stop both. Hard aport the helm,' he called hoarsely and concentrated his mind upon the next problem.

The *Kentucky Minstrel*, 470 feet in length, was now lying broadside across the channel and steadily bearing toward the spit of land sheltering the eastern end of the harbour. The dredged channel was narrow and, as the ship's head began to swing rapidly, he could see the shoal water bubbling over a series of sandbanks to lap against the long arm of the mole.

The ship turned in its own length as Turner lumbered back to the wheelhouse and took up his previous position. He squinted, lined up foremast and bow and waited until the net slung across the harbour entrance hove into view. He held up a hand.

'Easy now. Ease the helm.'

The wheel spun smoothly with a faint whirr of spokes. The chatter of the gyro slowed to a steady tickerty-tick. Turner chose the point of impact with care.

'Check her,' he commanded briskly.

The ship's head steadied.

'Steady on now, sir,' reported Jason.

Turner drew in a breath. 'Half ahead. Full ahead both, Mr Dean.'

The telegraphs jangled loudly. The engines surged with power as the screws bit into the water, thrusting the enormous bulk of the ship faster and faster. The bow wave creamed as the stem pushed the sea aside to form twin arrowheads. The wake was a turbulence of water, bubbling like a cauldron. And over all came the constant thunder of guns, the scream of shells and the roar of explosions.

Turner was aiming to hit the net a couple of hundred feet from the end of the mole. It should, he considered, be its most vulnerable point, where the eastern end of the heavy steel supporting cable wound round the drum of the lifting gear. There was also less danger of the anti-submarine meshes entangling themselves about the propellers.

Dean looked across the harbour, following the line of marker buoys until they became no more than a row of punctuation marks dotting the surface of the sea to stop short at the edge of the western breakwater. He raised his eyes above the headland. Tongues of fire licked heavenwards, illuminating the swirling black clouds with a ghastly glow. One of the clouds seemed to pulse with a fire of its own until he realised it was a rain of burning fuel oil. A series of explosions followed each other in quick succession and sheets of yellow flame gouted into the air carrying with them a miscellanea of flying fragments. He identified the barrel of a gun, still attached to part of its turret, turning end over end; the latticed remains of a tripod mast; jagged lengths of shell-plating tumbling like falling leaves; and other things spinning and floating through the air, ragged and misshapen like so many burst mattresses. Dean frowned, puzzled. Hammocks, he thought. The notion of hammocks flying amid that carnage seemed so incongruous that he found himself repressing an hysterical giggle.

With an effort he tore his gaze away and concentrated upon searching the surface of the sea.

The ship was bearing down upon the net. At the end of the mole figures danced and gesticulated wildly. Then he saw the mine, bobbing beyond the net, right in the centre of the channel.

Dean pointed. 'The second mine, sir. Four points off the port bow.'

'I see it. Thank you, Mr Dean,' said Turner. 'Keep her steady, quartermaster.'

The bows ploughed into the net and the giant steel hawser rose dripping from the sea. For a moment it seemed that it would take the strain. The ship shuddered and Mr Furlong, leaning perilously over the fore part, straightened, waved at the hands clustered on the fo'c'sle head, and threw himself flat.

The cable tore itself loose from the windlass of the lifting gear and flew high into the air. It hung suspended for a moment like some giant sea-serpent leaping from the depths. Then, dragged by the weight of the net, it danced across the sea to fall in a tangle of steel webbing across the mine swinging gently in the swell.

'Stop engines!' roared Turner at the same instant.

Dean swung the telegraph handles as the sea erupted into a boiling geyser of orange flame surrounded by a halo of water. The concussion almost lifted him from his feet, his head seemed to swell like a pumpkin and his ears rang and ached. He saw a mass of net and cable lift high into the air. It flailed toward them and clawed at the ship like some malevolent beast. A torrent of spray followed, hissing across the foredeck, and he felt the ship stagger under the hammer blow of the explosion. The net fell across the deck, gouging long groove in the steel-plating before wrapping itself around the foredeck rails and wrenching out an entire section. Then it slithered back into the sea dragging the rails into the depths.

Turner hastened to the wing of the bridge and peered down.

'That mine did us a favour. Blew the net clear. Full ahead both, Mr Dean. How's the head, quartermaster?'

Jason glanced at the gyro. 'Steering oh-four-oh, sir.'

'Bring her round to two-eight-five and let me know when she's on.'

'Steer two-eight-five, aye, aye, sir.'

Turner fished out Dean's packet of cigarettes, eyed the contents sorrowfully. 'Only two left.' He put one in his mouth. 'No matter, I'll savour the other later.'

'On two-eight-five, sir,' said Jason.

'Thank you, son. Keep her on that.'

'As she goes, sir.'

Turner inhaled deeply. 'Right, Mr Dean. Let's take her home.'

Quite suddenly silence fell, a silence almost oppressive in its stillness.

'It's all over,' said Turner softly.

Dean looked at the chronometer. A bare ten minutes had

passed. Ten minutes. It seemed like a lifetime. Glancing across at the headland he saw a vast wreath of smoke hanging above the naval base. It heaved and changed shape, swirling in the wind and drawing a dark veil across the face of the sun.

Rounding the headland they headed west. The sea heaved, leprous with mottled patches of oil and littered with flotsam. Broken spars; a shattered lifeboat, half-submerged; a hoist of multi-coloured signal flags turning in upon itself; the burned-out remains of a Carley float; and dead birds everywhere, gulls and land birds caught in the fury.

The ship ploughed through it all, sweeping aside the debris like so much driftwood.

They cleared the headland and had their first sight of Mers-el-Kebir. The water of the harbour was an oily filth erupting into evil pustules as air bubbled to the surface from sunken wreckage. Fires burned ashore from shattered houses. The lighthouse at the end of the mole had been pulverised into dust. Part of the jetty had slid into the sea. All that remained of a tug was a mast sticking forlornly above the surface. A battleship, its superstructure a tangled mass of wreckage, had run aground and was sinking by the stern. Another had capsized, while a third was but a glowing hulk surrounded by clouds of steam. A destroyer had jack-knifed with a broken back; another, her stern blown off, had been thrown high and dry on the beach. A few small boats moved about the harbour picking up survivors of the holocaust – a handful of desperate men floundering amid a sea of wreckage, coughing and choking from the poisonous effects of fuel oil.

Dean, sickened, looked away and down. Something moved and turned sluggishly and a grinning face looked up at him. The man seemed to be waving an arm. He started to grin back. Overcome by an enormous sense of responsibility, an overpowering urge to render help, to rescue something from the madness, he was reaching for a lifebelt when he became aware that the arm was bloodless and attached only to a bloodless shoulder and an equally bloodless head. Beyond was nothing. The remains, scoured by the sea, rolled over. The back of the skull was a dark cavern from which streamed a tangle of white worms. His stomach heaved and bile rose into his throat. The sea seemed to be filled with bodies, swaying and rolling, lurching in the wash of the ship. There seemed to be something familiar about them. Then he remembered the burst mattresses, the hammocks flying through the air. Rooted to the spot, unable to tear away his gaze, he stood and watched the ghastly parade float past. Some were blackened and charred beyond recognition; others, flayed by scalding steam, displayed an unnatural rosy red. One man, eyes bursting from their sockets, stared oyster-like at Dean; another, his lower jaw missing, lolled out a long tongue, while a third with no head at all, seemed to be sitting bolt upright and paddling with his hands. There were bodies without arms, bodies without legs, and bodies lying easily as though they had died in their sleep.

Dean finally closed his eyes, clung dizzily to the cab window and vomited over the side.

When he straightened he felt a fatherly hand patting his shoulder.

'Don't take it too hardly, son,' said Turner. 'That's what they were paid for.'

Dean wiped spittle from his chin and glared murderously at the impassive features of his captain.

Turner stared back. 'It's shock, son. Takes us all like that the first time. You think you'll never get used to it. But you will. Before this war's over, you will.' He transferred his gaze to the pall of smoke overhanging the harbour.

'My God,' he said softly. 'If that's a sample of what we do to our friends, then heaven help the enemy.'

CHAPTER TWO

CLOUD LAID aside his paint-brush and stared in awe at the figure standing majestically at the head of the companion ladder.

'Goddamighty,' he breathed. 'Don't he look a treat?'

Captain Turner had attired himself in shore-going rig, one which he often referred to as his gentleman's disguise. He wore a suit of heavy serge, short in the arms and long in the legs. His stomach strained at a tightly buttoned jacket, and the turn-ups of his trousers folded over a pair of thick-soled brown boots. A black tie with a bootlace knot revealed a brass stud holding in place a starched collar which encased his neck in a grip of iron. A bowler-hat clamped squarely upon his head and a pair of knitted woollen gloves completed the ensemble.

Jason also paused in his labour of over-painting the gleaming white derricks with a dirty battleship grey, to stare in fascination as a trim naval pinnace curved out from the dockyard to pull smartly alongside the ship.

A young sub-lieutenant in spotless white uniform, short trousers and pink knees hopped from the launch, lurched, regained his balance, then picked his way carefully up the canted companion ladder. Behind him the great slab-sided Rock of Gibraltar reared like a crouching lion to frown upon Algeciras Bay and stand guard over the entrance to the Mediterranean.

The sub-lieutenant paused before the apparition standing before him and raised a hand in a hesitant salute.

Cloud nudged Jason and the pair watched expectantly as they saw Turner's mouth opening and closing and the young man's hand fumble at the breast pocket of his snow-white uniform shirt.

'Cadging fags from the Navy now. Inn't he the limit?'

Jason nodded fond agreement. 'Good old Sloppy. Never misses a chance.'

Cloud grinned. 'I don't envy that lot ashore. They won't know what hit 'em.'

'Nor will you,' rasped a voice behind them, 'unless you get a move on.'

'Have a heart, Bos'n,' grumbled Cloud. 'We was only taking a breather and admiring Sloppy's thirty bob tailoring.'

'That suit never come from no thirty bob tailor,' pronounced the bos'n. 'I reckon the old bastard knitted it himself.'

They stood and watched the launch skim away to the shelter of the Rock. Turner was seated in the sternsheets, a battered attaché case containing the ship's papers clutched to his chest, a cloud of cigarette smoke puffing from his lips.

'God help the poor sods,' said the bos'n piously. 'They don't know what they're in for.' He fished out a turnip of a watch. 'Smoke-O in ten minutes. And I want those derricks finished by then as far as the goose-necks. So heave around and put your backs into it.'

Jason resignedly dipped a brush into his paint pot. 'Show willing, Cloudy, you hear what the man said.'

The *Kentucky Minstrel* lay inside the boom amid a huddle of ships clinging together like refugees from a storm. Across the Bay the town of Algeciras nestled against the brown foothills of Franco's Spain.

Mr Dean, lazing in a deck-chair, rewound his portable gramophone, and for the fifth successive time Al Bowley declared that someone was driving him crazy. "*What'll I do?*', he warbled. '*My tears for you make everything hazy. Clouding the skies of bloo-oo.*'

Cloud gave the last derrick a final pat of paint and stood back to survey his handiwork. He shook his head in disgust. 'Grey paint. Looks 'orrible.'

'It's supposed to match the sea,' said Jason. 'So the subs can't spot us so easy.'

'It's ugly.' Cloud wiped a forearm across his forehead and left a streak of grey paint to mark its passage. 'I like a ship to look like a ship. Painted in company colours. They look a treat.'

Lowrie joined them, put down his paint pot with a sigh

of relief, fished out a snakeskin tobacco pouch and commenced to roll himself a cigarette. He sparked a light from a Japanese lighter and inhaled deeply. 'Time for a blow.' He turned his head toward the boatdeck and Al Bowley's melodious tones. 'He's driving *me* crazy. Dinna Dixie Dean ken anither tune? He's played yon rubbish over and over ever since we left home.'

Cloud cocked his head appreciatively. 'I dunno, I reckon a nice piece of music helps while you're grafting.'

Lowrie snorted. 'You call that caterwauling, music?'

'Better'n bagpipes.'

'Wailing saxophones,' countered Lowrie.

The put-put-putter of the returning launch interrupted the promise of a long and fascinating argument. Walking to the shipside they peered down as the launch swung alongside the companionway.

Captain Turner rose to his feet, scowled blackly at the Rock as though it had done him a personal injury, clutched his attaché case, picked up a weighted canvas bag, tucked a week-old newspaper beneath his arm and stumped up the gangway.

'*You-oo are driving me crazy,*' sang Al Bowley as a breathless Mr Dean presented himself before Turner.

Turner thrust the canvas bag into Dean's arms. 'The whole damn world has gone document-crazy,' he pronounced. 'Stow that in me quarters, young man. We heave up and get under way in thirty minutes. Deck officers to report to the bridge immediately.'

'Aye, sir.' Dean scurried away up the boatdeck ladder and in a moment Mr Bowley's plaintive pleadings stopped in mid-flow.

Turner's gaze roved over the ship, lighted upon the three standing at the rail.

'Can't the bos'n find you anything better to do than hang around gaping?'

'Aye, sir. We've just finished, sir,' volunteered Cloud. 'We thought you might want a hand with your gear, sir.'

'Did you now? Three strong fellers to carry a newspaper. I think I can manage, thank you, Cloud. In the meantime you can occupy yourselves by swinging the gangway inboard. Then join the chain gang on the fo'c'sle head. I daresay the mate will be able to find something to keep idle hands busy.'

They watched Turner's departing back. 'Ye great gawp, Cloudy, can ye no keep your mouth shut? Can we lend a hand wi' your gear, sir?' Lowrie mimicked sarcastically.

The western seas were afire with the setting sun and the reflectors of Europa Point Light glowed ruby red as the *Kentucky Minstrel* slid out into the Straits.

Behind them the boom-defence vessel closed the gate and an anti-submarine trawler fussed about searching for invaders.

To starboard a destroyer cruised watchfully to seaward. Ahead lay Ceuta, the horned tip of Africa.

'Bring her round, Mr Furlong,' said Turner and made his way into the chartroom where the cold-faced Mr Potter was laying off the ship's course on a sectional chart of the Atlantic. To the south lay Tangier and the coast of Morocco. To the north stood Cape Trafalgar and the Gulf of Cadiz.

Potter glanced up and stepped back a pace as Turner entered. The weighted canvas bag gaped open upon the chart table, its contents stacked into neat piles. There were out-of-date *Notices to Mariners*, a summary of U-boat activity, *Instructions to Master in the Event of Attack*, instructions to Radio Officers in similar circumstances, Warnings of Minefields, of Magnetic and Acoustic mines, Silhouettes of Enemy Aircraft, and a heavily embossed, wax-sealed envelope *Most Secret. To be opened only by the Master.*

Potter referred to a typewritten sheet of paper. 'Once we clear Cape Spartel we are to head sou'west for ninety miles. Then we make a wide sweep out into the Atlantic, beyond the range of most of the U-boats operating from the French coast, and then enter home waters by way of the north-western approaches. The Jerries seem to have the south-west bottled up.'

'I know,' said Turner, and remembered the enormous map covering one wall of the conference room, and the grizzled lieutenant-commander of tired eyes and exhausted features making sweeping motions with his pointer out across the Bay of Biscay. 'Brest. Lorient. St Nazaire. La Pallice. These are the U-boats' hidey-holes. Their operational bases. Our latest information is that the enemy have about forty operational U-boats and more building. Of those forty, only five are long-range and capable of penetrating far out into the

Atlantic. They are the ones for you to keep watch for, Captain. The rest are of small displacement and capable of only short coastal missions. But they can do damage enough. Our shipping losses are high. Too high, Captain – so take no risks, that's a valuable cargo you are carrying. Advice: Should you sight a U-boat, immediately transmit an SSSS message in the form prescribed and turn tail and run. You have the advantage of superior speed. Should you hear a distress call do not – and I repeat – do not attempt to render assistance. Leave rescue operations to us. I know it goes against the grain, but U-boats have been known to hang around against such an eventuality. What else?' The Intelligence Officer had yawned without apology and fatigue lines had etched themselves upon his face. 'Oh yes – something to remember which might stand you in good stead: It is commonly believed that a U-boat is a submersible craft which only pops up to the surface to take a breath of fresh air. This is not so. A submarine is essentially a surface vessel which submerges only occasionally – when launching an attack or escaping a pursuer. A submarine spends more time above water than below, and that is when she is most vulnerable. Most submarine commanders prefer to sink with gunfire – they don't really relish being encased in an iron coffin.' The scarecrow face had creased into a smile. 'I should know. Served in 'em myself in the last shooting match.'

They had shaken hands and Turner had collected the canvas bag of documents and left the gaunt man staring with haunted eyes at the wall-map.

Potter stood politely awaiting his Captain's appraisal. Turner privately did not approve of the second mate. His work was meticulous and accurate and he kept a wide-awake watch. But not only was he a non-smoker and teetotaller, there was also something Uriah-Heepish in his attitude. Without being exactly deferential to his superiors, he did show a marked aptitude for readily agreeing with their opinions. He seemed to be a man entirely without an opinion of his own. Not, in Turner's view, the sort of man to be entrusted with command. He would always be an able lieutenant, but never a leader. Ambitious, certainly. As ambitious as a boatload of politicians, but lacking in bone.

Turner picked up the heavy envelope and broke open the seals.

'Getting married at the end of this trip, ain'tcha, son?' he asked conversationally.

'Yes, sir. We – Madeleine and myself – hope that you will accept an invitation to the wedding?'

'That's very kind of you and your intended. I'll give it a thought.' Turner up-ended the envelope and tumbled out two code books bound in green and embossed with heavy gold lettering. 'The Admiralty must have money to burn,' he commented, and tossed the books carelessly upon the desk. 'I reckon the best wedding present I could give you would be an extension of leave, eh?'

Potter hesitated. 'I would be reluctant to miss the ship's sailing date, sir.'

'Duty before pleasure, eh? Very commendable. Given thought to your honeymoon, have yer?'

Potter flinched before Turner's leer. 'Aye, sir,' he replied stiffly. 'We had considered touring Devon and Cornwall by motor car – we have a small Jowett, second-hand is all we could afford – but with the possibility of invasion . . .'

'The south coast is out? Very sensible. Very sensible. If I were you I'd head for the Yorkshire Dales. Bury meself in the country. Somewhere where there are no telephones and I could do me canoodling in peace and quiet without interruptions. Leave it to me, son, I'll have a word with Barraclough.' He tucked the code books beneath his arm. 'No doubt you think me a sentimental old fool, but when I see a young feller like yerself, with one foot on the ladder of promotion and all his life before him, I reckon it's the least I can do.' He spared a glance at the chart as he made his way to the door. 'Very neat. Very neat, Mr Potter. I like neat chartwork.' He opened the door. 'Promotion, young man. Promotion. Let that be your watchword. Don't give it another thought. Me and Barraclough will find you something.'

The door closed behind him and Mr Potter remained to chew over his Captain's words. Promotion. His eyes glowed at the thought. Promotion. That could only mean one thing. He had been singled out to be a first mate. He rapidly reviewed the Company's order of seniority. There was the dyspeptic Mr Furlong, for example. Long in the tooth and overdue for command. A little push in the right direction and he could easily be stepping into Mr Furlong's shoes. His thoughts turned to Madeleine's angular features with the faint betraying line of dark moustache upon her upper lip. No great beauty, perhaps, but then a man couldn't have everything in this world; and her father *was* a bank manager with prospects.

Clearing his mind of fanciful thoughts Mr Potter returned his full attention to the chart.

The *Kentucky Minstrel* made a wide sweep out into the Atlantic. In four days they had covered fifteen hundred miles at an average speed of 15.5 knots and were entering an area of drifting rain belts when the radio began to chatter. SSSS SSSS SSSS SSSS, it buzzed. Paddy Phelan scribbled rapidly while his left hand reached out to switch on the direction finder. The message stopped abruptly and became a long unbroken drone. Paddy clamped the D/F phones over his ears and spun the pointer. The signal howled in his ears. He searched rapidly, found the minimum, then the signal stopped.

'Bastards,' said Paddy, and rang the bridge.

Mr Potter answered the phone, checked the bearing against the gyro compass heading, called the Captain on his private phone, and strode into the chartroom.

Turner and Paddy Phelan arrived at the same time. Turner took the slip of paper from the Radio Officer's hand. 'Torpedoed. 44.40 north. 20 – ?' He glanced up. 'Is that all?'

Paddy nodded. 'The message broke off, then their Sparks screwed down the key. They were probably being shelled.'

'How accurate was your bearing?'

'Spot on.'

Turner grunted. 'That Sparks has earned his coppers.' He trudged through to the chartroom where Mr Potter was busy with parallel rulers plotting the stricken ship's estimated position. He drew a short neat line, then plotted the bearing, marking an X at the intersection. 'About here, sir,' he said, standing back.

Turner picked up the dividers and measured the distance. 'About fifty-five miles. If we can squeeze another couple of knots out of her we should make it in around three and a half hours.'

'Sir!' Potter looked affronted. 'The Admiralty instructions are quite explicit. A merchant ship must on no account attempt to render assistance.'

'I know. I've read 'em,' said Turner. 'And a feller in Gib told me the same thing. Only he wasn't hanging on to a piece of wreckage in the middle of the Atlantic.'

He walked through to the bridge and picked up the engine-room phone. 'Third Engineer? I want a full head of steam and all the revs you've got.' He glanced at the softly ticking gyro repeater. 'Bring her round to two-eight-three, quartermaster.'

'Steer two-eight-three, it is, sir,' Lowrie intoned impassively.

The ship's head swung through an arc of twelve degrees then steadied.

'Heading two-eight-three, now, sir.'

'Thank you, Lowrie. I suppose you heard all that, didn't you, son?'

'Aye, I did.'

'And what is your opinion?'

Lowrie shrugged. 'It might be our turn next.'

'And you would like to think that someone will come charging to the rescue? You are something of a romantic, Lowrie.'

Lowrie kept his gaze fixed upon the gyro compass. 'I don't know about that, but it inn't right to leave those poor sods floating around in an open boat.'

'There could be a German sub lurking about.'

'I'll tak' me chances,' said Lowrie doggedly. He took his gaze away from the repeater. 'In any case, it's nothing to do wi' me. You make the decisions. I mean, that's what you're paid for, inn't it?'

'No, son,' Turner replied gently. 'That's what I worked for.'

He walked away and poked his head into the chartroom. 'Mr Potter. Emergency stations, if you please. All hands to wear life-jackets. I want you and two A.B.'s on the docking bridge to keep a sharp lookout over the quarter. Two men to the fo'c'sle head, and one up the foremast. Roust out the watch below and inform Mr Furlong that I require all boats swung out. Mr Dean to the bridge. Got it?'

'Aye, sir,' replied Potter, and hastened away.

'Sparks – I'll let you have our position every half hour. Take yourself off to your shack and stand by.'

Phelan grinned. 'If you hear a thump, take to the boats, I'll be along later.'

Turner patted him affectionately upon the shoulder. 'No heroics, Paddy. I want to die of old age, even if you don't.'

A drizzle of rain swallowed the ship and hid the horizon from view. Pearl-grey beads ran down the wheelhouse windows and bow wave crusted with foam as the hammering engines thrust the ship forward with ever-increasing speed.

Mr Dean huddled miserably on the wing of the bridge. The cab windows were open and the sweeping rain stuck his eyelids together, trickled down his nose, soaked the protective towel wrapped around his neck and ran in runnels down his back. His oilskins rustled as he raised a gloved hand to wipe away droplets dripping from the peak of his uniform cap.

'Did you remember to bring your fags with you, son?' asked a familiar voice.

Dean summoned up a wet smile, tugged open the press-studs and fished out his cigarette case.

'And have one yourself,' said Turner affably. 'If me calculations are wrong it might be your last.' He ducked his head, cupped his hands and lit up contentedly. 'If I was that feller in the U-boat,' he mused, 'I wouldn't be hanging around on the off-chance. I daresay he's as well informed as to procedure as we are. In his shoes I'd be putting as much distance as possible between me and my victim before I found a destroyer breathing down my neck. That is,' he added sourly, 'if our fellers can find time to spare from shooting up our allies.' He drew deeply on his cigarette. 'That sub must be one of those ocean-going jobs. He's all alone in a big wide ocean, and a long way from home. What would you do, son, if you were in command?'

'The same, sir,' replied Dean without hesitation.

The frog features wreathed into a smile. 'If the rest of the Merchant Service takes after you, my boy, them bowler-hats in the Admiralty are in for a hard time.' He sniffed. 'They seem to think they own the seas. They don't, son. We do.'

The *Kentucky Minstrel* ploughed ahead leaving a froth of wake astern. The rain turned into a drum-beating downpour, beating the sea flat and reducing visibility to a few yards. The boats were swung out, cargo nets made fast to lee and weather rails and rolled into position. The relief lookout, cumbersome in oilskins and life-jacket, clambered up the foremast to take his precarious perch upon the cross-trees. At 4.40 Cloud, on the fo'c'sle head, spotted a red-and-white lifebelt floating past. The *Kentucky Minstrel* reduced speed and three minutes later they sighted an upturned life-boat with the bottom stove in. Then they sailed through a sea of debris: broken spars, a deck-chair, deck planking. The flotsam of what had once been a ship. The sea darkened into a leaden scum.

'She must have been a coal-burner,' said Turner.

The ship suddenly burst through into a bowl of washed-blue sky. Curtains of rain veiled the horizon. A school of porpoises broke the surface and put everyone's hearts into their mouths before cartwheeling lazily and plunging back into the depths. A faint breeze puckered the surface of the sea. A water cask bobbed in the now faint surge of the bow wave.

The lookout man climbed higher, up the swaying wire ladder until he clung just below the topmast truck.

Turner swung the telegraph handles to STOP. The ship rolled gently at the centre of a pool of silence broken only by the faint slap of water against the hull.

The lookout craned his neck and suddenly pointed: 'There awa-ay!' he yelled. 'Fine on the starboard bow. One – two boats!'

Turner raised the binoculars to his eyes. At first he saw nothing but the distant greyness of a rain cloud. But Atlantic rollers were deceptive. Out here a small boat, or a sub-marine's conning tower, could remain hidden from sight in the trough of a wave until the end of time. He swept across a short arc of the horizon. A movement caught his eye and then a boat's stern rose on the crest of a billow. A moment later the entire ship's boat hove into view, riding high, and he had time to glimpse the lop-sided lugsail and a handful of gesticu-lating figures before the boat slid down into the succeeding trough.

As the second boat climbed to the peak of the wave Turner held out the glasses to the quartermaster. 'Take a look-see, Conroy,' he invited.

Conroy brushed aside the binoculars and squinted into the distance. 'I got 'em, 'he said. 'Leave 'em to me.'

Turner was not affronted at this usurpation of authority.

He knew Conroy of old. A gnarled man of wizened features long blasted to bone and leather by the eroding winds of the sea. His long arms and bow legs giving him the shambling gait of a shrunken ape, Conroy was an old shellback wise in the ways of the sea. Bred in the latter days of sail he knew of no other home but that of a ship. He was a man to whose opinion even Matt Honest, the bos'n, deferred. In his hands a ship became a live thing, responding to every touch of the helm.

'She's all yours, Pat,' said Turner, and swung the telegraph handles to half ahead.

The boats rose and fell, becoming ever larger in the binocular lens as the ship drew closer. Turner watched them lowering the lugsails and made a swift count. Fifteen to a boat. Thirty men. He leaned through the open window and called down: 'Starboard side to.'

Mr Furlong, standing on number two hatch, raised a hand in acknowledgement. The cargo nets were unfurled and lowered and a Jacob's ladder tumbled over the side.

Turner rang the engines to slow ahead, then dead slow. The sun glinted from the mirrored facets of the sea. A stronger puff of breeze whipped a flurry of spindrift from the wave tops. He squeezed the binoculars to his eyes and carefully scanned the area yard by yard. They were rapidly approaching the point of maximum danger when the ship would be a sitting duck for a submarine lurking in the depths. *A ship hove to is the ideal target*, the man had said. He searched for the tell-tale feather of a periscope. *He'll go down to periscope depth, line you up, then break the surface. His ideal attack position will be about a thousand yards, half-submerged. If you see his conning tower, that will be the last sight you will have of him before you are hit.*

Conroy brought the ship round, keeping the boats in the lee. Turner stopped the engines as ship and boats drifted closer together. The bos'n threw a heaving line and Turner made a mental count as the figures scrambled over the rails and dropped to the deck. Captain, mate, second mate, third mate. The engineers. Cook and stewards. Seamen and firemen. Thirty-two, all told. *The latest torpedoes are driven by electric motors. No compressed air bubbles to betray their presence. But if they are close to the surface you might see their wake.*

Mr Furlong cupped his hands. 'All clear. All hands aboard.'

'Cast those boats adrift,' Turner called, and savagely rang the telegraphs to full ahead.

'Hard astarboard.'

Keep as small a profile as possible. Turn your stern to the expected direction of attack.

Port side, he thought. That's where he'll be. On the blind side while we are busy picking up survivors.

The ship swung through ninety degrees leaving a great curve of foaming wake.

'Steady on that,' said Turner. 'Steady as she goes.'

The spokes whirred under Conroy's hands. The ship steadied and headed for a dense cloud of mist and rain.

As the sun disappeared and the ship was once again enveloped in a protective cloak of drizzle Turner heaved a sigh of relief. Thus far theory had proved right, but putting theory into practice had been a nerve-wracking business. Unexpectedly he found his legs trembling and unconsciously he began to pat at his pockets. A polite cough at his side revealed the presence of young Mr Dean hesitantly offering his cigarette case.

'Thank you, son.' Turner steadied the young man's hand and summoned up a crooked smile. 'All over bar shouting, and we never even got our feet wet.' He glanced at the chronometer. Five o'clock. Twenty minutes since they first sighted the wreckage. It had seemed a lifetime. 'We'll resume normal watch-keeping, Mr Dean. Off you go and get your head down.'

Dean thankfully made his way below. On the boat deck he almost collided with a broad-shouldered man with a Viking beard and a Master's insignia on the sleeves of a faded uniform.

The newcomer clambered the ladder to the bridge, entered the wheelhouse and stuck out a hand.

'Cap'n Turner? I'm Bradley of the *Esmeralda.* We owe you our lives.'

Turner grunted and shook hands. 'Did you lose many?'

'Chief and fourth engineer. Donkeyman. A greaser. Three firemen. And two trimmers. Poor devils, they'd have been trapped in the bunkers.' Bradley fished in his pocket. 'Do you mind if I smoke?'

Turner eyed the pocket hopefully. 'I'm afraid I'm on my last cigarette now, but if you've brought a supply I'll be glad to join you.' He inhaled deeply and pitched the dog-end through the window.

'Cigarettes?' Bradley smiled. 'I never touch 'em.' He hauled out a tobacco pouch and an enormous meerschaum. Wadding a palmful into the bowl he struck a match and blew out a cloud of evil-smelling smoke. 'Can't stand cigarettes. Never could. After a pipe they taste like dried hay. Beats me what folks see in 'em.'

Turner scowled murderously. Pipe-smokers, in his estimation, ranked just below non-smokers. He coughed pointedly as a shower of hot embers flew from the pipe, but Bradley was already launched upon the seas of recollection.

'We were homeward bound from Rosario with seven and a half thousand tons of Argentine grain. He hit us amidships, smack in the engine room. No warning. We never had a chance. He surfaced and stood off about half a mile while we took to the boats. Me and the bos'n hung back waiting for Sparks. We got one boat clear then he started to transmit our SSSS. The murdering bastards opened fire. Shot the bridge to pieces. But she was an old ship. Built in 1912. No wireless rooms in those days. Sparks' shack was at the after end of the boat deck. Looked like a converted hen pen. We used to joke about it. Poor John Willie – cock of the roost, we called him. It took 'em a while to cotton on. John Willie came out running. A shell hit him plumb in the chest.' Bradley removed the pipe from his mouth and looked sick. 'Blew him to pieces. Murdering bastards!'

Turner wafted away wreaths of smoke.

'Aye,' he grumbled. 'It's a hell of a war.'

U-boat and ship sighted each other at the same time.

Mr Furlong had taken over the second half of his four-to-eight watch. A fiery sun had turned the mist to a blood-red haze, and the steward had just sounded the dinner gong, when the *Kentucky Minstrel* emerged from the screen of fine rain to find the submarine panting on the surface like some dinosaur of the deep.

Its foetid breath hung like a foul miasma, tainting the clean sea air with the mingled sour-sweet stench of fuel oil, bilge water, sweat, waste matter and battery fumes. Its flanks were scaled with rust and green with weed.

Two officers stood on the tiny bridge encircling the open conning tower hatch. On the long snout of the foredeck a couple of bearded ratings were daubing a thick coating of grease over the barrel of a wicked-looking gun.

The U-boat was undoubtedly a deep-water vessel. 700 tons and 240 feet over-all, it lay broadside on to the cleaving bows of the approaching ship.

Furlong had time to see the startled face of one of the officers turned toward him before the clamour of alarm bells sent the two ratings tumbling down the forward hatch. The two officers disappeared and the propellers kicked the water into twin churns of foam.

Furlong's shout brought Turner hurrying from the chart-room. He stared open-mouthed. 'Goddamighty! Ram her! Ram her, Jason. Ram her!'

Jason, standing transfixed at the wheel, could only nod his head. The *Kentucky Minstrel* was driving forward straight at the conning tower.

Turner and Furlong stood watching the rapidly decreasing stretch of water. Then the U-boat made a hard right turn. The hunter had become the hunted.

'Keep after her! Keep after her!' Turner's voice was hoarse with tension.

The U-boat's speed increased but it was no match for the ship's eighteen knots. They followed in its wake, inexorably closing the gap. Then the submarine dived. The foredeck became awash, then the after deck.

'The conning tower! Go for the conning tower!' Turner cursed as, with a bare hundred yards left, the U-boat fully submerged leaving but a whirlpool of water to mark its presence.

Jason spun the wheel, aimed at the centre of the swirling sea. They held their breaths as the *Kentucky Minstrel* ploughed across. There came a tremor, a distant grinding that vibrated throughout the ship, the grating of metal upon metal.

Furlong expelled a long-held breath. 'We've got him!' he whispered. 'We've got him!'

'We've shaken him up,' corrected Turner. 'Keep going.'

He stepped out on to the bridge and swept the area astern

through the binoculars. *If a U-boat can't catch you ahead, he'll try from the quarter. His top speed below the surface is no more than eight knots, so take evasive action.*

'Starboard the helm,' said Turner, and continued to watch the now placid sea.

He waited a minute.

'Port helm. Bring her back to course.'

The wake made a wide S. Then there was a roil of water and the U-boat lurched to the surface.

The magnification of the binoculars showed her to be in a sorry mess. The conning tower was a mangled twist of wreckage and the gun had been torn from its mounting.

An officer scrambled up through the forward hatch and began to clamber over the tangle of ripped and buckled plates. The periscope leaned drunkenly to one side and a gaping hole in the bridge housing revealed a litter of smashed steering wheel, broken pipes and the misshapen loop of the direction finder.

'They must have thought their last day had come,' exulted Turner. 'You should see that feller's face – he's livid.'

He watched closely as the officer squeezed himself into the battered remains of the conning tower. The man bent. Turner could see his lips move. Then the forward hatch slammed shut and the U-boat immediately kicked ahead. It altered course, sweeping through the chop of the sea. With ever increasing speed it manoeuvred into attack position off the ship's quarter.

If he's making a long shot, or aiming at a convoy, he'll fire a fan of torpedoes. Over a distance of four thousand yards a torpedo will run at about fifty knots. Turner's mouth ran dry. The voice pipe, he thought. He's conning the ship from the voice pipe. He concentrated his entire attention upon the man's face, willing himself not to alter course too soon. *Give him a clear shot. Tempt him into error, then swing away.*

The U-boat lay off the port quarter, its foredeck awash, its silhouette changing as it took aim.

'Stand by the telegraphs, Mr Furlong,' said Turner. He continued to watch and found himself consumed with rage at the thought of some loud-mouthed jackboot daring to attack *his* ship.

'Port easy,' he ordered, and saw the man lift his head and

bare his teeth in a grin of triumph as the ship began to swing broadside on.

The man concentrated his vision then, lowering his head, snapped an order into the speaking tube. A moment's pause. then a second order before straightening up to stare directly at Turner.

'Hard astarboard. Full astern starboard,' ordered Turner. The repeater telegraph from the engine room jangled immediately, the ship shuddered and turned in its own length as the starboard propeller flailed the sea into a smother of foam.

The submarine seemed to dance astern as Turner counted off the seconds and hurried through to the wheelhouse. He had reached 12 when a hail from Mr Potter on the docking bridge reported: 'Torpedo. Port quarter. Going away.'

'One,' said Turner.

The horizon whirled past as the ship spun on its heels.

'Torpedo track crossing astern,' yelled Potter.

'Two,' said Turner. 'Now it's our turn. Stop starboard. Midships the helm.'

The submarine reappeared on the starboard quarter and for a moment gave the illusion of racing ahead of the ship.

'Check her,' commanded Turner. 'Full ahead starboard.'

The horizon ceased its dizzy circling and the U-boat, now brought up dead ahead, lay wallowing in the trough of the sea.

He raised the binoculars to his eyes and once again focussed on the officer in the ruined conning tower. The man obviously realised the danger and was shouting feverish orders into the speaking tube. The submarine turned, lifted its snout over the wave and began to gather speed.

'Got her!' exulted Turner. 'They can't dive with that feller perched aloft. Keep after her, Jason.'

The U-boat officer evidently thought the same for he shouted another order, kicked off his heavy sea-boots, divested himself of jacket and scarf, clambered over the wreckage to the deck below and threw himself over the side.

A group congregated on the fore-deck watched fascinated as the man bobbed to the surface, spouting water and flailing his arms. The U-boat continued to make its turn, the swimmer saw the stern swinging inexorably toward him, pawed desperately at the huge bulk of the saddle tanks, then suddenly disappeared as though dragged down by a giant hand.

'He's a gonner,' said Albert, the cook.

Cloud pointed a long bony arm. 'No, he isn't. He's up again.'

The man momentarily reappeared in the boiling froth of wake. His arms clawed the air and a long scream of agony emerged from his gaping mouth. Around him the foam turned to creamy red, then bright pink.

'Christ!' muttered Cloud. 'The prop must have got him.'

'Chopped his bloody legs off,' crowed Lowrie. 'Serve the bastard right.'

'I told thee he wor' a gonner,' said Albert, with the air of a man whose word had been doubted. 'And gonner he is.'

'So is the sub,' said Cloud.

The U-boat was crash-diving once again. The sea boiled over her conning tower and she disappeared below the surface as the *Kentucky Minstrel,* throwing fountains of spray over her bows, crossed her track at an oblique angle.

'Missed 'em,' snarled Turner. He walked out to the starboard wing of the bridge and looked back at an empty waste of water. Something that looked like a tattered tailor's dummy slowly turned over and over in the distant wash of the wake.

'Bring her back to course, Mr Furlong. I doubt those jackboots will try that trick twice.'

He returned to the wheelhouse and picked up the radio room phone. 'Sparks. Transmit the following: Attacked by submarine position 44.40 north, 20.22 west stop survivors of – coded call sign *Esmeralda* – aboard stop request naval assistance in pursuit of damaged U-boat. End.' He replaced the phone. 'Lend us one of your fags Mr Furlong – I just don't seem to be able to give 'em up.'

Furlong smiled a dyspeptic smile and offered his case. 'Pursuit?' he queried.

Turner selected a cigarette, hawked and spat. 'Not likely. I just want the rest of those creeping squareheads to know what to expect when they attack a Minstrel boat.'

CHAPTER THREE

THE *Kentucky Minstrel* made the passage home under blue skies and with a flat calm sea without sighting anything more eventful than a spouting whale.

Fifty miles west of Tory Island they were met by a weather-stained armed trawler and escorted through the Western Approaches to the bottleneck of the North Channel.

Here they had their first glimpse of siege warfare. Coastal Command aircraft lumbered overhead; two destroyers weaved crazy search patterns; an armed merchant cruiser towered above a north-bound convoy: straggling lines of ships headed south. There were ships of all shapes and sizes: tankers, freighters, coasters; all painted a dirty grey and escorted by a motley collection of deep-sea trawlers and chunky corvettes with squat funnels and high fo'c'sle heads.

The *Kentucky Minstrel* rounded the Mull of Galloway, cleared the Point of Ayre at the northernmost tip of the Isle of Man, bore away from the unmistakable shape of Blackpool Tower and finally picked up the Bar Light Vessel guarding the bubbling shoal water at the entrance to the Mersey.

Above Liverpool the sky was smeared with the usual haze of mist and smoke through which peered the twin spires of the Liver Building. They paused long enough to pick up the pilot – a twenty-one-stone man as round as a barrel and as agile as a monkey, with a whisky-thirst and an appetite for gossip.

He greeted Turner like an old friend, offered a full-strength Capstan and beamed like a clean-shaven Father Christmas bearing good tidings. 'You'd be well advised to stock up with tobacco, Cap'n. There's a shortage ashore. Grub's rationed and the Luftwhuffer dropped a few bombs last night. Not like London – they've had quite a pasting –

but our turn will come.' He smacked his lips. 'I know just the thing for both of us. Where do you keep it?'

'In the chartroom,' said Turner. 'Help yourself.'

'Half ahead, Third Mate,' said the pilot. He singled out a black-and-white buoy marking the starboard hand of the channel. 'Keep that buoy fine on the starboard bow,' he told a gum-chewing Lowrie at the wheel, and disappeared into the chartroom, only to reappear within a minute with a half-tumbler of whisky. He swallowed generously and held the glass up to the light. 'This stuff is becoming as scarce as hen's teeth. You fellows don't know when you're well off. All the best, Cap'n.'

'Keep the bottle,' acknowledged Turner grumpily. He coughed explosively and inspected his cigarette. 'These things taste like fireworks. It's a poor exchange.'

The river was crowded with shipping: tugs fussed around their charges; ferryboats skirmished from shore to shore; destroyers and sloops lay at their moorings; the docks were forests of masts. The Liverpool shoreline seemed unchanged and unchangeable.

Even as Mr Dean hauled up the yellow, *I request pratique* flag, a tender was lunging out to meet them. The M.O.H. and a horde of rummagers swarmed aboard, gave the ship a cursory inspection and departed as quickly as they came.

'Things have changed,' said Turner. 'They used to hang around like a harbouration of parasites.'

'It's the war,' said the pilot. 'It's changed a host of habits.'

Things had changed. Liverpool had an oddly shabby look, rather like a decayed gentlewoman fallen on hard times. She bore herself bravely enough and her horde of bawdy children still clung tenaciously to her skirts, but the raddle of old age was beginning to show through hastily applied cosmetics.

The *Kentucky Minstrel* paid off in the domed Custom House building and, with bundles of crisp white five and ten pound notes sitting snugly in their pockets, the crew straggled across to the 'Flags of All Nations'.

The bar was crowded as Cloud shouldered his way back with a trayful of drinks.

'Beer's up a penny a pint,' he announced, handing out glasses. 'The Jerries bombed Bootle last night and knocked down a row of houses, and that yellow paint on the top of pillar-boxes turns green if there's a gas attack.'

Albert Hodges peered into the contents of his cardboard gasmask box. 'I reckon it'll be folks that'll turn green first.'

The bos'n took a satisfying draught of warm beer. 'They still serve a good pint,' he announced appreciatively. 'Are you coming back next trip, Albert?'

The cook lowered his beer. 'I doubt I'll have much say in the matter. I've been stuck wi' the *Kentucky* ever since Sloppy shanghaied me off a passenger boat. He's a rare fondness for his stomach, has Sloppy. Not that I regret it, mind thee. It's all go and little appreciation aboard a blood-boat.'

Matt Honest set up another round. 'You fellers won't let me down?' he queried. 'Yiz'll all be back next voyage? Same watch.'

Lowrie nodded. 'The Mate asked us.'

'The Mate knows how to pick a good crowd,' nodded Cloud sagely.

'He does,' agreed Jason. 'But who do you think picked him?'

'Good old Sloppy,' said Cloud, raising his glass. 'Here's to the fat old bastard.'

'Slopp'll see us through,' announced the cook.

'God help the Jerries,' said the bos'n piously.

'That U-boat lot must have thought their last day had come.' Lowrie licked a froth of beer from his lips. 'I've never kenned Sloppy in such a paddy. I reckon, given the chance, he'd have massacred them fellers with his bare hands. As it was, he near chopped them in two.'

'I wonder if they'll give us a gun?' asked Cloud hopefully. 'If we had a gun we'd have blowed 'em out of the water.'

'You'll get plenty of practice, Cloudy,' said the bos'n. 'This is going to be a long war.'

Cloud had his wish. On completion of discharging, the *Kentucky Minstrel* was towed into the graving dock.

Here the bottom was scraped and cleaned before being given a thick coat of boot-topping. Shipyard workers swarmed aboard. Be-goggled welders, haloed in eerie blue light, crouched amid showers of golden sparks while riveters beat staccato tattoos throughout day and night. The poop deck was a shambles of bent rails, lengths of rust-coloured angle-iron and splintered oak planking. The entire centre of the docking bridge had been removed and replaced with the circular shape of a gun platform, braced and strengthened above the after housing.

Amidships, radio room, chartroom and wheelhouse were in the process of being sheathed in armour-plating, while on each wing of the bridge a circular steel pill-box poked its mushroom head above the skyline and peered around through slitted lids.

Captain Turner, making one of his periodic forays, stared in wonder at a massive electric cable draped around the hull.

'What in hell's name is that?' he demanded of no one in particular.

Mr Page, the stand-by Second Mate, trotted across the narrow swaying gangplank, oblivious of the forty feet drop beneath, and joined Turner on the quay.

'The head drongo told me it was a degaussing system. It's supposed to de-magnetise magnetic mines.' Page was a tall lank young man with a long horse-face and an unruly forelock of hair tumbling from beneath the peak of a shapeless uniform cap. He wore working gear of dungaree trousers and a rumpled jacket with two gold bands upon the sleeves flapping open to reveal a coarsely woven seaman's jersey. His accent was unmistakably Australian and he bore himself with the easy-going, off-hand air typical of his countrymen.

'God love us all,' said Turner, at length. 'What will they be up to next?'

Page seemed to take the question literally, for he pointed to a party of naval ratings clustered about the gun platform. 'She's being fitted with a four-point-seven,' he replied laconically.

Turner trudged aboard and allowed Page to take him on a guided tour of the ship. The Second Mate was a sharp-eyed young man, Turner noted approvingly, and little seemed to escape his attention. As they made their way to the bridge he jangled a bunch of keys. 'I've kept the galley and accommodation locked – all except the saloon, the phone's in there – and I've had the devil's own job turfing out the card players and bookies' runners.'

He selected a key and unlocked the chartroom door. 'They set foot in here over my dead body. Given half a chance they'd nick everything that isn't nailed down.'

Turner stepped inside and blinked in surprise. The chart-room gleamed beneath a new coat of paint; chart table and drawers glowed and all brasswork had been polished to a mirror-like finish. The mingled odours of paint and varnish hung in the air. The chronometer screwed to the bulkhead ticked knowingly to itself.

Page was busying himself with the keys. 'One of these drawers was sticking, so I sanded the edge and gave it a smidgen of tallow. Hope you don't mind?' he asked, as though suddenly anxious that his motives be not misunderstood.

'Not in the least,' said Turner. 'All your own work, is it?'

'I was born restless,' replied Page. He yanked open drawers for inspection. 'Thought I'd give her a bit of a tidy. Scrounged the paint from one of those idle rat-bags below.' He seemed to think it explanation enough, stepped back and fished a packet of Gold Leaf from his pocket. 'I hear you are something of a smoker, Cap? I'm the same. Can't get by without a choke-stick.'

Turner selected a cigarette and tapped the end on his thumbnail. 'What happened to the man you replaced? The relief Second Mate?'

Page struck a match and held it out. 'Fell in the dock, I heard.'

'Not this dock?'

'No. Brocklebank. Next door. Coming back from the boozer, I heard.'

'Very unfortunate,' said Turner gravely.

'It was for him. They hauled him off to Bootle Infirmary and pumped him out.'

'And you providentially stepped into his shoes?'

'You might say I was lucky.'

'Very lucky,' said Turner drily, and turned his attention to an inspection of the contents of the drawers.

'Very neat,' he commented approvingly. 'You are a man of tidy habits, I see.'

The young man removed his peaked cap and rumpled a hand through his hair. 'Well,' he admitted, in the tone of one confessing to an inherent weakness, 'let's say I'm one of those characters who can't enter a room without wanting to put the pictures straight.'

Turner opened the locker door and peered inside. The

usual jumble of pieces of bunting, tins of bath-brick, colza oil, and lengths of worn signal halyard had been re-organised into regimented orderliness; the log line was neatly coiled; its log clock, governor and brass rotator cleaned and polished and placed inside the coil; its grapnel and line had been similarly treated before being bound together with a length of boat-lacing.

Turner spat out a fragment of tobacco. 'You're not a Company man, are you, son?'

Page shook his head. 'I joined a home-boat back in Melbourne. Thought I'd take a look at the Old Country before Hitler's war-wagons got on the move again.'

'Been on the beach long?'

The Australian rubbed his chin ruefully. 'Does it show?'

'Give me credit, son,' said Turner. 'An experienced Second Mate taking a cocky-watchman's job when any rust-tub that can float is being pushed off to sea, and certificated officers are as scarce as whores in paradise. Been in a bit of bother, have you?'

'I had a three months' suspension. Time's up in ten days.'

Turner eyed him thoughtfully. 'Want to tell me about it?'

'No,' said Page flatly.

'Prefer to carry your own burden. Very commendable,' said Turner easily. 'How's your navigation?'

'She's fair.'

'You'll be looking for a berth, then?'

Page shrugged. 'I'll find something.'

'I doubt you will find anything better than the Minstrel Line. Got your Mate's ticket, have you?'

'Aye, sir.'

'Easy as falling off a plank,' said Turner affably. 'I'll put in a word for you, if you like.'

'With the Marine Super?' Page shook his head. 'No hope. I've already had a run-in with him. He wants flunkies, not officers.'

'You mustn't pay too much attention to Barraclough, son. He's a bowler-hat, y'see, and all bowler-hats suffer from inferiority complexes. Just call him "sir" once in a while and you'll soon have him eating out of your hand.'

'We don't go for dog, back home,' said Page stiffly.

'Prickly young feller, aintcha?' Turner shrugged and

stubbed out his cigarette. 'Suit yourself, but remember the old adage: When in Rome do as Mussolini says.'

Page's features slid into a lop-sided grin. 'I'll try to remember, sir.'

'You're learning, son,' said Turner. 'You're learning.'

Page awoke early. A blade of sunlight had found a chink in the blackout curtains to slice across the unnatural darkness of the room. He rolled out of bed and padded across to the window. The curtain rings chinked and slithered along the brass rod as he threw the curtains aside. A lattice-work of light blazed into the room and drew a wavering pattern across the sleeping figure in the bed. Peering through bunched net curtains and window panes criss-crossed with protective tape he looked across the narrow street to the peeling stucco of an identical row of Georgian houses opposite, then down to the street and a milkman wandering from door to door.

The figure in the bed stirred, yawned, stretched and sat up. 'Morning, lover,' she murmured lazily. 'And how is my big bold Australian kookaburra feeling today?' She had a mane of red-gold hair, green eyes, and a wide mouth with sharp predatory teeth.

'A kookaburra is a laughing-jackass,' he told her absently.

'I know, lover, I know.' She gave her Cheshire-cat grin, threw aside the coverings, and beckoned invitingly. 'Back to bed, lover, you have work to do.'

'Awe, have a heart, Marge,' he pleaded. 'I gotta get back aboard ship. She shifts to her loading berth today, and I've trouble enough without missing her.' Nevertheless he obediently walked back to the bed and, hands on hips, stood looking down at her.

She moved languorously and her long lithe body rippled with shifting tiger-stripes of sunlight.

'I shouldn't be here,' he protested weakly. 'I'm on twenty-four-hour stand-by. It's only by greasing the nightwatchman to cover for me that I . . .' His mouth dried and he stopped in mid-speech as she reached out a cupped hand and began to gently fondle him.

'Awe, Marge – have a heart,' he repeated.

Her fingers were practised and dextrous. 'There,' she crooned. 'See what a handsome fellow he is. Standing there like a big brave soldier, all ready and eager to do his duty.'

'Marge – I gotta go.'

She tightened her grip. 'Don't you dare,' she warned and wriggled across the bed.

'Oh, hell,' said Page, leaning forward. 'Oh, hell . . .'

The little blue Jowett stood in the cobbled farmyard, a gathering of softly clucking hens pecking inquisitively at its tyres. A cow bawled in answer to its calf's plaintive bleating while a massive, splay-footed plough-horse nickered and neighed in sympathy.

In the tiny, rafted bedroom above, with its crooked ceiling sloping down to lattice-paned windows, Mr Potter lay on his back, groaned, and stared up at the angular features of his bride. Rat-tails of dank hair hung about her bare shoulders and she had drawn back her lips in a grin.

'Your Captain must be the most amiable and considerate of men,' she said. 'So thoughtful. I really must write and thank him for his kindness.'

'Yes, dear.' Mr Potter squirmed uncomfortably. 'But it is time we returned to Liverpool. I can't possibly let the old boy down,' he added hopefully. 'Not now.'

'Of course not, dearest,' she agreed. 'That man has a heart of gold.'

Mr Potter sighed. It was not, in his opinion, perhaps the most apt description of Captain Turner's vital organ. But during the past few weeks he had begun to doubt even his own sanity.

Captain Turner's wedding present had been a large manilla envelope containing a supply of petrol coupons, a large-scale map of the Yorkshire Dales, and advice to take themselves well off the beaten track.

Madeleine had been delighted and taken the advice only too literally. Petrol stations were few and far between, and with the absence of signposts – removed because of the fears of invasion – plus the reluctance of broad-vowelled inhabitants to divulge their whereabouts, they were now well and truly lost.

Not that the fact seemed to disturb Madeleine who looked upon their aimless wanderings as the bread of adventure leavened with the yeast of romance. Nor was that all. During the voyage he had conjured up a vague picture of himself and Madeleine walking hand in hand over hill and dale, pausing occasionally for a kiss and a hug before returning to the seclusion of a chintz-covered bedroom where Madeleine would be shyly submissive and becomingly grateful for his favours.

The reality had been entirely different. Madeleine, striding out like a dalesman, had marched him for mile after exhausting mile over hill and fell. Later, after tumbling bone-weary into bed, he had discovered that Madeleine had developed an unslakeable thirst for the torments of the flesh.

She looked down at him through the tangled veil of hair. 'Just once more,' she urged. 'Then we'll go for a nice long walk.' Her thin haunches rose and fell. 'Ooh,' she said. 'Oooh-ooh . . .'

As the water flooded into the graving dock, the *Kentucky Minstrel* rose buoyantly and Mr Page heaved a sigh of relief.

He had made it back to the ship with minutes to spare. The phone had already been disconnected and carried ashore and the berthing crew were straggling aboard as he hurried along the gangway to make his way to his cabin where he had rapidly changed into working gear.

By the time his fellow officers arrived he had made his rounds and was innocently pacing the bridge.

Turner and the docking pilot, sharing a taxi, had boarded the ship last of all. The gangplank was hauled ashore, the lock gates swung open and the tug's line taken inboard. Page was dispatched aft to his station on the remains of the docking bridge, bow and stern lines were cast off and the ship set off on her long slow haul into Langton dock, through Brocklebank to take up her berth in Canada No 2.

There had been no mishaps and the only disturbance the wail of air-raid sirens and the distant crump of gunfire. Barrage balloons rose like schools of silver porpoise to bob playfully at the end of their singing cables and a high-flying aircraft pencilled a thin vapour trail across a pale blue sky. Within half an hour the all-clear had sounded without what the newspapers euphemistically referred to as 'an incident' occurring.

False alarm, Page decided and, conscious that the Master's

eye was often turned in his direction, concentrated upon his work. Not that it was a particularly exacting task. The berthing crew under the charge of the shore-bos'n knew their job and, provided that he remembered to duck his head beneath the canvas-covered barrel of the four-point-seven as he crossed from side to side to check the sheer of the stern, there was little he needed to do beyond looking alert.

They slid through the first lock into Brocklebank with ample room to spare. Page stifled a yawn, watched the stern clear the stone buttresses, rang the docking telegraph handles to All Clear Aft, then allowed his mind to dwell upon Marjorie.

He remembered their first meeting with utter clarity. At a loose end one evening, bored with the seamen's pubs, he had boarded a tramcar picked at random. It had rattled its way out into the suburbs and deposited him at its Penny Lane terminus.

It was an area with which he was totally unfamiliar. He had wandered about aimlessly for a while, brooding over his misfortunes, when he suddenly realised that he was hopelessly lost in a maze of suburban streets with rows of identical suburban houses, each with its own neat suburban garden. It had been a golden summer evening with a heat haze glowing in the west and only the throaty notes of a blackbird to disturb the stillness.

Rounding a corner he had his first glimpse of her. She was posting letters at a round red pillar-box and had looked up with a smile as he hurried across to ask directions. Suddenly uncomfortably aware of a more pressing need than that provided by a jogging and swaying tramcar, he had changed his question in mid-sentence.

'The nearest pub?' she had repeated thoughtfully, as though trying to resolve a complicated problem in logistics. 'You must mean the Rose of Mossley. I am going that way, myself.'

He had fallen into step beside her and they had walked on silently for a while. 'Australian, aren't you?' she had asked eventually.

Long resigned to the fact that this was invariably the first question people put to him, he had agreed gravely that, yes, he was Australian.

'We thought of emigrating, once. But nothing came of it.

It was another of my husband's pet dreams. He thinks the world owes him a living. It doesn't. Anything you want in this life you have to grab while the grabbing's good. Maybe the Army will knock some sense into him.'

She had chattered on with something of the naïvety and frankness of a child confiding in a stranger. Her husband had been called up and was now stationed somewhere on the South Coast; one of the thin line of skirmishers hoping to repel the expected invasion. In the meantime she was living with her married sister and her husband. 'He's in a reserved occupation. A draughtsman at the aircraft factory. Doesn't know when he's well off. Fancies himself in uniform. He gives me the creeps. Always trying to touch me up. Thinks he's God's gift to women. It's not that I mind a bit of bottom-patting, but Ben is such a lecherous swine. I'm moving out as soon as I can find a place of my own.'

They had emerged into a long road with a small row of shops and a Methodist church. The pub stood on the corner, set back from the road, and with the swing doors latched back to allow a breath of sultry air to blow through the crowded saloon bar.

'Here's your oasis,' she had said, and led him through to a wide, open lounge with french windows leading to a bowling green beyond.

She had waved a cheerful greeting to a noisy group at a nearby table and then pointed him in the right direction. 'If you want to water your pony, the trough's through there.'

When he returned she was seated with the group, her head thrown back and her throat rippling with laughter. He had stood uncertainly for a moment, aware of the English dislike of the intrusive stranger, but she had waved a hand and hallooed him across.

They went through the complicated ritual of exchanging names and he had been found a chair between Simon, a middle-aged man with a fund of atrocious jokes, and Jeff Lowe, a solemn, tweedy young man with a tiny wisp of moustache.

They were heavy drinkers and the evening passed quickly in a haze of alcoholic bonhomie. At a quarter to ten the landlord had called, 'Time, one and all', and thrown the towels decisively over the pumps.

They had lurched out of the jumble of noise and stifling

air into the cool blue dusk of a June evening. It seemed expected of him so he had walked her home, back the way they had come, past the red pillar box and houses already drawing their blackout curtains, until they reached a small garden gate of white-painted palings. A name plate identified the house as *Bensholme*, a point emphasised by a second plaque bearing the inscription: *No Hawkers, Canvassers, Circulars.* A thick privet hedge, carefully trimmed to an arch over the gateway, gave the pebble-dashed house an oddly cloistered look.

He had stood shifting awkwardly from one foot to another, trying to prolong the moment. Finally she had held out a hand: 'Good-bye, and thank you for your company,' she had said formally.

'Shall I see you again?' he had asked hopelessly.

She had paused in the act of turning away, cocked her head and eyed him reflectively. 'Why not?' she said decisively. 'Six o'clock. Outside the shop.'

'Which shop?' he had called after her.

She had turned and laughed. 'Of course – I never told you. The Bon Marche. Side entrance.'

He had lingered a moment watching the flaunt of her hips as she tipperty-tapped up the path to the front door. In the front room a curtain parted to reveal the pale blur of a prying face. Then the door opened and a man with abnormally long arms, simian features and thick, bushy eyebrows appeared. He had time to intercept a malevolent glare from the ape-man, then the door closed behind her.

The following evening they had met as arranged, greeting each other with a mixture of shyness and boldness, each aware that the first dangerous step had been taken. He had taken her to Reece's Grill where she had eaten with a voracious appetite and they had indulged in an exchange of confidences.

From that moment the affair had progressed with the inevitable formality of a preordained ritual. They met again and again. Held hands, kissed, squirmed against each other in darkened shop doorways, until one evening, strolling aimlessly from one pub to another, they had seen a notice: *Flat to Let. Fully Furnished.* They had stopped, struck by the same thought. 'Will you share with me?' she had asked, adding by way of face-saving explanation: 'Estate agents don't like to let to women alone. It would need to be in your name.'

Within the week they had set up house together. The war, with its looming threat of total destruction, took care of the future and easily assuaged their consciences. They lived each moment as though it were to be their last and tomorrow would never come . . .

The ship angled into Branch No. 2 and Page was kept busy checking the mooring lines as the stern nudged alongside.

The cranes were already nodding over open hatches and, as the berthing crew tramped ashore, the first sling-loads of cargo were dropping into the holds.

On the bridge, Turner owlishly surveyed his officers. 'It will be cargo-watching twenty-four hours a day, so you'd best share out the duties between yourselves. Mr Page will lend a hand. Won't you, Mr Page?'

'Aye, sir,' Page answered uncertainly. Cargo duties were the responsibility of watch-keeping officers.

'Mr Page is thinking of joining us, aren't you, son?'

'Ah,' said Page.

'I never interfere, and I'm the model of tact. Noted for it.' Turner waved an expansive arm. 'These fellers will tell you the same. But if you want my advice, you'll not go looking gift horses in the mouth. Beggars can't be choosers, and after three months on the pebbles no doubt you'll be feeling the pinch, so if you want the job report at the shipping office tomorrow, ten o'clock, sharp. We'll be opening Articles then, and I want you signed on before that old woman Barraclough can stick his oar in. Can't understand that man,' he added darkly. 'He plays favourites, y'know.'

They watched him roll away, a porcine figure in bowler-hat and heavy tweeds. Page expelled a breath. 'Is he always like that?'

Furlong twisted his features into the grimace of a grin. 'Our Sloppy is a human steamroller.' He stuck out a hand. 'Welcome aboard.'

CHAPTER FOUR

THE DEMS gunner was a corporal from the Royal Artillery. A grizzled man with no neck and a head like a bristling cannon-ball, he slammed around the deck in iron-shod boots, springing to attention and barking '*Sir*!' every time an officer walked past, until the bos'n took him aside and explained gently that barrack-room discipline was unknown aboard a merchant ship and merely served to amuse the hands and embarrass the officers.

For the first few days Corporal Jackson wandered about the ship in a state of bemused inarticulacy, barely able to comprehend a swirl of activity which constantly threatened life and limb. He tripped over wires and hawsers, was cursed by dockers and rescued from near-decapitation by a sling of cargo by a grinning Cloud. The ship lay port-side to. 'When you're heading forrard, use the outboard alleyway, starboard side, and watch out for the sujee-mooji gang, they're not too particular where they slosh the stuff.'

This gibberish left him more confused than ever, for the seamen, he quickly learned, communicated in a language he could barely understand. As a result he took to spending his time on the gun platform, polishing and cleaning until barrel and mechanism gleamed and glittered in the sun.

He came to life only when the gun crew shambled aft for their training session and stood sheepishly around their new toy while Corporal Jackson initiated them into the mysteries of his calling.

'This here gun,' he began, patting it affectionately and speaking in the monotonous tones of one who has learned his lecture by rote, 'is known as a 4.7 breech-loading QF

4.7 inches being the diameter of the bore, breech-loading for the hobvious reason that the shell is no longer rammed down the muzzle as was the case of our forefathers at Trafalgar, ha-ha. QF means quick-firing, the method requiring no more than a quick depression of this here brass lever upon which I will now place my hand.'

He gave a sharp flip of the wrist and the breech block swung smoothly open. A second flip and it closed.

'When do we have a go?' asked Cloud.

'We'll have a practice shoot without ammo once you have familiarised yourselves with the basics,' Corporal Jackson promised.

The basics consisted of being hustled and bustled into position while Corporal Jackson, now in his element, stamped his feet, squared his shoulders and bawled instructions in a parade ground voice.

'You dozy, useless, idle lot!' he yelled. 'Move, move, move! You, there! Cloud, you shambling drink o' water – break to the right! Right, right, right, I said! Loaders, stand by to take the ammo! Ammo party, pass the ammo! No!' he screamed. 'First the shell, *then* the charge! Shell – charge. In that order, you dizzy, hopeless crowd o' washerwomen!'

The gun crew had eagerly volunteered to a man, under the impression that a daily half-hour's exercise with the gun would be a welcome release from ship routine. At the end of an hour they hated the gun and had acquired a deep and inexpressible loathing for Corporal Jackson.

'We'll try it once again,' said Corporal Jackson.

They tumbled wearily down on to deck and stood waiting for the shrilling of their tormentor's whistle.

'If he calls me a Scotch 'addock just once more, I'll murder the bastard,' snarled Lowrie, doubling his fists.

The whistle shrilled. 'Clear for action!' yelled Corporal Jackson. 'At the double, at the double!'

'I'd like to double him and stuff him up the spout,' grumbled Cloud. 'Him and his bloody gun.' But obediently he scrambled up the short iron ladder to the gun platform, hit the quick-release lever which dropped the safety rails and ran to his perch on a steel-ribbed seat fixed to the gun mounting. He squinted through the sighting telescope, turned the horizontal wheel and lined up an idling docker in the cross hairs.

'On, on, on . . .' he intoned.

'Louder!' bawled Corporal Jackson. 'I can't hear you!'

'Then pull the bloody trigger,' answered Cloud. 'We've just sunk a docker.'

'I only 'ope he's not shooting back,' said Corporal Jackson scathingly.

Jason stood at the left of the gun, turning twin dials. 'Sights moving. Sights set,' he announced mechanically.

'Breech open,' growled Lowrie. 'And hurry it up with that bleedin' ammo, Lofty.'

Lowrie's function was to open and close the breech. Lofty, a lantern-jawed, buck-toothed seaman, mimicked staggering under the weight of a non-existent shell. 'I just dropped it,' he explained, grinning hugely.

'Then you've just blowed us all to Kingdom-come,' snapped Corporal Jackson. 'So stop arsing about and ram it home.'

Lowrie scowled at Lofty. 'I'll sort you out bleedin' later, mate.' He slammed the breech shut. 'Breech closed,' he reported sullenly and stood waiting for the corporal to call '*Fire!*' and click the trigger.

Instead Corporal Jackson stood arms akimbo steadily surveying Lowrie. Then he pointed a finger. 'Bang, you're dead,' he said.

Lowrie took a truculent pace forward. 'Wha' d'ya mean – I'm dead?'

Jackson buried his cannon-ball head even deeper into his shoulders and leered roguishly at Lowrie. 'Well, perhaps not dead,' he admitted. 'But you'd be wishing you were. The recoil has just knocked your balls through your arse. How many times do I have to say it? Always stand to one side of the breech!' he roared. 'You stupid man! You great Scotch 'addock!'

Lowrie, goaded beyond endurance, hurled himself at the monster only to discover that the experienced corporal had turned his back and moved away.

'Turn round and put yer fists up, ye slobbering English toad!' he howled, gibbering with rage.

Corporal Jackson turned a mild gaze upon the prancing Lowrie. 'Keep that up and you'll find yourself on a charge, lad,' he rebuked mildly. He fished out a turnip of a watch, consulted the dial and replaced it. 'On ship you can be pigs in your own midden, but up here I'm cock o' the walk, and don't none of you forget it. Gather round and I'll tell you why.' He squared his shoulders, straddled his legs and clasped his hands behind his back.

'The Jerries will have up-to-date armaments. All we got is an ancient old cannon that last saw action in the First World War. *They* use coupled range-finders. *We* bang away and hope for the best. *I've* got a few hours to bring you up to the mark. *They've* got months of discipline and training behind 'em. *They* are professionals and you lot are amachoors. So I got to bear down on you. Do you follow?'

They nodded dumbly.

'We've got one advantage,' continued Corporal Jackson. 'They've been having it all their own way, so far, and won't be used to having sixty pounds of high explosive thrown at 'em.'

'No more are we,' said Jason.

'That makes us even-Stevens in that respect. Now *I* would call that a decided advantage. A second factor is that a near-miss from us will scare the shit out of 'em. All we got to do is puncture 'im and he'll sink like a stone.'

'They'll not have much bother puncturing us,' grumbled Cloud. 'I mean, look at the size of a ship compared with that of a sub.'

'Don't be daft, lad,' said Corporal Jackson cheerfully. 'They'll be aiming at the gun, not the boat.'

The *Kentucky Minstrel* shouldered aside a huddle of barges and slid out into the river to tail on to the end of the long line of a slow-moving convoy.

Mr Page, leaning against the shipside rail, glumly watched the docks gliding past. His head ached abominably. He and Marjorie had celebrated until the early hours of the morning. If a spitting cat-and-dog fight could in any way be described as a celebration. She had never really accustomed herself to the fact that there must come a time when the halcyon days must end. He had tried to explain that once he had signed Articles he was bound to the ship as though in wedlock, but she had tossed back her mane of hair in a stubborn refusal to accept the inevitable. 'You only want me because I'm sexy, not because you love me,' she had accused. 'You have tired of me, and now all you want is to run off to sea.' Her impeachment had been so uncomfortably close to the truth that all his efforts to placate her had foundered on the rocks of her intuition. She had stormed, wheedled and cajoled until, having drunk themselves into a state of maudlin insensibility, they had tumbled into bed and slept like logs, arms and legs intertwined but too emotionally exhausted to make love.

The imperative clamour of the bedside alarm had dragged them both from sleep and the argument had continued while he dressed and shaved. He had done his best to reassure her but she would not be comforted. Eventually he had left her, a slumped, softly-weeping figure, convinced she would never see him again.

He had set off back to the ship with the spring of relief in his step and wondering what could possibly have caused the egregious Mr Potter to miss the sailing date . . .

Albert Hodge soon enlightened him. The cook had rolled up to stand beside Page in silent appraisal of the landscape.

'It's a reet friendly town, is Liverpool,' he observed at length. 'Tha can allus find summat to suit all tastes.'

Page agreed absently. 'Sometimes it can be too friendly.'

'Ah, tha has tha mind on that red-headed lass, no doubt?' The cook scraped at the bowl of a blackened pipe and knocked the dottle out into the palm of his hand.

Page stared at the round cherubic face. 'What red-head?'

'Striking young woman, I thought. Very handsome figure. But if tha wants to keep tha peccadilloes to thissen, Second Mate, tha shouldn't take her boozing for all to see. I daresay she'll be fretting for thee, by now?'

'Well,' said Page, 'I never really expected to sail. I thought the regular Second Mate would turn up.'

'Then tha's reckoned without Sloppy,' said Albert. 'He inveigled me much the same road.'

'Oh?'

'Happen young Mr Potter found himself stranded in Yorkshire, so I heard.'

'Stranded?'

'Run out of petrol, and then found there was summat wrong wi' his coupons. So I heard.'

'The cunning old devil,' said Page.

'He's all of that,' agreed the cook. 'Happen he's took a fancy to thee, so take good care tha don't rub him up the wrong way. He can be a demon when he feels afflicted, can our Sloppy.'

'I'll remember,' Page promised.

Once clear of the Bar Light Vessel the escorts bustled about shepherding their charges into some semblance of formation.

The convoy consisted of 40 ships in columns of four, each vessel keeping station 3½ cables apart from its neighbour, the entire formation covering about fourteen square miles of sea, and plodding along at the speed of the slowest ship. The laggard in this case being the *S.S. Bolsover*, an ancient rust-tub riding high out of the water and belching a black pillar of smoke from a tall thin funnel.

To Turner's fury the *Kentucky Minstrel*'s allocated position was in the rear rank alongside the *Bolsover*, with the result that whenever the wind swirled, or the convoy altered course, the *Kentucky Minstrel* was smothered in choking black fumes and a deposit of gritty ash.

'God love us,' he swore, wiping streaming eyes. Her owners should have been strangled at birth. Just look at her wallowing all over the ocean. She must be fifty years old if she's a day.'

He stumped off to take refuge in the chartroom, leaving Mr Furlong to keep an eye on one of the pair of escorting destroyers manoeuvring close to the *Bolsover*. A loud-hailer demanded that the culprit stop making smoke, only to receive a strangled obscenity by way of reply. The destroyer sheered off, picked up speed and took off in a huff as though mortally offended. Mr Furlong warped his features into a sour grin: he could readily understand the destroyer's anxiety, a prowling U-boat would sight the *Bolsover*'s smoke long after the convoy was hull down beyond the horizon. Not that the *Bolsover*'s engineers could do much about it. She was old and neglected, probably burned the cheapest coal obtainable, and her flues would be choked with the accumulation of years of soot.

Nor was the *Bolsove*r alone. Pacing the bridge Furlong counted eight coal-burners staggered about the pack. At the end of each watch they would need to clean their fires when dense clouds of smoke would pour from their funnels. It would be worse by night. Then flames would lick from their funnels as though lit from the fires of hell below. Mr. Furlong was not a religious man but a dimly remembered passage from the bible wormed its way into his mind: *Thou leddest them in the day by a cloudy pillar; and in the night by a pillar of fire.* He shrugged off a sense of foreboding, checked that they were keeping station astern of the ship ahead, and wandered into the chartroom.

Turner was surveying the chartroom with a benign expression. 'I've been having a bit of a nose around. Very meticulous, very neat. Place for everything and everything in its place. Got an obsession for detail has our new Second Mate. What do you think of him, Harold?'

Furlong winced. Turner, he knew, counted it as a mark of especial favour to address a subordinate by his forename. At the same time, however, he succeeded in keeping familiarity at arm's length by never descending to the use of the diminutive. As a result those unfortunates blessed with parents of more imagination than common sense tended to prefer Sloppy in tyrannical rather than benevolent mood.

'A bit rough-and-ready for my taste,' answered Furlong guardedly.

'He's certainly one of our wilder Colonials from the cut of his accent, but he does seem to have a certain primitive instinct for self-preservation. Give him time, Harold, give him time.' He laid a fatherly hand on Furlong's shoulder. 'We mustn't judge by appearances. Without me finery would you take me for a Master Mariner?'

Turner had not yet troubled to change from his shore-going rig. He modestly stroked the threadbare sleeve of his jacket. 'Look every inch a businessman in me civvy suiting, don't I? It was a good year for tweed, was 1925.'

He guided Furlong out on to the bridge. 'We mustn't stand here gossiping, Harold,' he said affably. 'Idle watch-keeping makes for a slack ship.'

A blast from the escort's siren choked back the rejoinder rising to Furlong's lips. A rash of flags broke out from the destroyer's signal yard, whipping colourfully in the breeze.

Furlong read them off. 'We are to commence zig-zagging,' he reported.

For the remaining hours of daylight the convoy exercised making emergency turns.

On paper the theory worked. In practice the result was chaos.

At a signal from the Commodore in the leading ship the entire mass was expected to turn in unison. Masters swore blasphemously as they tried to avoid collision with their neighbours. Some ships were sluggish in answering the helm, others were quick to respond. Ships lurched and blundered, crowded together, bumped and bored like a herd of frightened cattle.

Then no sooner had they settled into some semblance of order but the whole business started over again.

Their progress was agonisingly slow: it took nine hours to bring up Chicken Rock Light, a lonely barren outpost south of the Calf of Man; then they made their staggering way north until the sun setting behind the soft greens of Ireland put an end to their tribulations. They re-formed into two lines and headed north-west between Scotland and Northern Ireland.

At six bells in the forenoon watch of the following day they plodded past the mist-enshrouded hills of the Mull of Kintyre, sighted Islay to the north, then turned due west and swept out into the battleground of the wild Atlantic.

CHAPTER FIVE

TWO HUNDRED miles west of Northern Ireland the destroyers handed over their charges to the care of an armed merchant cruiser and turned to foam away to the east, sheets of spray bursting over their narrow foredecks.

The A.M.C. had seen more graceful days as a trans-Atlantic passenger liner. Now requisitioned by the Admiralty, she flew the Blue Ensign and bristled with six-inch guns. A hybrid, neither flesh nor fowl, she faced a hopeless task. No match for the German surface raiders she was expected to repel and as vulnerable to torpedo attack as the ships she was there to protect, there was little to recommend her presence beyond the loan of an air of false-security.

Page voiced the opinion of them all. 'She'll be as much use as a fart in a thunderstorm,' he pronounced sourly and concentrated his attention upon keeping clear of the *Bolsover,* already pitching and yawing wildly in the deep Atlantic swell.

The U-boat, hunting alone, had sighted the convoy as a smudge of smoke above the horizon. Increasing speed she closed the distance until the smudge translated itself into a moving forest of masts. Her commander carefully searched for signs of an escort. Finding only the patrolling A.M.C. he altered course and swept in a wide arc to lie ahead of his prey.

Submerged to periscope depth he waited until he could hear the drumming beat of engines, the steady pounding of a mass of propellers, and the leading ships loomed like mountains in the eye of the periscope.

The U-boat attacked from the blind side and raked the unprotected flank with a spread of four torpedoes.

The shock wave of the first explosion rippled through the convoy and the surrounding sea flamed red as the third ship in the first line suddenly broke in two, her bow and stern rising like a giant pair of scissors as she collapsed and sank. The sea boiled over her grave and the following ship, reacting too slowly, ploughed through the debris. There were no survivors. Forty men died in an instant.

Seconds later the fourth ship in the third line erupted into a sheet of yellow flame and rolled over on to her side. Then, keel up, her screw still churning, she slid beneath the surface leaving a trail of flotsam to mark her passing.

A torpedo leaped like a long slim fish across the trough of two waves, smashed into the rising wall of water, shot high in the air and exploded into a sheet of yellow flame. The concussion shattered the *Kentucky Minstrel*'s cab windows and flying fragments rang against the armoured pillboxes.

Mr Page ducked his head. 'Jesus!' he half-whispered. He was gingerly raising himself to his full height when the fourth torpedo struck. The ship ahead suddenly shuddered and stopped. Then she reared up and slewed to starboard to lie across the *Kentucky Minstrel*'s course.

'Hard a-port!' he shouted to the helmsman, rang the telegraphs to full ahead and gave a prolonged blast on the whistle.

The ship abreast on their port side was already swinging away as the *Kentucky Minstrel*, responding to the thrust of her twin propellers, plunged for the gap between the two ships.

'Easy – ease the helm.' He glanced at the quartermaster, a young seaman of freckled face and carrot hair, his lips moving as though in prayer as he stared glassily at the narrow canyon of heaving sea between the high stern and thrashing propeller of the portside ship and the slowly sinking stern of the stricken vessel.

'Bring her round easy, son,' said Page as calmly as he could. 'Starboard easy. Nice and easy now.' He spoke as though gentling a horse and was relieved to hear the faint whirr of spokes as the helm was put over and the bows began to swing through the slowly widening gap. For a few moments he felt as though he and the ship were fused into one living thing. Through the telegraph handles he could sense the pulse of the engines matching the beat of his own heart. Without conscious awareness he calculated drift and speed, rang the starboard engine to slow ahead and watched the wreck gliding passed. Her decks were already awash and he could see a group of men trying to lower a lifeboat as their ship listed to port. She rolled sluggishly as a wave lifted her stern and the lifeboat smashed to matchwood against the shipside. He saw men with life-jackets leaping over the side. The *Bolsover*, following in the *Kentucky Minstrel*'s wake, bore down upon the swimmers like an avalanche of steel, her bow wave burying them in a choking welter of water. Then the shipside chopped into the trough and they were no more.

The long drawn-out wail of the dying ship's whistle changed to a bubbling sigh as superstructure and funnel disappeared beneath the waves and the sea folded over to draw her down to the ocean floor a mile below.

The *Kentucky Minstrel* cleaved through a sea littered with wreckage and took up her position in the gap left by the sunken freighter. Page rang the telegraphs to slow ahead and expelled a long-held breath. 'Jesus Christ Almighty!' he swore softly.

'Amen to that,' said a voice at his shoulder. Page turned, startled, to find Turner's bulk looming in the wheelhouse door. 'No point in interfering,' he commented approvingly. 'Not when you had everything under control.'

'Thank you, sir,' said Page and fished out his cigarettes.

Turner selected one, exhaled a satisfying lungful of smoke, and surveyed the remaining ships of the convoy, rising and falling, butting their way through the long Atlantic rollers.

'Turns your stummick, don't it, Hubert?' He nodded toward the AMC fussing around the flock of ships. 'Unless that bowler-hat has his wits about him, he's going to get us all massacred.'

Page agreed. 'We're like ducks in a shooting gallery. We'd stand more chance on our own.'

A flutter of colour broke out from the AMC's signal halyards. Page raised his binoculars and read off the signal. 'Disperse and proceed independently,' he translated.

The convoy opened like the wide spread fingers of a hand,

the ships increasing speed to head for the illusory freedom of the sea.

'Full ahead,' said Turner, taking command. 'Steer one-eight-five.'

'Steer one-eight-five,' repeated the freckle-faced quartermaster, visibly relieved to be liberated from the task of keeping station among a hustling and jostling crowd of ships. Already the puffing and panting *Bolsover* had become his private nightmare. He spun the wheel and listened to the fast ticking of the gyro repeater as the ship's head swung to point at the wide empty horizon.

The *Bolsover,* as though seeking company, laboured astern, clouds of smoke belching from its funnel, its boilers straining under the pressure, its ancient frame shuddering from the clamour of its thundering engine.

The U-boat broke the surface and singled out his next victim.

The *Kentucky Minstrel* was moving away at speed, showing her stern and presenting a difficult target. The *Bolsover*, however, must have loomed up like a haystack for the torpedo hit her amidships. It punched a hole through her side and exploded in the bunkers. Hatch covers flew into the air, a shattered lifeboat hung from its davits. The funnel crumpled and the masts snapped in two. The explosion pulverised the bunker coal to dust: a vast dark cloud which hung for a moment above the ship and then, ignited by the fierce heat raging below, turned into an enormous fire-ball expanding at tremendous speed and incinerating everything in its path. Men seemed to burst into flames even as they ran; one, jumping over the side, became a flaming torch as he fell into the sea; an officer on the tilting bridge raised his arms preparatory to diving and was charred black in an instant; a group on the foredeck slumped and fell, melting like burning waxwork figures.

The surrounding sea flattened, hissed and boiled like a witches' cauldron. There was the rumble of an undersea eruption as the boilers exploded. Then the fire-ball rose high, spinning in its own vortex until it became a roaring column of fire surmounted by a swirling umbrella of smoke.

On the *Kentucky Minstrel*'s gun platform the gun-crew stood at their stations staring hypnotically at the cataclysmic destruction of the *Bolsover*. Only Corporal Jackson seemed unaffected as he continued to scan the restless sea for a sight of the enemy.

For a while the dustbin shape of the U-boat's conning tower remained hidden in the trough of the waves, then a flurry of spray betrayed its presence.

'Close up!' Corporal Jackson bawled. 'Load and train!'

Lowrie swung open the breach as Cloud wriggled into the trainer's seat, squinted through his telescope and rapidly rotated the traverse wheel.

Lofty rammed home shell and charge. 'Ready!'

'Breach closed!' yelled Lowrie. 'Sink the sodden bastard!'

Corporal Jackson estimated the distance. 'One thousand. Down fifty,' he told Jason, and lined up the bobbing conning tower in his sights.

'One thousand. Down fifty. Sights moving. Sights set,' Jason responded, turning the calibrated dials.

'On – on – on – on!' howled Cloud. 'Hurry up and bloody fire – I can't hold her here for ever!'

The ship's stern lifted and corkscrewed in the swell. Cloud lost sight of his quarry for a moment. 'Hang on a minute!' he shouted. 'I can't see the bastard! Christ, it's like trying to find a floating pillar-box!'

'Just tell me when she's on,' said Corporal Jackson calmly.

'On! I got her! On! On – on – on . . .' Cloud bellowed excitedly.

Corporal Jackson squeezed the trigger.

The gun erupted into a thunderclap of sound which almost ruptured their eardrums. A sheet of flame licked from the muzzle and, caught by the following wind, blew back to scorch skin and hair with its fiery breath.

The shell, packed with sixty pounds of high explosive, tore through the air at a velocity of two thousand feet per second and raised a fountain of water a couple of hundred yards beyond the U-boat.

'Over,' said Corporal Jackson laconically. 'Down a hundred.'

'Down a hundred,' repeated Jason, dazed. He moved like an automaton, his brain fogged with shock. The others were in a like state of near-paralysis. With the exception of Corporal Jackson there was not a man aboard who had ever experienced the ear-splitting thunder of a gun fired at close quarters. It came to them as a smashing madness of sound that scrambled a man's brains until he could no longer think.

A trained and disciplined gun-crew would continue firing steadily although the world around them was a bedlam of sound and a holocaust of fire. But the *Kentucky Minstrel*'s crew had long been subject to a different discipline, that of self-reliance cemented by the mortar of mutual understanding, so they stood stock-still, numbed with shock until Corporal Jackson's voice brought them to their senses.

'Load and train!' he barked. 'Load and train!'

There was a lick of orange flame from the U-boat followed by a thrumming overhead.

Corporal Jackson's jaw bulged. 'The sod wants a fight. He's shooting back. Move, you bleedin' donkeys – move!'

Galvanised into action they reloaded even as a succeeding shell threw a torrent of water over the ship's stern. The gun crashed again and again as they laboured like demons, ramming home shell and charge, oblivious of the roaring concussion and the choking reek of cordite, aware only of the demanding appetite of the gun.

Lowrie, who had developed a healthy respect for the savage recoil, took care to stand to one side and shuffle around as the gun traversed first one way then the other as both U-boat and *Kentucky Minstrel* took avoiding action. He opened and closed the breach, only pausing to bawl at the sweating Lofty to shift his lazy carcass, when a shell from the U-boat crumpled the starboard samson post and screamed over the bridge to explode in the sea a quarter of a mile ahead.

Only Corporal Jackson and Cloud witnessed the fall of shot. The U-boat, looming large in the magnification of their sighting telescopes, seemed to be surrounded by fountains of water. To the inexperienced Cloud every burst of spray appeared to be a near-miss, so he cursed and concentrated all his will on holding the wallowing cigar-shape in his sights while the ship's stern rose and fell and sky and water merged into a blur of foam-streaked waves and wind-riven scud. The submarine danced in and out of his vision like something demented, so he yelled '*On!*' when he should have held his peace, and called down maledictions upon the heads of friend and foe alike when the U-boat momentarily stood out blackly against the cross-hairs of his sights.

Corporal Jackson, on the other hand, had a cooler head. He watched the gouts of water leaping around the submarine, some falling ahead, some astern and many far too short. They were firing wildly, he realised, but all the steadiness in the world would not compensate for the battle-lust of a crew shooting from a jumping and bucking platform which gave an equal chance to a hit as a miss.

So Corporal Jackson continued to prime the breach with a detonator taken from his cartridge belt and methodically squeeze the trigger until a shell from the German's high-velocity 88 struck the port shipside rail and plunged into number 5 hatch. The force of the explosion blew the hatch covers into whirling splinters and hurled one of the massive steel supporting beams high in the air. The hold was stowed with crates of machine tools, the 'tween deck with Manchester cotton goods. Howling fragments of red-hot metal ripped jagged holes in the deck plating, a sheet of flame roared through the cratered opening and turned the 'tween deck into a raging furnace as the bales ignited.

The close stowage of her cargo saved the *Kentucky Minstrel* from further destruction by confining the force of the explosion to number 5 hold. Even so the blast warped the hatch coaming, sprung the shipside plates and brought the main topmast crashing down in a tangle of wire stays and standing rigging.

Able Seaman Lopez, a staunch supporter of Everton, invariably wore a bright blue shirt with the name of his favourite football club emblazoned across the back. He was a tubby little man of little imagination who functioned as one of the two ammunition suppliers. His mate was passing up another shell from the lockers at the base of the gun platform and Lopez was reaching for the cordite charge when his entire torso turned bright scarlet. Lopez died instantly as a length of splintered hatchboard ripped into his back, tearing through heart and lung before bursting through the chest wall in a froth of blood and bone.

His mate, Able Seaman Parslow, leaned away and vomited over the deck. Lofty, leaning down to take the cordite charge, saw it rolling away toward the wall of flame roaring from number 5 hold.

'The charge!' he yelled. 'Get the bleedin' charge!'

Parslow, raising a dazed head, gazed dully at Lofty's gesticulating arms then, suddenly alert to the danger, turned, stumbled toward the scorching heat, scooped up the charge and threw it to the waiting Lofty. Then, coughing and reeling, blackened with smoke and spattered with blood, he returned to his task of passing the ammunition.

Behind him the bos'n was already leading his fire control party to deal with the conflagration. The hose leaped and bucked like a live thing as the pumps sent a torrent of sea water gushing from the nozzle. Steam, mingled with smoke and flame, poured in a huge cloud from the shattered hatchway and, blown by a quartering wind, wreathed the entire midships section in a choking cloud of fumes.

Lopez's body lay in an ever-widening pool of blood which spread crimson tentacles as the ship rolled in the swell and shook from the renewed pounding of the gun. Then a couple of white-faced stewards hurried along and with averted faces dragged the body away while Ordinary Seaman Mason shakily took Lopez's place and bent to the work of handing up the heavy shells.

There were two types of shell stowed in the ammunition lockers. One, which they had been steadily firing, was of direct impact HE. The other was semi-armour piercing. It was one of these that Mason handed up.

Mason's shell – at it became known – was rammed into the breach, followed with its charge of cordite. The breach was primed, the detonator fired. The cordite exploded and the shell was propelled along the barrel of the gun. The lands of the rifling gripped the driving band of the shell and spun it faster and faster, flighting it through the air at twice the speed of sound. It took three and a quarter seconds to reach the U-boat. Then it struck just abaft of the conning tower, drilled a hole through the armour plating and exploded in the motor room.

The *Kentucky Minstrel*'s gun-grew saw a sun-burst of orange flame suddenly bloom against the slate-grey sky and immediately broke off the action to indulge in a bout of self-congratulatory cheering.

'Keep firing,' ordered Corporal Jackson. 'He isn't done for yet.'

As though to lend emphasis to his words the 88 spat

viciously again and again. Spouts of water clustered about the *Kentucky Minstrel*'s stern. One shell ricochetted from the surface and like a duck-stone skipped from wave to wave, turning end-over-end slowly enough for those on the bridge to follow it. It rose forty feet in the air and somersaulted high above the ship's foredeck to plunge into the sea off starboard bow.

'A miss is as good as a mile,' said Turner with more confidence than he felt, but knowing that the weight of responsibility demanded that he should appear clear-headed and calm.

Young Mr Dean, on the other hand, was feeling the strain. The incessant noise and nervous tension were wearing him down. He felt shaken and physically exhausted to the point where he could barely concentrate. His throat was dry and every thump from the 4.7 made him jump like a marionette on a string. The smoke from the now dully blazing number 5 hold made his eyes smart, and the sporadic flashes of light from the U-boat's gun made him grip the rail until his hand cramped as though welded to the metal. Part of his brain was praying that the awful din would stop, the terrible danger cease so that he might safely return to the arms of Olwyn. He had met her on leave while being dragged around by his proud parents on interminable visits to regiments of admiring friends and relatives. She was blonde, blue-eyed, as shy as a faun and plump as a partridge. Equally spellbound they had instantly tumbled headlong into the abyss of love-at-first-sight and, on his last night, kissing stickily in the discreet shadow of a dusty laburnum tree, she had sworn eternal fidelity and promised to write every day.

Dean clung to her image as a drowning man would clutch at a raft. She was the only centre of stability he could find in a world gone mad so, although every nerve shrieked for him to take refuge in the armoured pill-box, he remained at his post, peering through the swirl of smoke and willing himself to report on the progress of the battle, leaving his Captain free to concentrate on manoeuvring the ship.

A smoke-blackened Mr Page, his cap tilted at a rakish angle, trotted up the companion ladder, grinned at Dean and made his report to Turner.

'She'll do,' he stated laconically, and jerked a thumb toward the burning number 5 hold where he had been making an inspection. 'The fire's contained to the 'tween deck and the bos'n's party have it well under control. Blew off a few hatchboards, but no serious damage, apart from one man killed.'

'Who?'

'Lopez. I've had him hauled away and covered. He's a bit of a mess. Might put the others off their grub.'

Turner eyed Page thoughtfully, wondering if the young man was as callous as he seemed.

The Second Mate fumbled in his hip pocket and produced a cigarette packet. 'Smoke, sir?' he asked, then stared in surprise at the soaked and crumpled packet.

'Looks like a bale of wet hay,' commented Turner. 'How'd it happen, son?'

'I dunno,' said Page. 'I reckon I must have got drenched going below.' He crumpled the soggy cardboard and threw it away.

'I daresay Mr Dean can oblige us.' Turned raised his voice. 'Can't you, Mr Dean?'

Dean levered himself away from the rail and fished for his cigarettes. 'Aye, sir.'

Turner pointed to Page's left arm, the jacket sleeve charred and the hand red and swollen, raw with blisters. 'I wasn't referring to your Gold Flake, son. I meant that.'

Page gazed dumbly at his injured hand and shook his head. 'I've no idea. It must have been the ladder.' He took one of Dean's cigarettes, propped it between his lips, and leaned forward for a light.

He's as shocked as I am, Dean thought, and experienced a tremor of relief at the realisation that the gibbering ghost of terror poked fingers at others besides himself.

Turner helped himself to a lungful of smoke. 'Take him below, Mr Dean, and see to it that that wound is attended to.'

'Not on your life, sport,' said Page. 'I'll find my own way.' He marched away nursing his injured arm as a woman might cradle a baby.

'A promising young feller,' said Turner. 'Typical colonial. A heart as big as his boots.' He raised his binoculars to his eyes. 'Not like that feller. I reckon he's had enough.'

It was true. The U-boat had suddenly broken off the action and turned tail. Her Commander had been faced with a difficult decision. Although disabled and no longer able to dive he could still manoeuvre on the surface but, designed as an attack vessel, the U-boat's armament had been placed forward, so turning away meant he could not return the merchantman's fire. With seas slopping through the hole in the casing, the motor room a wreck with its attendant ratings mashed to pulp, there was only one logical decision left: to escape and fight another day.

The gap between the two adversaries widened as they moved apart at a combined speed of thirty knots. Then suddenly there was an additional thunder in the air. Great columns of water spouted around the fleeing U-boat as the A.M.C. joined the battle.

From the *Kentucky Minstrel* they could see the armed merchant cruiser's silhouette high above the distant curve of the horizon, her upper-works sparkling with twinkles of light as her six-inch guns flamed and boomed.

The first salvo straddled the U-boat. The second found its target. There was a bright flash just below the conning tower then, like some huge ungainly harpooned fish, the submarine rolled over and sank in a moil of air bubbles and oil. A subterranean explosion from below drove a final cascade of oily water upwards; then there was silence.

'Cease firing,' said Corporal Jackson.

Cloud leaned back in the trainer's seat and wiped his eyes. 'We got 'im,' he said hoarsely. 'We sank the bastard.'

Corporal Jackson thought otherwise but held his tongue, sagely considering that the illusion of success could harm no one while adding a fillip to morale.

The gun-crew stood around silent and uncertain in the sudden peace that had descended over the ship. Their chests heaved and they shook with fatigue. Stripped to the waist their bodies were rosy with flash burns and speckled with powder marks. They felt no exultation, only a great weariness that lidded their eyes and lent them the blank glassy stare of automata. One by one they lowered themselves to the gun-deck and sat or sprawled, languid and silent, absorbing the cooling breeze of the sea and the basking warmth of the sun while a last curl of smoke eddied from the muzzle of the gun and behind them the hose spluttered and hissed as it extinguished the final flickering glow of fire.

By evening new tarpaulins had been stretched over number 5 hold as a temporary measure until the carpenter could fashion new hatchboards; the engineers had inspected the jagged tears in the deck plating and almost completed their task of welding patches over the holes; Mr Page, with a neatly bandaged arm, had a more piratical look than ever; Mr Dean had written a long and loving letter to Olwyn; and Able Seaman Lopez, sewn into a canvas shroud, a plank of timber as his bier, waited to be launched into eternity.

The ship lay hove to, rolling gently in the Atlantic swell, silent except for the lap of the sea and the faint keening of the wind through the rigging. With the exception of the essential watch-keepers the entire crew had assembled to stand as mute witnesses to the ceremony.

Captain Turner's voice rose and fell like the surge of distant tides as he read from the Book of Common Prayer: 'We therefore commit his body to the deep,' he intoned, 'to be turned into corruption, looking for the resurrection of the body, when the sea shall give up her dead, and the life of the world to come, through our Lord Jesus Christ. Amen.'

He closed the prayer book with a snap and rolled his eyes heavenward as though seeking inspiration. Then he nodded to the bos'n and carpenter holding the inboard end of the plank.

'Dump him,' he said briefly.

The body slid forward and tumbled into the embrace of the sea. A trail of bubbles gulped to the surface; then there was nothing but the wide grey wilderness of water and the blue dome of the sky.

Turner returned his ancient cap to his head and squinted into the distance. 'He's joined a more select company than the Banjo Line,' he said. 'Carry on, gentlemen.'

Cloud looked aggrieved as he watched Turner stump away to his quarters and the engine responded to the ring of the telegraphs. 'Dump him!' he complained disgustedly. 'Dump him. What a way to go!'

'I thought he read a very nice service,' asserted the cook. 'He has a lovely reading voice, when he chooses to use it, has Sloppy.'

'Dump him,' Cloud repeated. 'What an end! He deserved better than that.'

'A more select company,' Albert mused reflectively. 'I thought Sloppy put that very well. He has quite a talent for expression has our Sloppy.'

CHAPTER SIX

THE *Kentucky Minstrel* swayed through the night, butting aside the marching seas.

Mr Dean, elbows propped on the bridge rail, watched the dark outline of the forecastle rising and falling against the oncoming ranks of white-topped waves. Beyond the pale blur of the crests there was complete darkness with only an occasional star pricking through thickening cloud to distinguish sea from sky.

The wind soughed, gaining in strength, and a hiss of spray rattled across the foredeck. The engines beat their steady muted rhythm and, high on the foremast, snug in the newly acquired steel crow's nest, the lookout man raised his voice in a softly lilting melody.

And thanks again, for leading me on
The road to Paradise.
We lost our way,
But still I must convey,
My thanks.

A door opened and the stuttering stammer of incoming morse signals confused the night air. Then the door closed and a bulky shadow moved against the dim outline of the bridge housing.

'Cloud is in good voice,' said Paddy Phelan.

Dean grinned. 'No doubt dreaming of the luscious Sonia.'

'I wonder if she really exists?'

'I doubt it. According to Cloud she has legs like Betty Grable, more top hamper than Jane Russell and the appetites of a Messalina. A figment of the imagination.'

'Either that or he keeps her under the stairs and only lets

her out to bay at the moon.' Phelan held out a pale rectangle of paper. 'Got a CQ for you, Third Mate.'

Dean squinted into the darkness. 'What does it say?'

'We're in the path of a storm front. Heavy weather on the way.'

'They are a bit out of date,' said Dean. 'The wind's been strengthening over the past hour.' He hunched his shoulders and turned up the collar of his bridge coat as the wind growled and the sea rose like an many-fanged beast. 'How are your two oppos making out?' he asked conversationally, hoping to lure Paddy into whiling away a dull half-hour.

'Blossom is still a bit green about the gills,' said Phelan. He jerked a thumb toward the wireless shack. 'I've been keeping an eye on him. First trip and fresh from wireless school, he takes down morse as though trying to decipher the Rosetta stone.'

Flower and Martin were two new additions to the ship's complement. Until the outbreak of war the ship's radio communications had been handled solely by one operator who worked a complicated routine, his hours being governed by G.M.T. which was invariably well out of step with ship time. With the opening of hostilities, however, it became essential for all ships to keep a continuous listening watch. As a result the wireless schools were bursting with eager young men, crammed into a six months' course and then launched as junior Radio Officers to be scattered far and wide over the oceans of the world.

Of such were Flower and Martin, Third and Second Radio Officers respectively. Young Flower had been immediately christened Cherry Blossom because of a girlish complexion which tended to acquire a damask blush at moments of stress.

Martin was of different calibre. A swarthy man of saturnine features, he had spent three years at sea as a steward and, an opportunist to the fingertips, recognised the demand for wireless operators as a short cut to the much-coveted officer status. He was inclined to give himself airs and graces and bully his unfortunate junior who would blush like a rose at Martin's pointed sarcasms.

'My Second is the problem,' said Paddy. 'He's a bastard. Runs poor Cherry Blossom ragged.'

'I shouldn't worry,' said Dean philosophically. 'There's a bad apple in every barrel. Sloppy will soon sort him.'

'He won't,' replied Paddy firmly. 'It's my department and that makes him my pigeon, not Sloppy's. Goodnight, Third Mate.' He stalked away to disappear into the darkness.

Dean sighed. The war seemed to make everyone touchy. He wandered into the comparative warmth of the wheelhouse, stared unbelievingly at the face of the chronometer, a pale shape illuminated only by the blue pilot light. Time seemed to be standing still. The gyro repeater was ticking faster as the ship pitched and yawed, dipping thunderously into the troughs and rising again over the increasing weight of water pushing against the bows.

'She's taking a half turn of port hellum,' said Lowrie helpfully. He raised his unblinking stare from the shaded light of the binnacle compass. The bows smashed into an unseen roller and a ghostly fountain rose twenty feet into the air. 'The trouble is, I canna see a bleedin' thing ahead.'

Dean understood. A good quartermaster, given a view of the sea, could anticipate the lift of every wave and, by paying off the head, allow the ship to slide down the larger troughs and ease over the crests. It made life easier for everyone. Saved the ship from buckled plates, the engineers from the laborious task of keeping the revolutions steady as the propellers thrashed clear, and allowed the watch below to sleep undisturbed by the constant clanking of the steering quadrant. The Q.M.s were professionals and took a pride in their skills. The surly Lowrie would swear and curse and fight the ship as though every comber were a personal enemy to be defeated at any cost. Old Pat Conroy, on the other hand, would croon softly to himself, 'There, my beauty, up you go, over and over you go,' and the ship would respond to his gentling touch.

'Do your best,' said Dean and drifted back to the bridge to dream of the seductive Olwyn as the wind screamed out of the black night and the sea leaped in fury at the unattainable sky.

By one bell, as the stand-by man called the twelve-to-four watch, the sea had risen in a fury of leaping, jarring wave crests. It surged high over the weather rail to roar across the foredeck in a welter of foam. The wind had acquired an eldritch screech and the night darkness was an inky black smeared with streaks of white. The ship laboured and took enormous bites out of the onrushing waves. Spindrift rose as high as the bridge and lashed Dean's face with a thousand icy whips.

A wail from the engine room voice pipe took him back into the temporary refuge of the wheeelhouse.

'We'll need to drop back a few revs,' said a disembodied voice.

'If you are afraid of the damp down there, I'll ring down to half,' said Dean. As the Fourth Engineer was little more than Dean's own age he calculated that he could afford the occasional witticism.

The voice chuckled. 'Just stop bumping us about, sonny,' it said, 'and remember – if you hear frogs croaking, we're ashore.'

Dean swung the telegraph handles and prayed that the resultant jangling would not arouse Turner from his slumbers.

He was soon disillusioned. An apparition appeared on the bridge. It wore an ankle-length bridge-coat, a relic of a bygone age, over a woollen dressing gown. Striped flannel pyjama ends peeped slyly from frayed cuffs and spilled over knitted bedsocks and a pair of thick-soled carpet slippers.

'A bit wild on top,' Turner commented as though commending the Third Mate for a particularly gratifying rearrangement of natural forces. 'There's not many young fellers of your limited experience who would have hesitated to roust out the Master at the first sign of a blow, passing on the responsibility to older and wiser heads.'

'I was about to give you a call, sir,' said Dean, unsure whether to accept the remark as a compliment or a reprimand.

'Just remember that it will always get worse before it gets better,' said Turner mildly.

The sea roared and thundered, the deck canted beneath their feet and the constant spray became a cloud of blinding mist. The ship creaked and groaned, while the watch below swallowed tin cups of hot sweet tea and buttoned themselves into oilskins in readiness for yet another battle with their old enemy, the sea.

At eight bells Dean thankfully handed over his watch to

Page and stumbled below with the wind gusting to gale force.

By two bells driving rain had added to their discomfort. Hissing across the decks in icy sheets, it drummed on the taut lifeboat covers and enveloped the hot funnel casing in clouds of steam. Around them was nothing but the wastes of the ocean; a spongy greyness whipped into streaks of white foam; and beyond it the chaos of the night.

Page, wearing oilskins and sou'wester, glistened like a wet fish. He banged gloved hands together and bent at the knees to ease the cramp in his calves. His feet felt like leaden weights encased in blocks of ice, his shoulders ached with constant hunching and his face seemed to have been flayed to the bone by the whiplash of wind and rain. He ducked as a towering greybeard loomed ahead, broke over the forecastle head to pour over the foredeck in twin torrents. It smashed against the midships housing with a shock that shuddered throughout the ship and hurled a vast sheet of salt-laden spray high over the bridge. The ship bucked and reared, threw long sluices of water over her sides, then lifted her bows to smash into the next oncoming wave.

Page stole a glance into the wheelhouse and the fire-fly glow of a cigarette which, momentarily illuminating Turner's face, lent him something of the look of a pudgy Mephistopheles.

One of the bridge phones rang. 'I'll take it,' said Turner and flapped across to the Radio Room phone. He spoke briefly then trudged to the open wheelhouse door. 'God love us,' he said. 'I don't envy you fellers. It's cold enough to freeze the marrow of an unborn child out here. Second Sparks on the phone. Says he's got a message for us. Most Secret, he says, but it's probably one one of them bowler-hats reminding us to douse all lights at sunset. Off you go Hubert, I'll take the bridge.'

Turner returned to his vigil in the shelter of the wheelhouse while Page fumbled his way around to the Radio shack.

He pushed open the door, stepped into inky blackness and the crackle of morse as the light switched off automatically. Closing the door tripped the switch and the unaccustomed glare from the solitary bulb almost blinded him.

He shook his head and blew away the raindrops trickling

down his face. A puddle of water formed at his feet to darken the worn carpet with a widening stain. The atmosphere was stuffy and hazy with cigarette smoke. The morse signals spluttered and whined, rising and falling as the main aerial swayed with the pendulum swing of the masts.

Second Radio Officer Martin sat at his ease, sprawled comfortably in his swivel chair, headphones draped loosely about his neck and one leg stretched out on the desk. He treated Page to an unctuous smirk and waved a hand to a message pad.

'Don't stand there dripping, Second Mate, you make the place look untidy.'

He probably meant it as a pleasantry, but Page had little liking for Martin whom he privately considered to be a smarmy-natured dingbat too big for his boots.

He scowled murderously at the lolling figure, squelched toward the desk, removed his gloves and splattered Martin with a shower of droplets.

'Be careful,' yelped Martin removing his leg and dabbing at his shirt.

'Get stuffed,' said Page and quickly read the printed block capitals of the message.

'You dragged me around here for this?' he demanded.

'I can't leave the wireless room,' said Martin sullenly. 'You know that.'

'What's the matter with the phone? Or can't you read your own writing?' Page was justifiably irritated. He had lost his night vision and, partly thawed out, would now need to re-acclimatise himself to the ferocity of the storm.

'It is prefixed Urgent and Most Secret,' Martin protested. 'Strictly speaking, it is for the Master's eyes only.'

'In which case you should have hauled yourself off your arse and humped it around to him,' snapped Page.

'I can't leave the wireless room unattended,' repeated Martin obstinately.

'Come off it. You're just bloody bone idle.' Page tore off the sheet from the message pad, unbuttoned his oilskin and stuffed it into his uniform jacket. 'And self-important,' he added. 'Next time, read it over the phone.'

Page blundered out into the wild darkness and, groping ahead like a blind man, found his way back to the wheel-house.

He made his way to the chartroom followed by Turner.

Page took off his oilskins and sou'wester and spread the chart on the chart table.

'It's a change of destination, sir. Instead of proceeding to Halifax we are to rendezvous with convoy HX84 at position 51.25 north. 43.22 west.' He busied himself with ruler and dividers. 1,338 miles. Course nor'east by east. E.t.a . . .' Page shrugged. 'The Admiralty expect us to make contact at noon, November 5th.'

'Typical of bowler-hats,' said Turner. 'They think the ocean's a billiard table and a ship runs on wheels like a train.' He examined the chart as the ship heaved and lurched and the barometer swung crazily in its gimbals. 'We'll never make it, Hubert, not in this weather. Lay off a course to bring us up a day's run ahead of them. They should have escorts scouting ahead. Shouldn't be too difficult to find us, even for gold-braided bowler-hats.'

By noon the following day the worst of the weather had blown itself out. The sea still heaved, foam-flecked and angry, but the wind had dropped and shifted to the south-west. A watery sun broke through the ravaged sky and painted tattered banners of cloud in soft pinks and yellows. The *Kentucky Minstrel,* now laden with case oil from Philadelphia and a miscellaneous cargo of dried eggs, evaporated milk, tinned bacon, lard, and canned meats from New York and Boston, pushed steadily north-east.

On the fourth day they arrived at their self-appointed rendezvous with a giant sun setting in the west and turning the sea into a lake of fire. Stars as sharp as crystal began to glitter in the deepening sky. A northerly wind blowing straight from Greenland smelled of ice and cut like a knife.

'It'll be as black as the inside of the devil's boots in half an hour,' commented Turner. 'Too late to find 'em now. I'm off below for a thinks. Call me if you bump into anything, Harold.'

Furlong bade him 'goodnight', and concentrated upon searching the horizon through his binoculars. There was nothing but the long oily swell of the sea and the pale wash of the ship's wake as she moved at half speed, crossing and re-crossing the expected path of the oncoming convoy.

Dean relieved him at eight bells with the great wheel of

stars pricking the velvet blackness. He, in his turn, passed an uneventful watch until Page arrived. Then, as though it were the witching hour, the heavens spun a web of gold and lowered a curtain of fire to cover the northern skies.

Page and Dean stood spellbound as the Aurora Borealis curled and shimmered, changed shape and colour. Spectral folds swayed as though moved by an invisible wind. Drapes of amethyst and malachite hung above their heads. Striations of sapphire and topaz glowed with an unearthly light. The world fell silent. Only the muted rhythm of the engines and the faint susurration of the bow wave broke the stillness.

For twenty minutes the ship sailed across a purple sea, then, as suddenly as it had begun, the display ended. The vast curtains disappeared as though whisked away by an omnipotent hand leaving only a quiet arc of softly pulsating white light far to the north.

Dean left the bridge and retired to his cabin where, rocked in the cradle of his bunk, he listened to the lullaby of the sea and planned a masterly seduction of Olwyn. Nestling in the bottom of his suitcase, carefully gift-wrapped, were an assortment of feminine fripperies calculated to weaken the resolve of any but the most adamant of young ladies. He fell contentedly asleep to dream of a bewitching Olwyn, caparisoned like a May horse, leading him through a forest of magic trees to a bower frothing with lacy lingerie.

He awoke to a new day and the steward's insistent voice.

'Seven bells, sir. Guy Fawkes day. And I've brung your tea. Norrer cloud in the sky and no sign of the convoy. Pussenly speaking I'm not sorry. 'ad enough of convoys, outward bound. I reckon we're best off on our own. 'ash, griddle cakes and bacon-'n-egg for breakfast. Are yiz awake, sir?'

Dean, dragged from Olwyn's willing arms, mumbled that he was, levered himself from his bunk and began to lather his face from the can of hot water left by the steward.

Promptly at eight bells he relieved the Mate, resolutely banished all thoughts of Olwyn from his mind, checked the ship's head against her new course and entered the chartroom to study the chart. The ship's course was neatly plotted showing that they were steaming in a series of Zs, altering to a new leg every two hours.

Returning to the bridge he climbed to the monkey island

and carefully scanned all around the horizon. To the east a saffron dawn mottled the sky. A solitary tuft of cloud chased its own shadow across the sea. The wind blew bitingly cold. The surrounding ocean was a vast saucer, empty, as smooth as glass with only the ripples of the bow wave to disturb its surface. Of the expected convoy there was no sign.

The winter sun rose a few degrees above the horizon, its feeble rays barely of sufficient strength to dispel the rime of hoar frost coating the rails and running gear.

Cloud relieved Lowrie at the wheel. Dean altered course from S.E. to N.W. Turner stumped on to the bridge, silently smoked one of Dean's cigarettes, then returned to his private lair below.

At midday, with the sun reaching its zenith, the officers congregated on the bridge to take the noonday sight and Dean thankfully handed over the watch to Page.

Turner scowled at his sextant. 'Enough is enough,' he pronounced decisively. 'One of them bowler-hats has made a cock-up. Lay off a new course, Mr Page. We're heading for home.'

'Bring her round and steer due east,' Page told the Q.M. and rang the telegraphs to Full Ahead.

In the chartroom, plotting their new course, he tried to stifle a sense of guilt at the recollection of himself and the Third Mate totally absorbed in the display of the northern lights. The convoy could easily have passed unobserved. The ocean was big enough to swallow an entire fleet. The convoy could have sailed past unnoticed just beyond the rim of the horizon. A few short miles would have been sufficient to hide it behind the curvature of the earth. But a sharp lookout might have spotted something: a curl of smoke blotting out a star; the gleam of a mast etched against the blackness: the muffled drumming of distant engines.

With the growing conviction that the convoy must lie somewhere ahead he concentrated upon the task of calculating its probable course, speed and position. At length, satisfied that he had left nothing to chance and secretly hoping that he be proved wrong, that the small Armada would be trailing somewhere astern, he marked their noon position, drew a neat course line on the chart and instructed the buck-toothed Lofty, leaning somnolently over the wheel, to steer oh-six-four. Then he took to perambulating the length of the bridge, trudging from one side of the ship to the other as though performing a ritualistic penance for a mortal sin.

The pale sun crawled like a yellow eye rolling in an empty socket. The wind freshened slightly and ruffled the sea into a network of wrinkles. To the north-west a smear of cloud promised rain before nightfall.

At six bells the steward brought him a cup of tea and two arrowroot biscuits. He drank the tea and gave the biscuits to the helmsman. Ten minutes later the lookout man, staring through misted binoculars from his perch high on the foremast, reported sighting a ship.

'About three points off the starboard bow. Hull down over the horizon. Heading on the same course as us, I reckon. She's a motor ship. Three island. Looks like a Scandahoovian. A Swede from her lines. Hang on . . .' His voice squawked triumphantly through the telephone. 'There's another . . . and another . . . We've found 'em. It's the convoy!'

Page thanked him, told him to keep a sharp lookout for the accompanying escort and cradled the phone. He bent on their recognition signals and their convoy number, HX84, and ran up the flags to the signal yard. Then he rang down to the Captain's quarters, repeated the information and, picking up the powerful three-inch telescope, swung up the vertical ladder to the monkey island above.

The dusk was already drawing across the eastern sky and Page found time to thank his lucky stars that the sharp-eyed lookout had spotted the convoy just in time. Otherwise they might easily have overtaken it in the dark or, worse, have blundered into the rear ranks.

Steadying himself against a supporting stanchion, he peered into the gathering darkness until his eyes watered and his vision blurred. Where in hell's name are the bloody escorts, he wondered, and then, suddenly sharp and clear, he found the answer.

The superstructure of a large passenger liner loomed large and clear in the magnification of the lens. He caught a flicker of blue from the ensign flying at the stern. The ship was turning beam on and evidently making a sweep toward them. He recognised her immediately from her many visits to Australia when, with bunting flying, bands playing, her decks packed with passengers and emigrants, she steamed between Sydney heads.

Page took his eye from the telescope and found that he could now sight her as a speck on the horizon to the north of the convoy. He called down to Turner on the bridge below.

'Only one escort, sir. An AMC. Looks like one of Aberdeen and Commonwealth's Bay boats. I think she's the *Jervis Bay.*'

The AMC soon became visible to all as, standing high out of the water, she headed toward them.

Turner scanned her array of decks through his binoculars and counted off her armament of seven 6-inch guns, four mounted forward and three aft.

'God love us,' he muttered. 'Thirty-odd ships huddled together like a gaggle of geese with nothing to protect them but a floating gin palace.'

The AMC acknowledged the *Kentucky Minstrel*'s recognition signals and ordered her to close the convoy and take station at the rear, then she made a 180-degree turn and swept away to the north to resume her former station.

It took *Kentucky Minstrel* an hour to overtake the plodding convoy. They were making their approach from the port quarter when Page spotted a blink of light flickering from the *Jervis Bay*'s searchlight.

'She's signalling,' he said. 'Calling someone up.' He screwed the telescope to his eye and focused carefully, first on the AMC then slowly to the north and east. The horizon leaped and danced emptily across his vision, then suddenly a long, sleek grey shape swam into view. He focused critically until every detail stood out sharp and clear.

'Oh, Jesus,' he breathed. 'Oh, dear sweet Jesus!'

He turned an ashen face toward Furlong and Turner, tried to articulate through a mouth suddenly as dry as a lime kiln.

'It's a Jerry,' he almost whispered. 'A Jerry pocket battleship.'

Even as he spoke the thunder of the AMC's siren broke the stillness and the entire convoy turned and wheeled to the south, fanning out like radiant spokes from a central hub.

'No point in following 'em,' said Turner. 'He'll pick 'em off like sitting ducks.' He singled out the growing mass of rain cloud to the north-west. 'That's our best bet. Hard aport, quartermaster. Mr Furlong, ring the engine room for as many revs as they can give us.' He jabbed a finger on the alarm button. Bells pealed and the crew came tumbling out to take up their pre-arranged action stations.

The *Kentucky Minstrel* made a wide circle, leaving a trailing crescent of foaming wake to mark her passage. The convoy was now a scatter of ships plunging south to escape the murderous guns of the German raider. The AMC lay off their starboard beam, smoke belching from her funnel as she raced toward the enemy.

'Christ Almighty!' said Page. 'He's taking her on!'

'He don't stand a prayer,' said Turner. 'Not with those pop-guns.'

The *Jervis Bay* dropped a trail of smoke floats and opened fire with her 6-inch guns trained at their highest elevation. At a distance of eight miles her shells fell far short. But the attack was enough to divert the battleship from her prey. She turned on her tormentor with the full fury of her 11-inch guns.

The contest was hopelessly unequal. In a few moments the *Jervis Bay*'s bridge disappeared in a smother of fire and smoke. Her gunnery control was smashed to pulp. Hit after hit pounded her upperworks into a tangle of steel and rubble. And still she tried to close with the enemy, the thump of her remaining 6-inch guns reverberating across the open sea and mingling with the crash of the battleship's broadsides.

Engulfed in flame and smoke she refused to sink but continued to hold her adversary at bay while the convoy raced to the sheltering darkness of the encroaching night. The surrounding sea, erupting into fiery fountains, reflected a furnace glow as torrents of steel poured into the stricken ship. Then, with her steering shot away, her engine room flooded, all but one of her guns silenced, the *Jervis Bay* reeled like a punch-drunk boxer, lost all headway and from being a fighting ship became in an instant a motionless, burning hulk.

'It's all over,' said Turner softly. 'God help them.'

Furlong emerged from the chartroom carrying a volume of ship identification issued by the Admiralty. 'She must be the *Admiral Scheer,*' he told them. 'Pocket battleship. 10,000 tons. Carries an armament of six 11-inch guns in triple turrets and a secondary armament of eight 5.9s. Top speed believed to be in the region of thirty knots.'

Turner gazed at the dim shapes of the scattering convoy. 'With that speed and range he'll be in among 'em like a fox in a hen-house.'

The *Admiral Scheer*'s silhouette stood out clearly against the blazing inferno that was once the *Jervis Bay*. Unaccountably the German continued to fire at his helpless foe as though in a blind rage at being opposed by so presumptuous a challenger. His guns continued to blaze and hammer long after the *Jervis Bay* had been reduced to a shambles of tormented metal and the stench of blood and burning wreckage rose in a funeral pyre of flame and smoke.

But every crashing broadside gave the widely scattering ships an added margin of safety.

'That feller's a raving maniac,' Turner growled angrily. 'He'll earn no medals this trip.' He turned abruptly to Page. 'Mr Page, tell Sparks to transmit an RRRR message: Convoy HX84 under attack by enemy pocket battleship *Admiral Scheer*. Send it in clear and give our position. Got it?'

'Aye, sir,' replied Page, his heart stumbling into his mouth as he understood the implications.

'It's the least we can do,' said Turner heavily. 'That bowler-hat has earned his coppers today. Poor devil, he must have had the heart of a lion.'

Page made his way to the radio room and found a white-faced Martin hovering by the door.

'What the hell's going on?' he asked anxiously.

'It's a Jerry battleship shooting up the convoy,' Page told him brutally. He walked to the desk and scribbled the message on the pad. 'You are to send this. Plain language. Full power.'

Martin stared at the signal. 'A battleship? I can't . . . The moment I start transmitting he'll blow us out of the water!'

'Hard luck,' said Page unfeelingly. 'Some poor sods out there have just died to give you the opportunity, so get on with it.'

Martin reached below the desk and ran up the rheostat. The alternator hummed and the enormous power valves lit up and glowed behind their little glass portholes. He stretched out a shaking hand toward the key and then stopped.

'I can't.' He looked piteously at Page. 'I can't . . .'

The door opened and Paddy Phelan rolled in. 'He's still knocking hell out of the poor old *Jervis Bay*,' he began conversationally, then his eyes took in the situation. 'What's the problem?'

Page jerked a thumb. 'He is. Sloppy wants this message transmitting. Your Second thinks he knows better.'

'Shift your carcass,' snapped Paddy, hauled Martin from the chair and took his place. He drew the message pad toward him, settled his rimless spectacles firmly upon his nose, and commenced to transmit at a cool, calm and measured pace. The high-pitched *parp-parp* of morse filled the room as Martin, green with the sickness of fear, lurched out on to deck.

'See you, Paddy,' said Page laconically with his stomach churning and bile rising into his throat.

'Save a place for me,' returned Phelan without a break in the rhythm of his keying.

Page left him, a fat Irish leprechaun hunched over the desk, his hand tapping out a steady stream of morse.

He returned to the bridge feeling the prickle of rain on his face to find that the *Admiral Scheer* had at last broken off combat and was now in hot pursuit of the convoy.

'She's left it too late,' Turner enunciated with satisfaction.

The words had barely left his mouth when a star-shell turned night into eerie day. Spouting flames were leaping from the *Scheer's* guns. The *Jervis Bay*, now reduced to a blazing hulk, rolled over, capsized and sank. The fleeing ships of the convoy suddenly stood out stark and clear as the pocket battleship bore down upon them like a wolf upon the fold.

A ship exploded into a mass of blazing incandescent fragments. A tanker swung off course, swallowed in flame. The star-shell spluttered and died as it parachuted into the sea. Then the long fingers of the *Scheer*'s searchlights wandered across the dark face of the sea and singled out another victim. A rain of shells from one of the triple turrets smashed her into oblivion.

Spouts of fire illuminated the darkness. A second, third and fourth star-shell burst in the sky. A column of water soared high off the *Kentucky Minstrel*'s quarter.

'Can't reach us,' Turner pronounced. 'He carries his heavy

stuff forward. Only to be expected from the Nazis – put all their eggs in one basket.'

A fine mist of rain drifted across the sea. Star-shells bloomed like evil flowers. The Scheer's guns crashed and crashed again.

Turner swung his binoculars toward the distant convoy. Around one ship the sea boiled with shell-splashes. Then suddenly she erupted into a gush of flame and seemed to fall apart and disintegrate into a volcanic spew of debris. The concussion rolled over the waves and rattled the wheelhouse windows in their frames.

'Ammo ship,' grunted Turner and transferred his gaze to the *Scheer.* The long lean shape was now about seven miles distant, the gap between them steadily widening. After the first couple of half-hearted ranging shots with her secondary armament she had ceased firing upon the lone *Kentucky Minstrel* and now concentrated all her attention upon the remaining thirty-seven escaping ships. Then, beneath the yellow brilliance of the star-shells, he saw the *Scheer*'s silhouette change as she made a fast turn to starboard.

She's coming for us, he thought, and his stomach muscles tightened into knots as he waited for the warning flame of her forward guns followed by the approaching shriek of her devastating 11-inch shells. He continued to stare fixedly at the swiftly changing outline while his brain, as though already separate from his will, calculated trajectory, distance and time. *Seven miles. Each shell climbing to a height of about a mile. E.t.a., say twenty seconds. Three shells bracketing the ship. Wait until they fire, then shorten the range. They'll not be expecting that.* But he knew it to be hopeless. The second salvo would catch them even as they turned. Modern range-finders and director sights could calculate faster than any human brain.

Turner straddled his legs, clenched his fists behind his back, pulled in his chins and prepared to face the enemy. Then unbelievingly he saw the warship's turrets swinging away to point in the opposite direction. Her heavy guns flashed and boomed and he realised the purpose of the *Scheer*'s manoeuvre.

'He's trying to outflank 'em,' he stated. 'But he's left it too late. If he'd had his wits about him he could have collared the lot.' He sniffed disparagingly. 'But what can you expect from a feller who takes his orders from a prancing half-wit who looks like Charlie Chaplin?'

The rain closed in and turned to sleet. Clusters of star-shells probed the sky, weaving a web of ghostly luminosity beyond the swirling curtains of white snow. The *Scheer*'s broadsides were a distant thunder, the rate of fire slackening and then ceasing altogether leaving an eerie silence with only the faint glow of burning ships to signpost its passing.

'Got three or four, but he's lost the rest.' Turner wafted drifting snowflakes from his vision. 'This front is moving north and east. We'll stay with it as long as possible. We got other worries besides tin-pot battleships.'

Paddy Phelan ambled on to the bridge. 'Message transmitted and acknowledged,' he announced cheerfully. He jerked a thumb towards the wireless room. 'It's bedlam in there. Everyone's joined in. Jammed his D/F. I'll bet his W.T.O.'s are going crazy. They'll think they've stuck their heads into a hive of bees.'

'Good work, Paddy,' said Turner. 'Now our fellers can hunt him. Give him a taste of his own medicine. I suppose you didn't bring your cigarettes with you?' he asked hopefully. 'It's a rare solace, is tobacco, on these occasions.'

The sleet turned to snow and by daybreak the *Kentucky Minstrel*'s decks were piled with drifts; a fine white powder which crunched and squeaked beneath the feet and blew miniature whirlwinds between the housing; it stung their faces, numbed hands and feet and gathered in folds and drapes about masts and rigging. The wind came fitfully in sudden gusts and lulls. The sea chopped at steel plates coated with ice and the spray froze in mid-air.

Cloud slithered to the foot of the foremast, grabbed one of the rungs of the steel ladder and felt the bite of cold through his gloves. He climbed rapidly, his oilskin billowing about his legs, until he disappeared into a white world. At the head of the ladder the trap door in the crow's nest opened and Lowrie's muffled features peered down.

'Where the 'ell have you been?' he demanded. 'You're a minute late. It's bloody freezin' up here.'

Cloud heaved himself up by the grab rail and kicked the trap shut.

'You don't know when you're well off,' he said cheerfully. 'It's a bobby's job up here.'

'I canna see the sense to it,' grumbled Lowrie. 'Ye canna see a blind thing and it's cold enough to freeze the balls off an alleycat.'

'It's marvellous,' said Cloud. 'Just like Christmas. And here you are, all on your tod, snug as a bug in a rug, and no toffee-nosed officers to bother you.'

Lowrie raised the trap door and lowered himself through the opening. 'It's Dixie Dean's watch,' he said grumpily. 'And Dixie Dean don't never bother nobody.'

'It's Sloppy's watch as well,' Cloud reminded him. 'Mind your head.' He dropped the trap door and was rewarded with a yelp and a string of curses from the descending Lowrie. 'Sorry mate,' he grinned, and settled himself comfortably in his tiny enclosed world.

The crow's nest was a semi-circle of steel welded to the mast. It measured six feet at its widest and its height reached to a man's shoulders. The forepart was given added protection by a canvas dodger over which the lookout could peer at the surrounding sea. Above his head hung a roof of armoured steel. His only communication with the outer world was an old-fashioned magneto phone connected to the bridge. It was, in Cloud's view, a peaceful world made the more desirable by being insulated from prying eyes by a blanket of snow.

He peered out into a fog of whiteness with visibility down to zero. Satisfied, he unfastened his oilskins and removed a length of canvas wrapped around his body like a cummerbund. Making one end fast to the grab rail, the other to one of the small dodger stanchions, he quickly slung a makeshift hammock. Settling himself comfortably Cloud fished out a copy of *Men Only*, lit a cigarette and exhaled a curling spiral of blue smoke.

'Perfect,' he murmured contentedly. 'Perfect.'

Four days later the depression swung away to the east and the *Kentucky Minstrel*, bearded with ice and snow, broke out into a sea of glass glittering beneath a turquoise sky. The sun glared with a brassy eye, the wind dropped and the air temperature fell to twenty below. The long, slowly rolling billows sluiced over the shipside and froze the rails into bulwarks of ice, setting the crew the unending task of hacking and chipping with axes and scrapers, knowing as they toiled that their bone-numbing misery would start all over again as each wave lipped the deck.

The cold cut through to the marrow. The bulkiest of clothing seemed to offer no protection. The exposed skin of their faces became blistered and seared as though burned by fire. They brought out steam hoses and the ice melted and reformed into translucent layers of molten glass. There was no moisture in the air, no heat in the sun. The ice held the ship in an unrelenting grip until even her engines seemed to be panting for life.

This was their real enemy. The empty, mindless sea. The war no more than an unwelcome interlude in their age-old battle with a foe that knew no mercy.

It was Conroy who first sighted the mermaid. A heavy scarf wound around his wizened monkey-face, eyes puckered against the cold, he stood in the crow's nest, rhythmically shifting his weight from one foot to the other, his gaze continually searching every ripple of water from horizon to horizon.

He picked up the phone and rapidly wound the handle. 'There's something over to starboard. Bearing about four and a half points. No more'n half a mile. Can't quite make it out. Might be a dead fish, belly up.'

'What is it, Mr Dean?' asked Turner as the Third Mate cradled the phone.

'Conroy reports an object about four points on the starboard hand, sir.' Dean lifted the binoculars dangling against his chest as Turner walked across to join him. Turner raised his and together they scanned the wide expanse of sea.

At first they saw nothing beyond a freezing wilderness of water; then a swelling billow raised her gently into view.

She waved and smiled, beckoning siren-like with a long white arm. Dean's blood ran cold as childhood fantasies rose from the deeper recess of his mind. *Oh, my God,* he thought. *It's a bloody mermaid*!

The figure, unmistakably female, lolled in the ocean as though it were her natural element. Long golden tresses, combed by the sea, swayed about her shoulders as she rose from the wave and plunged beneath the surface with the flip of an unmistakable tail. She reappeared tail first and slid down the trough of the next wave with wide-open arms.

'Poor creature,' muttered Turner. 'War's a damnable business. Especially for women. Put those glasses down, boy!' he snapped abruptly. 'Haven't you ever seen a naked body before? Let the lady rest in peace, God rest her soul.'

Dean slowly lowered his binoculars realising that it was no mermaid, but a natural woman, unclothed by the long slow caress of the sea. Only one stocking remained, elongated and unaccountably wound around both legs, the toe and heel giving the appearance of a small flipper. Preserved by the cold, washed by the waves, the body rose and fell, waving stiff arms as though in a long farewell.

An hour later they came across the crystal boat. At first they took it to be drift ice; a tiny, miniature iceberg, sparkling in the sun. It slid past close enough for all to see. The chippers and scrapers stopped work and lined the shipside to stare at the grisly tableau.

It was a ship's boat encased in ice. They counted a dozen figures, some seated on the thwarts, bowed as though frozen in the act of rowing with invisible oars; others curled in the bottom boards in attitudes of eternal sleep; one sat in the sternsheets, the tiller still in his hand, leaning forward as though exhorting the rowers to greater efforts. They wore long beards stiff with ice and their bodies gleamed with an unearthly green pallor, glittering in the sun like many-faceted diamonds.

The boat moved steadily away, bobbed in their wake, and disappeared from view.

They never knew who they were; where they came from; of what nationality; whether their ship had been torpedoed; or foundered due to one of the natural perils and hazards of the sea.

They continued to head north and east. The wind shifted and whipped the sea into a fury of foam and spray, but it also brought relief in a torrential downpour of rain which melted the ice and washed the decks clean.

Five days later they arrived off the North Western Approaches without further incident. They cleared Malin Head with a wintry sun chasing fleecy clouds across a cerulean blue sky. Rounding the angled green hills of Rathlin Island they entered the North Channel, and steamed past a line of ships heading south. They were evidently the remnants of a battered Atlantic convoy: one was down by the stern, her plates buckled and smashed, but still managing to keep afloat; another's bows were ripped open as though by a giant tin-opener; one sailed with her superstructure blackened by fire; yet another had lost half of her bridge and most of her funnel, her dead laid out like parcels on number 2 hatch.

But they bore themselves proudly, blood-red ensigns fluttering defiantly in the breeze as they fought their way over the last few miles with their precious cargoes intact. Engine rooms half-flooded; shored bulkheads straining against the pent-up weight of water; steering shot away; upperworks blasted into tangles of charred spars, they panted and laboured and obstinately refused to sink.

They were merchantmen returning from the bloodiest battleground of all.

'I wonder if we'll get Christmas at home?' asked Cloud hopefully.

'Not a hope,' answered Lowrie morosely. 'It'll be discharge, load, and off again before you can give your cock an airing.'

'Poor Sonia,' commiserated the bos'n. 'She don't know what she's missing.'

'Oh, every day is Christmas day with Sonia,' said Cloud. 'She has a very generous nature has my Sonia.'

'What's this bint like?' asked Jason. 'I mean, really like?'

'Pulchritudinous,' said Cloud. 'Very pulchritudinous.'

'I'll believe it when I see her,' said Lowrie. 'I think she's got cross eyes and a wooden leg. If she exists at all.'

'Oh, she exists,' said Cloud. 'But she's too couth for you lot.'

They were standing on the forecastle head, idly watching the shoreline gliding past as the ship nosed its way up-river.

'Stand by. The tug's coming, lads,' announced the bos'n, breaking into their conversation.

'It's no' that I mind missing Christmas,' said Lowrie. 'It's just that I dinna fancy spending Hogmanay at sea wi' a shipload o' heathen Sassenachs.'

They berthed at four in the afternoon alongside a transit shed no more than a tangle of wreckage and with the stench of charred and smouldering timber hanging over all.

CHAPTER SEVEN

THE FOLLOWING day was bitterly cold with sombre skies. The trees stood stark and bare and the boating lake had frozen solid enough for a few venturesome skaters to try their skills. They were no more than a handful and Dean listened to the scuff and rasp of their skates as he crossed the park and made his way to the tram stop at the park gates. It was a sign of the times, he thought, practically everyone not in the Forces was engaged in war work. Another sign of the times was the disappearance of the ornate wrought iron gates, taken away to be melted down to aid the war effort. All that now remained were the sandstone posts and the famous Calder Stones, a circle of greyish white slabs whose origin was lost in myth.

A number 7 tram waited at the terminus and Dean, smart in superfine uniform topped by a high-collared, full-skirted bridge coat, boarded the tram and sat opposite a young housewife who immediately rolled hopeful eyes in his direction. Dean, however, armoured by fidelity, ignored her blandishments and clutched his parcel the tighter. He was already filled with misgivings. His carefully planned seduction of the delectable Olwyn, so easy aboard ship when he could bend fantasy to his will, now seemed liable to founder on the rocks of simple human curiosity.

'And what have you brought for Olwyn? Such a dear sweet girl,' his mother had asked, after crooning over her own present of a box of perfumes and powders bought at the last possible moment in New York.

'It's a surprise,' he answered quickly and, hoping to divert further questioning, 'How do you find the tobacco, Dad?'

His father was stoking up his pipe from a half-pound tin of Prince Albert. 'Rich, very rich. Take a bit of getting used to after St Bruno.' He had smiled affectionately at his son. 'But I'll persevere. Probably acquire a taste for it and never switch back.'

'It's the shortages,' his mother had complained. 'You have no idea. Queue for everything. And rationing. One and tenpence worth of meat, two ounces of tea, eight ounces of sugar and only four ounces of bacon. Your father can eat more than that for his breakfast. I am sure I don't know how we can be expected to survive.'

'It's fair, though,' his father had interposed judiciously. 'You must admit it's fair. Same rations for rich or poor alike. Mind you, the restaurants seem to have plenty for those who can afford it.'

'We make a point of dining out once a week. It is the only possible way of eking out our rations. How poor people manage is quite beyond my understanding.' His mother had shaken her head in grave commiseration for the less fortunate.

'No defeatist talk in this house, if you please, mother.' His father had puffed placidly at his pipe. 'Of course you missed all the excitement while you were away, David. We gave Hitler and that fat Goering the fright of their lives. They sent their bombers over in waves. Thousands of 'em. In broad daylight, mind. They must have been mad. Our boys shot 'em out of the skies by the hundred. Sent the rest back with their tales between their legs. Then we bombed Berlin, to give 'em a taste of their own medicine.'

'Reprisal raids.' His mother, a normally placid woman with an abhorence of violence, had nodded her head determinedly. 'We'll give that Hitler a bloody nose and bomb his cities to smithereens.'

'What is more we repelled the invasion.' Mr Dean laid a finger to his nose and winked knowingly. 'The newspapers tried to hush it up, but it's common knowledge. I have it on good authority from a colleague whose brother is an ARP warden on the South Coast. He said he saw thousand of bodies in German uniform littering the beaches. He says that they tried to cross in barges but our lads were waiting for them. Gave 'em hell. Set fire to the Channel . . .'

'Roasted them alive, the fiends,' Mrs Dean had added with relish.

'They'll not try that game twice. Of course Corporal

Schickelgruber doesn't understand the meaning of sea-power.' His father, who to Dean's certain knowledge knew as little of the sea as a Tibetan lama, had wagged his head sagely. 'But no doubt David understands what command of the seas means only too well. After all, we have a sea-dog in the family now.'

There had been a conversational pause and, looking at their expectant faces, he had realised that he was being invited to recount his own exploits. Recollecting the slaughter in the Atlantic, and not wishing to add to their anxieties, he had painted a picture of a minor skirmish.

'Sank a U-boat, eh?' Mr Dean had gazed upon his son with pride. 'Wait until I tell 'em down at the Post!'

His mother, intercepting a puzzled look, had explained: 'Your father is a Warden.'

'I try to do my bit. And so does your mother. She is quite a big wheel in the WVS. Out at all hours ladling out soup to the bombed-out.'

'Do you get many raids?' he had asked, remembering shattered warehouses along the dock road, shops and houses collapsed into heaps of rubble with here and there a lone chimney poking into the air like warning fingers.

'Terror tactics. Cowardly night attacks. Bombing helpless women and children, the poor mites.'

'A hundred and fifty came over last night. A real firework display.' A cloud of smoke curled from Mr Dean's pipe. 'But our ack-ack drove 'em off. No real damage. Flattened a couple of streets in Everton. I daresay they'll be back tonight. If they do, I want no false heroics, young man. It's off to the garden shelter with you. That's an order.'

That had been last night. No air-raid sirens had disturbed his sleep and he had lain long in bed until the hall clock chiming ten had roused him from his slumbers. He had bathed, shaved, eaten a large breakfast with a guilty conscience, telephoned Olwyn to learn from her mother that she was now employed as secretary to an official in the Ministry of Food and usually returned home at around six o'clock. He had been given Olwyn's telephone and extension number and she had squealed with delight at the sound of his voice and made him promise to call at seven sharp. 'TTFN' she had added mysteriously and hung up.

Now with the tram lurching along the hedge-lined grass

tracks he had time to ponder over the information he had been able to glean. It was evident that social habits had undergone a radical transformation during his absence. There was a scarcity of entertainment, cinemas closed at ten, public transport was disrupted and people flocked home to the suburbs to avoid the worst of the bombing raids.

By the time the tram had wound its way to Penny Lane he had arrived at the gloomy conclusion that in war time the path of the would-be seducer was beset with obstacles.

Wrapped in thought, he couldn't be bothered with changing trams for the short distance. With his beribboned package tucked beneath one arm he walked up to the Clock Tower whose pointing fingers reminded him that he was early. The Lamb and Flag offered promise as a temporary refuge so he crossed the road and made his way through to the bar. Asking for a Scotch he was met with a hostile refusal from a crab-faced barman with a seamed unhappy face who added the surly information that there was a war on.

Sipping a glass of insipid beer he finally faced the reality of Olwyn's unassailable virtue and sadly consigned the project to his private limbo of unfulfilled dreams. He drained his glass and ordered a second while wondering what the hell he was going to do with the parcel of pretties. The thought gave him goose-pimples. He swallowed the rest of his beer and ventured upon a third glass. It tasted as foul as the others but lent him a counterfeit courage. He hadn't battled his way across several thousand miles of ocean to be intimidated by the snooty Mrs Trotter. Olwyn would have her present, come what may.

His glass of beer looked and tasted like the bottom of a fish pond. He left it on the counter and, pushing aside the double blackout curtains, stepped outside into freezing winter cold.

The wind was backing sharply to the north-west. The clouds were scudding away to leave patches of open sky. A bone-white moon was rising quickly to paint gabled roofs with silver. A darkened tram rumbled around the corner and droned away toward the city centre.

A brisk ten-minute walk brought him to Thingwall Road and a row of semi-detached houses hedged in privacy. The Trotters' house stood aloof from its neighbours in detached superiority. Mr Trotter, a self-made man, had paid highly for the privilege and advertised the fact with a surrounding screen of tall poplar trees.

He marched boldly up the path and jabbed a finger upon the bell push. The peal coincided with the measured chimes of the hall clock. There came the clickerty-clack of footsteps across the parquet flooring, then the door opened and Mrs Trotter subjected him to a basilisk stare and death's-head grin.

'Ah – David,' she cooed. 'Do come in. We have been expecting you.' She made it sound as though they had been anxiously pacing the living-room in anticipation of his tardy arrival.

He stepped inside and sneezed involuntarily as he inhaled the powerful aroma of Mrs Trotter's perfume. She switched on the light and he noticed that she was dressed to kill in a long gown of turquoise blue French brocade. A collar of watered silk plunged to a deep neck-line and a rope of pearls encircled her throat. Her hair, curled and piled into a fashionable Pompadour coiffure, added to her statuesque height. She had a small bird-of-prey head, her mouth a red slash beneath a beaked nose. 'Do take off your coat, David,' she commanded, adding, as he fumbled with the row of brass buttons, 'Let me take your parcel.'

He hung hat and coat on the antlered hall-stand and followed her into a room of carpeted comfort, fringed and tasselled with heavy swagged curtains and chintz-covered furniture. A low fire slumbered behind a gilded fireguard and wall sconces shaped like sea-shells floodlit rough-cast walls.

Mr Trotter bounced across the room to shake him warmly by the hand as though greeting a long-lost friend. Mr Trotter was a tubby man of breezy manner and generous heart, already perspiring from the restriction of a black bow tie, starched shirt and stiff collar. 'David, my boy! Good to see you, good to see you! Come leching after me daughter, have you? Can't say I blame you. I said, I can't say I blame you. But you'd best watch where you put your feet – she takes after her mother, does our Olwyn – gracious living and don't muss up me hair. Have a cocktail and make yourself at home. We're just off to the Adelphi. Got me dressed up like a dog's dinner, the pair of them.'

He released David's arm, beamed upon his spouse who

was carefully placing David's parcel upon an onyx occasional table, winked at his daughter, trotted across to a cocktail cabinet loaded with an array of mirrored bottles, and occupied himself by briskly rattling a silver shaker.

Olwyn was seated demurely upon the settee. She wore a dark dress, tight at the waist and with a short billowing skirt with a frill of white lace peeping coyly out below. She treated Dean to a smile reserved for a comparative stranger and primly tugged her skirt fractionally lower.

'Good evening, David, so good of you to call,' she announced coolly, and immediately turned her attention to her parents.

'Must you go, Mummy? I mean, the bombing has been perfectly dreadful these last few nights. I shall worry about you the whole evening.'

'Don't give it a thought,' said her father cheerfully. 'Nuisance raids, that's all. They knock down a few houses and then pee off somewhere else.'

'Don't be coarse, Edward,' chided Mrs Trotter. 'I am sure I don't know where you pick up such expressions.'

'On the building sites, that's where.' Mr Trotter poured amber liquid into frosted glasses with the care of a chemist dispensing a prescription. 'We've got plasterers with more names for a trowel than you'll find in any dictionary.'

'Well, I am sure we don't want to hear them in this house,' responded his wife coldly. She bent like a crane and peered at the inscription on the parcel. 'Why, Olwyn – I do believe this is for you.'

She carried it across to her daughter and placed the package carefully on her lap.

'Oh, David – how kind!' Olwyn began to fumble at the ribbons while Dean hastily sought for another topic of conversation.

'The cloud's are clearing,' he ventured. 'It looks as though it might be a bombers' moon.'

Mrs Trotter sniffed. 'I have no intention of having my social life disrupted by a grubby little house-painter!'

'We could do with him over here,' said Mr Trotter. 'He'd make a first-rate foreman. Keep some of those Irishers in line, they're a Bolshie lot.' He passed the cocktails around. 'Sup up, lad. That's a Ted Trotter special. Guaranteed to put hairs on your chest.' He made a mock bow in the direction of his wife. 'Saving your presence, ma'am.'

Dean had packed Olwyn's presents in a cardboard shoe box, layered the contents in tissue paper and wrapped the whole in paper decorated with tiny roses. He swallowed Mr Trotter's special at a gulp and waited, stomach curdling, while Olwyn carefully unpicked the bows of pink ribbon. He remembered choosing the garments, aided and abetted by Bert Page who had been embarking upon a similar shopping expedition. Together they had wandered into Greenwich Village and discovered a shop with a window display of exotic feminine fripperies. After a short session in a nearby bar they had hilariously entered the premises and bought armfuls of flimsy garments ranging from suspender belts to fancy garters, from wispy scanties to sheer silk stockings.

Dean's heart lurched into his mouth as Olwyn removed the wrapping paper and raised the lid. In a moment of alcoholic madness he had added a couple of frothy extras. Minute triangles edged with lace and designed to reveal rather than conceal. One was lemon-coloured, the other black. Each embroidered with a pierced heart and the legend, *This Side Up*.

Mrs Trotter took a bird-like sip from her drink and craned forward. Mr Trotter hospitably refilled Dean's glass. Olwyn let out a chirrup of delight. 'Stockings! Silk stockings! Oh, David, you blessed angel!'

'Most considerate,' said Mrs Trotter glacially.

'A dozen pair!' crowed Olwyn. She burrowed deeper. An apple-blossom blush appeared on her cheeks. 'Dozens of pairs,' she corrected hastily. 'Oh, David, you darling!' She closed the lid. 'I'll just take these upstairs and put on a pair especially for you, David.'

She hurried away, flushed and excited, hugging the package like a mother hen with a precious chick.

'That's the style, my boy,' said Mr Trotter. 'Keep the ladies cossetted, and you'll keep 'em happy. Just take care you don't ladder them when you're fumbling in the dark, eh.' He guffawed and poked Dean in the ribs.

'Don't be vulgar, Edward.' Mrs Trotter peered down her nose. 'The poor boy is positively blushing with embarrassment.'

The door bell suddenly emitted a peremptory peal.

'That'll be the taxi,' announced Mr Trotter. He drained his glass, picked up his wife's mink wrap and draped it carelessly about her shoulders. 'Come along, Margaret, the meter's ticking over.'

'Have a nicc time,' said Dean.

Mrs Trotter collected her gold lamé purse, apologised for rushing away, expressed the hope that he would be a frequent visitor, adding ominously that they must have a long and serious talk, reminded him that Olwyn was an only child and had not yet attained her majority, announced that public transport was *so* unreliable, that they did *so* miss the use of the limousine and that taxi-drivers' impertinence knew no bounds, flicked a glance over the room as though counting the spoons and finally bade him farewell.

He waited until the diminishing sound of the taxi's engine signalled their departure, then shakily poured himself a generous helping of one of Mr Trotter's Specials.

The room seemed uncomfortably warm. He mopped his face and nervously awaited Olwyn's reappearance. He imagined her stalking in, haughty with anger, to pitch the offending articles into his face. She was a delicious little bundle and he was a fool. He'd muffed his chances. She had given him a cool enough reception as it was, greeting him with a smile borrowed from her mother and only showing hypocritical enthusiasm for the benefit of her parents. He thanked his lucky stars that she had had the wit to smuggle those offensive articles away before the revelation of his perfidy was exposed to the affronted gaze of the starch-faced Mrs Trotter.

He was loosening his collar and moodily shifting his feet when the door opened and Olwyn peered in.

'Have they gone?' she whispered.

'Yes,' he answered hoarsely, bracing himself for the inevitable outburst.

'Oh, you darling, darling,' she cried and flung herself into his arms. Her body, soft and pliant, squirmed unashamedly against his rising stiffness. A tongue ferretted into his mouth and ran around like a little wild thing. She moved rhythmically, rubbing and swaying against him until he thought his heart would burst.

She stepped back, pushing him away. 'That is quite enough of that,' she announced severely. 'I really don't know what to make of you, David. I think you are an evil, wicked monster, filled with evil thoughts.' She patted her hair and smoothed her dress, then suddenly giggled. 'This Side Up! Mother would have had a fit!'

He gazed at her, enraptured. This was a different Olwyn from the memory he had taken away with him. The war-time diet had played its part by trimming away the puppy fat and changing a plump, pert young maiden into a nubile young woman. An immature shyness had also given way to a coquettish boldness, an indefinable undercurrent of recklessness.

She stretched out a leg, hoicked up her skirt an inch or two, and narcissistically drew a hand from her calf to her thigh. 'Real silk,' she murmured. 'Aren't they beautiful, David? Clara will be green with envy.'

'Beautiful,' he acknowledged thickly, lurching toward her.

She skipped nimbly away from his grasp. 'I think you have ideas beyond your station, young man. The present of a pair of stockings does not automatically give you the right to put them on. That is a right you must earn. And I warn you, it will be a long and hard apprenticeship.'

Mr Trotter's Specials were making their presence known by making his eardrums ping.

'I don't care who puts 'em on,' he told her daringly. 'As long as it is me who takes 'em off.'

She lowered her eyes demurely. 'Really, David, I think you take far too much for granted. I am not one of your cheap foreign trollops.'

'No, no,' he hastened to reassure her. 'No, no. I only meant...'

She gave him a prim smile reminiscent of her mother and quieted him with an upraised palm. 'As long as we understand each other, we shall say no more about it. Now pour me a drink before the others come.'

'The others?' He had imagined that he was going to have her to himself for an hour or two.

'Two very dear friends. They are taking us to the Rocket for drinks.'

'Oh.'

She pouted. 'Don't look so disappointed. It is very kind of them to offer. Fred works *extremely* hard at the Ordnance Factory.'

'Oh.'

'In a managerial capacity.'

Bully for Fred, he thought, as he picked up the cocktail shaker and clashed it in time with the beating in his skull.

She took her drink and raised the glass: 'I'm going down now, sir. Don't forget the diver,' she announced in a strangely lugubrious voice, and swallowed Mr Trotter's Special at a gulp.

A cheerful ring-a-ding from the front door bell drew a delighted yelp from Olywn. 'That will be Fred and Clara. I'll go.'

As she pattered away to the front door Dean took the opportunity of pouring his drink back into Mr Trotter's evil concoction, while wondering how Olywn had managed to acquire such a strong head and stomach for alcoholic mixtures which would send the average drinker hiccuping and reeling in the sawdust. On his last leave she had spent one entire evening sipping delicately at a gin and orange juice and later, snuggled in his arms beneath the shadow of the garden tree, had whispered that alcohol made her positively dizzy.

He heard voices boisterously echoing through the hall.

Olwyn: 'Can I do you now, sir?'

Screeches and guffaws.

A man's voice: 'After you, Claud.'

A woman's voice: 'No – after you, Cecil.'

The front door closed and the trio erupted into the lounge, arm in arm, and kicking their legs in the mock semblance of a chorus line.

'It's That Man Again,' they sang. 'It's that Man Again.'

'Everything tickety-boo?' enquired Fred Lambert as they shook hands.

'How do you do?' said Dean politely.

'Wizard show,' said Fred and introduced a dimity blonde, with shoulder-length hair topped by a pert pill-box hat, as the feather-plucker who lived with the man who kept her.

Fred had a thatch of red hair, a cheerful carbuncular face, evidently looked upon himself as the life and soul of the party and lost no time in hustling them away, beaming like a fairy godfather bearing priceless gifts.

'I think it will be That Man Again tonight,' he told Dean jovially. 'So we'd best press on regardless and down a few scoops before Mine Host uses it as an excuse to turn off the tap.'

The four walked arm-in-arm along the wide tree-lined pavement with a high white moon splashing the houses with jade. A darkened goods train rumbled beneath the road bridge, the will-o'-the-wisp glow from the engine's fire-box flickering against the greater darkness.

They crossed the road and entered the pub by way of the lounge entrance. Fred pushed his way through to a corner table, calling: 'Gangway, for a Naval Officer. Make way for the walking wounded, if you please!'

Dean found himself wedged between Olwyn and Clara, while Fred disappeared in the direction of the bar. Olwyn and Clara leaned across and embarked upon an animated conversation which seemed to be conducted entirely in a baffling mixture of acronyms and unfamiliar catch-phrases. He soon abandoned all attempts at maintaining polite interest and settled back to take stock of his surroundings.

The lounge bar was oak-panelled, hazy with smoke, and already crowded with a motley collection of noisy drinkers. Army uniforms seemed to be in the preponderance, with here and there a sprinkle of Air Force blue. A couple of Land Army girls in bosomy sweaters were screeching happily in a corner surrounded by a group of hopeful males. A cluster of nurses from the nearby Broadgreen Hospital perched at one end of the bar chattering like magpies. A few civilians bobbed about like so much flotsam adrift in a tidal backwater; the men, mostly middle-aged, tended to sport plus-fours and Fair Isle pullovers, while their ladies were bright as parakeets in floral dresses, fox furs and cloche hats.

People seemed to congregate much earlier in the evening than pre-war days and, he noticed, they not only mixed more freely, but drank with the dedicated ferocity of confirmed topers.

Dean was musing over the phenomenon when Fred returned carrying a tray above his head like a music hall barman.

'Bombs away,' he called and distributed eight glasses of beer about the table. 'Waste not, want not,' he announced, draining a glass in one long satisfying swallow. 'I have it on good authority that the bitter will be off in half an hour. Chin-chin, one and all.'

'I don't mind if I do,' said Clara fruitily.

'Glug-glug,' said Olwyn taking a deep draught. 'Good beer.'

'Keeps a fair cellar,' said Fred. 'Sup up, David.'

'Cheers,' said Dean taking a manly gulp.

Fred picked up his second glass. 'Same again?'

'I don't mind if I do,' said Clara emptying the contents of her first glass.

'A health to Cardinal Huff,' said Olwyn following suit.

Dean watched fascinated as Olwyn tilted back her head and swallowed the remainder of her beer. She up-ended the glass and blew out her cheeks. 'God bless Cardinal Huff,' she announced. 'Who's in the chair?'

'Can't resist a challenge,' said Fred, draining his second glass.

'Going down now, sir,' said Clara. She returned the empty glass to the table and looked expectantly at Dean.

'Down the hatch,' said Dean struggling with his first glass. He had never been anything but a moderate drinker and began to wonder how he could stand the pace of such determined tippling.

'Hard luck, David,' said Olwyn. She snuggled closer and gave him goose-pimples by rubbing her instep against the calf of his leg.

'Your chair,' Fred told him cheerfully. 'Double up, and press on regardless.'

Dean detached himself from Olwyn, picked up the tray and made his way across to the bar amid a hubbub of chatter and a fog of tobacco smoke.

The evening passed in a nightmare recollection of absorbing oceans of liquid until his stomach expanded and threatened to erupt like some long-dormant volcano. Snatches of surrealist conversation impinged upon his consciousness. At one point Clara had glanced slyly at him and mysteriously advised Olwyn to take particular care if she should see someone called Kay tonight. Olwyn had then flushed, bridled somewhat at the advice, assured Clara that she was well able to take care of herself, snuggled even closer and tickled the palm of his hand, adding the information that David was a gentleman and therefore to be trusted.

'A gentleman to his fingertips and takes his weight on his elbows, eh, David?' Fred had laughed coarsely then suddenly erupted into a bout of explosive hiccups. 'Scuse, please.' He lurched to his feet. 'I think I need a guide dog. Are you coming, Dave?'

Dean thankfully followed him through to the aseptic coolness of the gents. Fred, standing in the next stall, leaned his forehead against the tiles and expelled a sigh of relief. 'One of the few tax-free pleasures left, and I suspect you have the other one well under way, you lucky dog.'

'Me?'

'Who else? Clara likes her oats and screws like a rabbit, but I'd swap a dozen Claras for one bold thrust at young luscious-legs.'

'Who?'

'Olwyn of the lovely limbs. My God, what a magnificent pair of pins. Those and her other endowments. What a pair of bumpers! The way they wobble is enough to give a man a throbble. Hey – did you hear that? I've just composed a poem: "The way you walk, the way you wobble, is enough to give a man a throbble." Oh, my God, I think I'm going to throw up!'

Fred heaved himself away from the wall and staggered away to the cubicle from where Dean could hear him heaving, retching and swearing, and calling blasphemously upon the Almighty.

Fred eventually reappeared, sunken-eyed and whey-faced, tottered wordlessly to the basin, gargled fiercely and dowsed his head in cold water.

'Oh, Christ,' he said, drying his face. 'I feel like death warmed up.' Fishing out a comb he ran it through his hair and bleared into the mirror. 'Jesus! I look like Dracula on a diet. It's all right for you bold sailormen but some of us poor landlubbers have work to go to.'

'Work?'

'I'm on at two,' said Fred. 'So if it's okay with you, old man, I'll collect my bedmate and high-tail it for the old homestead.' He sighed. 'Although from the tenor of their conversation I doubt either of us will get much sleep. I gather both of us are in for a rough ride.'

'Oh?'

'You must have heard 'em. Chattering away in female doubletalk. 'If you see Kay tonight.' He snorted. 'They must think us a dim-witted pair.'

'Oh – ah – of course,' said Dean dimly.

'Back to the fray,' said Fred, straightening his shoulders.

Dean trailed after him into the lounge to hear the landlord bellowing: 'All those with homes to go to – go! Time, if you please, ladies and gentlemen!'

They collected Olwyn and Clara, who rose from the table, embodiments of sobriety, to walk ahead with the graceful gait of a pair of racehorses stepping over invisible objects.

The night air was ice cold and Olwyn's teeth chattered as she huddled into her melton cape and linked Dean's arm.

'Remember what I told you, if you see Kay,' said Clara conspiratorially to Olwyn.

'We'll bid you farewell,' said Fred. 'TTFN.'

'Goodnight,' said Dean to Clara. 'See you next trip.'

It was a seafarer's commonplace, but it brought a startled glance from Clara and a guffaw from Fred.

'See you next trip! Caught you there, girl, eh?' Fred clapped Dean upon the shoulder. 'Rich. Oh, very rich. I must remember that one.'

Clara gave a war whoop of laughter. 'Nothing personal, I hope?'

Olwyn's eyes glittered in the moonlight. 'Clever,' she said admiringly. 'Coarse, but clever.'

She linked Dean's arm and they parted on a note of hilarity, Fred and Clara making for Bowring Park Road, Dean and Olwyn heading in the opposite direction.

They wandered on in silence for a few minutes, Dean mulling over the peculiar reception given to his harmless figure of speech. Unable to make either head nor tail of it he came to the conclusion that his companions had been subject to the manic phase of intoxication, and concentrated his attention upon his head which seemed to be filled with tiny trip-hammers beating a steady rhythm inside his skull.

Olwyn eventually broke the silence. 'A very nice couple, don't you think?' she mused.

'Oh, very,' he agreed.

'Although they can be – well – rather crude at times.'

'Ah.'

'They seemed to think it a huge joke.'

'Yes.'

'You really did put Clara in her place.'

'Oh, well –'

Olwyn giggled. 'She looked as though she'd been hit in the mouth with a wet fish.'

'Oh? I thought she found it amusing.'

'She covered up quickly enough, I grant you, but Clara won't try that game twice. Not with you, David.'

She gave him a quick hug. 'We'll keep that code to ourselves. When we write to each other. You must be awfully good at it.'

He stole a glance at her. She did not appear to be demented. Codes, he thought, what the hell was she babbling about?

'Of course, Clara is my best friend, and I would not hear a word against her, but she really does not make the most of herself. That hat! Well – I ask you!'

Privately he had thought it a charming example of feminine frivolity, but wisely keeping to safe ground, gave her an affectionate squeeze.

'She lacks the style to carry it off.'

'And so thin.'

'Skinny. Thin as a rake.'

'Knobbly knees.'

'Not in the least like yours.'

'Do you like them?'

He took a leaf from Fred's book of synonyms. 'Luscious legs.'

'Do you really think so?' The description evidently pleased her for she snuggled against his arm with an unmistakable feminine pressure. 'Yes, people do say that my legs are my best feature.'

The gambit was so transparent that he barely hesitated before plagiarising Fred once more.

'Oh, I don't know,' he said. 'The way you walk, the way you wobble. Is enough to give a man a throbble.'

His reward was a gurgle of delight and a quick probing kiss on his ear.

'You darling!' she crowed. 'You clever, clever darling!' She preened herself, pouting like a pigeon. 'Wobblers! What a lovely name. We'll keep it just to ourselves. They are nice, though, aren't they?' She proved it by pushing one closer to his arm.

'Beautiful.' His heart seemed to have changed position and crept into his throat.

'And all for you,' she whispered.

As they turned into Thingwall Road the sirens emitted a banshee wail and searchlights began to weave spectral patterns across the sky. There came the distant crump of guns as the outer ring of the ack-ack barrage opened up; then the unmistakable drone of approaching bombers; bursting shells bloomed like evil flowers; shrapnel began to fall like the Devil's hailstones.

'Run!' said Olwyn and ducking their heads, they scuttled like a pair of demented beetles for the security of the house.

Dean imagined that they would rush for the safety of the air-raid shelter in the rear garden, but Olwyn led the way to the front door, scrabbled for keys in her bag, and then dragged him inside.

He clung blindly to her hand as she hurried him through the pitch-dark hallway, hauled him up a flight of stairs, opened a door and, throwing off hat and cape, scurried to the window.

'Isn't it exciting!' she exclaimed. 'Do hurry, David, or you will miss everything! You get a wonderful view from here.'

He stood blinking, adjusting his vision to the light filtering through the drawn curtains, and took stock of his surroundings.

Wandering searchlight beams, backed by a pallid moon, threw a shifting pattern of light and shade across the room, picking out a solitary bed with a pink ruched bedspread and pink pillows edged with lace. From a corner niche a fat Buddha smiled benignly. A dressing table in white and gold held an array of cut glass perfume bottles, powder bowls and silver-backed hairbrushes. He caught sight of a startling, saturnine image of himself reflected from oval mirrors set into the gilded panels of a built-in wardrobe. A duplicate image leered back from the dressing table mirror. It seemed to wink knowingly as he removed cap and bridge-coat and walked across to join Olwyn.

She was kneeling on a padded window seat, her nose pressed against the window pane like a hungry child outside a confectioner's shop. He kneeled beside her and peered out between the interstices of th anti-blast tape.

Her bedroom was at the rear of the house and they were gazing out at the sprawling expanse of the city. Toward the docks and the river the dull glow of fires loomed against the jagged outline of roofs and chimney stacks. The barrage had opened in full fury and the crash of a nearby battery shook and rattled the windows in their frames. He flinched and encircled her waist with a protective arm.

'Isn't it marvellous!' she breathed. 'Oh – look, we've caught one!'

A searchlight beam, flickering across a jumbo-sized barrage balloon, lighted upon a silver fish apparently hanging motionless in the sky. Instantly a dozen other beams locked on and the silver fish hung haloed in light, while the ack-ack guns roared and bellowed their anger and tiny puff-balls of smoke popped and burst into fiery rosettes.

Dean heard the distant long-drawn-out whistle of falling bombs as the pilot jettisoned his cargo and took evasive action. He held his breath and clutched Olwyn the closer as the whistle became a shriek. Then the ground shook and shuddered as the bombs fell and burst in a random pattern. The shock wave and concussion rocked the house and his immediate impression was that at least one must have fallen in the front garden. But a mile away a row of houses was obliterated and a gas main erupted into a sheet of yellow flame, to continue burning fiercely amid the overhanging pall of smoke and dust.

The silver fish swooped in a long shallow dive, changed contour and became a silver moth trapped in a dazzle of light. It waggled its wings and whined plaintively. Pin-pricks of light twinkled around it. Then suddenly it became a sunburst of red and yellow flame. Bits and pieces flew off to tumble through the air. The searchlights crossed and crisscrossed excitedly and then, as if the moment had broken their concentration, moved apart and resumed their earlier aimless wandering, poking probing fingers across the firmament while the remaining invisible bombers droned on and the guns thundered and gouts of fire rose from the darkened city.

Olwyn detached herself from his encircling arm and slipped away. 'Keep looking,' she called. 'Let me know if anything else happens. I shan't be a moment.'

Fascinated, he kept his gaze glued to the panorama of raging fires and weaving searchlights. In the far distance yellow flames licked the sky. 'I think a timber yard has just gone up,' he reported.

In a moment she was back to curl up on the seat and lay

her head against his shoulder. 'It's like the end of the world,' she whispered. 'Fire and brimstone raining down from heaven.'

He returned his arm to her waist and met the scalding touch of bare flesh. Glancing down quickly, past her raised head, her parted lips and the long rippling line of her throat, he discovered that she was attired only in the more seductive items of his gift parcel.

She treated him to a shy smile. 'I put them on straight away,' she whispered. 'I've been wearing them all evening. Especially for you.' She followed the direction of his gaze. 'You are reading it upside down.' She began to fumble shakily at the knot in his tie. 'Now it's your turn. I mean – it's only fair, isn't it?'

It was not, he thought, quite the way he had planned, but as a substitute had much to commend it.

Bombs poured down upon the city as though aimed by blind men. The docks burned and warehouses tumbled into heaps of rubble. The river glowed red, reflecting the glare like an ever-moving polished mirror. Ambulance bells shrilled their imperatives and the bombers turned to drone away, leaving the city to lick its wounds and count its dead. The barrage stuttered to a halt and the searchlighs winked out, battery by battery, until only the moon, serene and clear, looked down from the cloudless sky.

Dean heaved himself upright and, gasping and perspiring, rested his head against the pillow and gave up the struggle.

'Are you mad at me?' asked Olwyn softly.

'No,' he said untruthfully, grimacing into the darkness.

Lying beside him she lightly ran her fingers down his chest. 'I mean,' she said. 'We are not even engaged. Not properly.'

'We'll buy a ring, tomorrow,' he promised ardently and slipped his arm about her shoulders.

'Nice,' she purred, dancing her fingertips on a tour of exploration. 'Very nice,' she murmured a moment or two later. 'Just wait until we are married!'

Dean doubted he could wait a minute longer and still retain his sanity. Olwyn had at first proved bewitchingly amorous, by turns ardent and pliant, shivering with excitement and wriggling like a snake as she helped him slough off first one tantalising garment then another, until all that remained was the filmy triangle of lace with its embroidered exhortation. But at that point she had displayed an adamantine streak of obstinacy which had resisted all his blandishments. He had coaxed and wheedled, begged and pleaded, tugged and fumbled to no avail. The flimsy wisp of chiffon remained firmly in place as though rivetted to her hips.

The gibbous moon sent skeins of light slanting across the room. They fell across the edge of the bed and picked out a mosaic pattern of intertwined bodies in the wardrobe's oval mirrors.

Idly he watched the reflection of his hand gliding along her thighs to pat her silken rump. Then suddenly he sat bolt upright.

'Christ!' he said.

'What...?'

'Did you hear the All Clear?'

'What?'

'There are no searchlights. The bloody raid is over!'

'It will be all right,' she answered. 'Mummy and Daddy will be simply hours and hours yet.'

'Listen.'

They both heard it: the unmistakable purring of the taxi's engine; a murmuration of indistinct voices; footsteps crunching up the gravel path; the snick of a key in the lock. A voice echoed through the house: 'Are you there, Olwyn?'

'Oh, Christ,' he whispered hoarsely, out of bed and scrabbling for his clothes. 'Its your bloody mother. She's coming upstairs!' Panic seized him by the throat. 'Stop her! For God's sake, stop her!'

'I've just been having a bath, Mummy. I shall be down in a moment.'

'Where's David?'

The voice was coming nearer. Where to hide? In the wardrobe? Under the bed. But where in blazes was his tie? His cap? His bridge-coat. His shoes?

'He left just before the air raid started,' said Olwyn conversationally.

'You poor darling. Were you here all alone? It must have been simply dreadful for you.'

Olwyn waved a frantic arm and he huddled behind the door as she opened it to step out on to the landing. She closed it firmly behind her. 'Not too bad,' she was saying, calm and self-possessed as he hunted about the near-dark room like a demented squirrel. He found Olwyn's bra, stubbed his toe against the bedpost, discovered a treasure trove of shirt, socks and underpants.

'I stayed with the Lamberts – in their air raid shelter. I've not long been home.'

'We worried about you all the time. Your father insisted we took a taxi the moment the All-Clear sounded.'

'Did you have a nice time?'

'Dreadful. Simply dreadful. The dinner party was utterly ruined.'

'Margaret! Can you spare a moment?' Mr Trotter's voice mercifully demanded his wife's attention.

'I'll be down in a minute, Mummy,' said Olwyn and skipped back into the room.

Dean found his trousers and babbled hysterically as he pulled them on back to front.

'Hurry!' hissed Olwyn. 'Or we'll have them both up here!'

He hauled his braces over his shoulders and thrust his feet into his shoes. 'My tie!' he clamoured. 'I can't find my tie!'

She helped him into his jacket and feretted about the room. 'Here it is,' she said, stuffing it into his pocket.

He climbed into his bridge-coat, put his cap on his head, and looked about wildly. 'How the hell do I get out?'

'This way,' she gestured, opening the sash window.

He leaned out and stared horrified at the drop into the darkness. 'I'd break my bloody legs,' he said aghast.

'There's a drain pipe. But for heaven's sake, be quiet, the living-room is just below.'

A blast of cold air swept into the room.

'Hurry,' she whispered urgently. 'I'm freezing!'

He ducked his head, swung a leg over the window sill, and reached for the drain pipe. It was slippery and encased in rivulets of ice that numbed his fingers. He stretched for a foothold feeling that he was being slowly torn apart. Then, with the buttons popping on his reversed trousers, he found one of the clamps holding the pipe to the wall. He hauled the other leg away from the sill and clung desperately to his temporary refuge.

'Be quick,' hissed Olwyn. 'Give me a ring tomorrow.' She blew him a kiss and firmly closed the window.

He hung in space for a few moments, then commenced to

slither down, inch by terrifying inch. His cap slid from his head and sailed away into the darkness. His bridge-coat rucked up to his shoulders giving him the appearance of a petrified Quasimodo. Finding the second clamp, he was stealthily lowering himself to the level of the living-room window when, to his horror, Mrs Trotter appeared and gazed thoughtfully out into the garden. He clung to the pipe, not daring to move and expecting that at any moment she would turn her head and catch him in full flight. Then she yawned, stretched both arms and, to his intense relief, drew the curtains together.

Dean slowly eased down another foot. His right shoe fell off and brought from the nether regions a screeching caterwauling that raised the hairs on his scalp. Looking down he was just able to discern the shape of a marmalade cat, back arched and spitting fury at the offending object. The sound was followed by the rapid clump of footsteps and the rasp of bolts sliding back. He pushed himself out from the wall, offered up a short prayer, and launched himself into the night. He landed in a flower bed. His right foot plunged into an ice-bound puddle with the sound of shattering glass. Then, as the back door swung open, he dived for the shelter of a nearby rhododendron bush.

'Puss, puss, puss,' called Mr Trotter. 'Where are you, puss?'

The cat sat, licked a paw and stared wih jewelled eyes at the bush.

'Shoo!' Dean willed silently. 'Shoo – shoo – shoo!'

The cat hunched down, lashed its tail and growled deep in its throat.

Mr Trotter took a couple of paces forward. 'Puss, puss. Where the hell are you, cat?' A note of command entered his voice. 'Come in, you ginger-haired bastard! Tiddles, Tiddles, Tiddles. Din-dins, you monkey-faced monster! Gawd, I'm bloody freezing!'

The cat continued to stare flatly in Dean's direction. Dean stared back, equally motionless.

Mr Trotter bawled into the darkness: 'Come in at once, or stay out all night!'

It was either the finality in his voice, or a draught of warm air from the open door that enticed the cat from its prey. It turned its head, delicately sniffed the air then, mewling and mincing disdainfully, made its way to Mr Trotter and purred a greeting. Mr Trotter, evidently no animal lover, snarled: 'One day I'm going to make a fur handbag out of you, you little horror,' swung a boot and slammed the door.

Dean straightened up, waited a breathless moment, then searched for his missing shoe and cap. He discovered the shoe in the flower bed and his cap perched on a rose bush. Squelching into his shoe he hobbled across the lawn, blundered into the privet hedge, found the wicket gate and stepped out into a ploughed field.

An overhanging tree gave concealment from the darkened houses and he took the opportunity to reverse his trousers. He fastened the two remaining fly buttons, tucked in his shirt, knotted his tie about his collar and took his bearings.

There seemed to be no way out beyond skirting the edge of the field. The moon glinted from shards of ice, a rime of frost dusted the hedgerows and ankle-wrenching furrows stretched away as far as the eye could see.

Dean turned right and stumbled on like a sleepwalker in the throes of a nightmare. Evenutally he found a five-barred gate topped with barbed wire. Scrambling over he emerged into Queens Drive. The broad, deserted thoroughfare stretched interminably before him. Bruised in body and spirit he turned his back on the Trotters and their maddening daughter and set off on the long weary trudge home.

CHAPTER EIGHT

THE *Kentucky Minstrel* sailed for Oporto leaving behind a skyline that seemed substantially unchanged. Along the waterfront the pinnacles of the Liver Buildings still towered over the Pier Head. The floating landing-stage was undamaged. The Customs House with its domed cupola still stood four-square, even though an avenue of fire had raged through old Sailortown leaving the hulks of charred and gutted buildings to mark the passing of the bombers. The docks, built by the Victorians from blocks of granite, bore a few minor scars, although transit sheds and warehouses had collapsed into tangled heaps of wreckage.

The following day the Luftwaffe had switched its attack to Bristol, Birmingham and Southampton. Then the weather closed in and, during the lull, the *Kentucky Minstrel* had completed loading, signed on her crew and joined a north-bound convoy.

Now that there was a respite from the threat of invasion the convoy escorts were strengthened. Forty ships protected by two destroyers and six corvettes rounded northern Ireland and headed westward, while the U-boats gathered in strength and began to hunt in co-ordinated packs.

On the morning of December 10th the *Kentucky Minstrel* detached herself from the convoy and, escorted by a lone corvette, bore away to the south and the wider reaches of the Atlantic.

A hundred and fifty miles west of Slyn Head the corvette wished them good luck, turned away and, pointing her bows towards the setting sun, set off to rejoin the main body.

Watching her departure Turner heaved a sigh of relief. 'Now perhaps we'll be allowed to go about our business in peace and quiet. I've had enough of bowler-hats to last me a lifetime. Full ahead, Mr Furlong, we've been dragging our heels long enough.'

The bow wave creamed and the wind sang through the rigging as the twin Doxfords, rising to full power, thrust the ship through the grey Atlantic waters at her maximum speed.

They led a charmed life. 'Sloppy's luck,' they called it, as day after day the sea remained empty of all but the ever-restless waves, lifting and heaving in long, undulating ridges crowned with spindrift.

Triumphant U-boats returning from successful sorties, others leaving their bases to throw their weight into the increasingly savage battle, must have crossed and re-crossed their course time and time again. But the *Kentucky Minstrel* was left miraculously alone with nothing to disturb her passage but the turbulence of her wake and the steady throb of her engines.

They made a wide sweep out into the Atlantic, altered course and made their easting for Leixões, Oporto's deep-water port. A couple of hundred miles from neutral waters they had their one and only sight of the enemy.

It rode high out of the water, wallowing slowly in the deep Atlantic swell. Corporal Jackson and his gun crew loosed off a couple of ranging shots. It was enough. The U-boat, filled with dead and dying, its conning tower crushed as though squeezed by a giant vice, turned away and, leaking oil like the life-blood of a wounded beast, limped away toward its distant lair.

They passed through the outstretched arms of Leixões' breakwater and berthed alongside the quay.

The small, enclosed harbour was filled with neutral shipping, mainly Spanish and Portuguese coasters, but there was also a Swiss cargo ship boldly painted with the words SUISSE at either side of an enormous reproduction of the national flag.

It had not saved her. She lay at anchor, down by the stern, with a swarm of boats huddling about her weather-stained sides in an effort to pump out her after holds.

'The Jerries scatter mines wherever the fancy pleases them,' said Commander Davis. 'And mines are no respecters of neutrality.'

Commander Davis was the Naval Attaché and had come

aboard bearing gifts of a box of cigars and a case of Sandeman's port. 'Compliments of the management,' he told Turner.

Turner locked the cigars in a drawer. 'I can find a good home for those.' He gazed hopefully at his visitor. 'Personally, I'm a cigarette addict. Can't seem to be able to give up the habit.'

Commander Davis produced his cigarette case. 'Only local weeds, I'm afraid. Strong enough to choke a goat, but you are more than welcome to try your luck.'

Turner inhaled, spluttered and stared in disbelief at the cloud issuing from his lips. 'Goddamighty! Green smoke! What do they put in 'em?'

'Not for us to reason why,' said Davis cheerfully. He savoured his glass of Turner's Scotch and listened thoughtfully to the tale of the damaged U-boat.

'One more we can chalk up. They've been trying to penetrate the Straits, but we've given them a plastering. Sunk three, including one of their aces.'

'And last month, in the Atlantic, they sank three hundred thousand tons of shipping,' said Turner. 'So don't look so smug, young man.'

The Commander was neither young nor smug and was well aware that merchant captains tended to be a touchy lot, and not without reason, so he smiled amiably and got down to business.

'You'll be loading with cork, olive oil and sardines. I gather people back home have developed quite an appeiite for sardines.'

'People back home,' said Turner sourly, 'have developed an appetite for anything that goes into the stomach.'

'Ah, yes, of course, rationing,' said Davis, uncomfortably. 'Must make life very difficult for the chap used to kidneys and bacon for brekker.'

He wilted beneath Turner's stony gaze and realised that he had put his foot in it again. He tried a new tack. 'Portugal, being neutral, is stiff with Germans.'

'Spies,' said Turner. 'But when it's our lot we call it Intelligence.'

'They garner information from many sources, chief of which are brothel-keepers. Need I say more?'

'It's a barmy way of collecting it, but I'll bear it in mind.'

'All is grist to the mill,' said Davis. 'And the enemy is pretty good at sifting fact from fiction.'

'They've had plenty of practice with spying on one another in Nazi-land. Very well, we'll see if we can't keep 'em occupied with a few ill-found rumours.'

At the end of the bar a mournful lady with a husky voice plucked at the strings of a guitar and sang a sad fado:

Há sempre tanta tristeza,
No coraçao de quem sente,
Que até a alegria às vezes,
Tem pena de estar contente.

'It sounds like the tune the old cow died on,' said Cloud. 'She's got a good voice for selling coal.'

Replete with plates of grilled sardines and crayfish, they sat at a corner table drinking from bottles of Dão, the dark red wine of the Douro. It was heady stuff and, encouraged by their *inamoratas*, they swallowed it down with the practised tempo of confirmed beer drinkers.

Cloud looked from Jason's slender, wide-eyed senhorita to the pock-marked face of his own companion of the night. 'How is it,' he complained, 'that I always get the ugly one?'

'You got to stay faithful,' said the bos'n, one massive arm looped about a diminutive Circe.

'We're saving you for Sonia,' grinned Jason.

Lowrie's girl had protruding rabbit teeth and hennaed hair. 'They're all the same wi' the light oot,' he said.

'Mine isn't,' said Cloud. 'She's been eating garlic.'

Jason up-ended his bottle into his glass. 'Your shout, Cloudy.'

Cloud snapped his fingers. 'Oy – Mozo. Same again. Todos round, eh?' He turned to his girl. 'What's your name, kid?'

She pointed to herself. 'Me chamo, Arrabella.'

'Miriam Araby,' translated Cloud. 'I'm beginning to get the hang of this lingo. I'll call you Mary, for short, eh?'

The girl smiled accommodatingly and pointed to her companions. 'She – Juanita. She – Carmen. She – Mercedes. All good pokey-pokey.' She snuggled closer to Cloud, drained her glass and showed a row of discoloured teeth. 'Me very good. Plenty shag, eh?'

'Christ,' said Jason. 'They come right out with it, don't they?'

'Horrible,' said Cloud. 'It's enough to put you off your stroke.'

The waiter arrived and banged down four more bottles. 'No moço,' he hissed angrily. 'Me – criado. Criado de mesa.'

Cloud paid him and added a generous tip. The waiter bowed his thanks. 'Obrigado.' He wagged a finger. 'No moço, pliss? Me Jaime.'

Cloud refilled his glass. 'What's he on about?' he demanded.

His companion helped herself from the bottle. 'Moço not good. Jaime criado.'

'I know he's crying about something,' said Cloud. 'But what?'

A broad-shouldered man with close-cropped hair turned from the bar. 'Moco is ovensive. The vaiter is prefer criado vich means vaiter. But it vill please him to be called Chaims. That is his name.'

'Chaims,' said Cloud. He raised his glass. 'Jeers, then.'

'Cheerio, pip-pip,' said the man. 'I am Svenske. Svedish businessman. You are English, no?'

'No,' said Lowrie. 'They're Sassenachs. I'm frae Dumfries.'

'Ah,' said the man blankly. He held out his glass at arm's length. 'Happy and glorious.'

'I'll drink to that,' said Cloud. 'And stuff Hitler.'

The man smiled vaguely, drained his drink and returned to his identical twin at the bar.

'A pair of crop-heads,' said the bos'n. 'If he's a Swede, I'm a Chinese opium-eater.'

Arabella squeezed Cloud's arm and leaned closer. 'You go 'way, soon?' she whispered.

Cloud counted on his fingers. 'Mañana, mañana, mañana, mañana.'

'One-two-t'ree – four days. Where you go?'

'Bootle,' said Cloud.

'Boa-tel?'

'Where the fleas wear clogs and the barmaids eat their young.'

'Boa-tel.' She squirrelled away the information. 'I 'member.'

Juanita learned from Jason that they were bound for Otterspool Gardens on the Gold Coast.

Carmen gleaned the knowledge that the bos'n's next port of call would be Fiddlers Green. 'Where all good sailors go,' he told her.

'Auchtermuchty,' said Lowrie.

'Que?'

'Auchtermuchty, ye heathen. Have ye no sense o' locality?'

She looked at him uncertainly. 'You mak' chiste?'

He put his fingers to his lips and nodded toward the two ment at the bar. 'Ssh – even the walls have ears.'

Her quick glance across confirmed his suspicions. He chucked Mercedes under the chin. 'You are worth your weight in gold, hinnie,' he told her. 'I'm going to hae one of them Nazis for breakfast.'

Lowrie did not have long to wait. One of the pair detached himself from the bar and made his way through a doorway marked: *Cavalheiros*. Lowrie gave him a moment or two then sauntered in the same direction.

Within a minute he returned, licking his knuckles and smiling broadly. He walked across to the man's friend and tapped him on the shoulder. 'Excuse me – but yer mate's just met wi' a nasty accident.'

'Vasa?'

'Fell over and hurt hisself.' Lowrie jerked a thumb. 'He's in there, sleeping it off.'

He returned to the table. 'We'd best be pushing off. I've just thumped one of them Nazis. Then I put the boot in. He'll never be the same again.'

'You mad Scotch git,' said Cloud. 'I've just spent half a week's pay getting little Miriam here in the mood.'

'Suit yersel',' said Lowrie. 'But I've just tell't his mate where to find the body.'

'You're a bleedin' nutcase,' said the bos'n. He heaved himself to his feet. 'Back aboard, lads, unless you've a fancy for a Portugee calaboose.'

Cloud stuffed a handful of escudos down the front of Arabella's dress and ran out after the others.

They made their way breathlessly back to the ship, roundly cursing a cock-a-hoop Lowrie.

'I was looking forward to a couple of quick jumps,' complained Cloud as they trudged up the gangway. 'That Miriam would have been a bit of all right with a sack over her head.'

'I've done yiz all a favour,' said Lowrie. 'I bet they was all poxed up to the eyes.'

'You can console yourself with that thought while you chip and scrape every plate on the ship,' growled the bos'n. 'Starting tomorrow.'

Commander Davis came aboard the following morning, a newspaper tucked beneath one arm. 'I hope, Captain, that you will see to it in future that before your crew go ashore they are able to distinguish between friend and foe.' He unfolded the newspaper and pointed to the thick black heading above a half column on page one.

Turner put on his spectacles and shook his head. 'Can't make head nor tail of it. Typical of foreigners – always write in a language no one else can understand.'

The Commander grinned. 'According to this newspaper report a Swedish businessman made the mistake of speaking English last night. It seems that he was having a quiet drink with a colleague when he was set upon by an English hooligan. The gentleman received cuts and contusions to his features and severe bruising to his ribs. The assailant then decamped accompanied by his three companions, believed to be English seamen.'

'Spoke English, eh? No doubt with an accent you could chop with an axe.' Turner sniffed. 'Just where was this bar?'

'On the waterfront.'

'Oh? And what were a couple of respectable Swedish businessmen doing in a sailors' pub?'

'A question I have been asking myself. It does enjoy something of a seedy reputation.' The Commander smiled wryly. 'Probably having a night out on the town and got more than they bargained for. Under the circumstances I doubt they will be anxious to press charges.'

Turner reflected a moment. 'Very well. I'll keep all hands aboard until we sail.'

Davis nodded. 'Very wise.' He passed Turner a sealed envelope. 'Your orders, sir. We are spreading the rumour that you are bound for Gib. In fact you will sail at nightfall, head north and west, and pick up a homeward bound convoy at the rendezvous indicated in your orders. Loading will be completed by the twenty-first.' He shook hands and took his leave. 'Good luck, Captain.'

They passed through the breakwaters into a turbulent sea and sailed beneath leaden skies toward a horizon smeared with red from the dying rays of the setting sun.

They steamed south for the benefit of watchers on the shore then, when the blanket of darkness fell, laid off a new course for their rendezvous.

By eight bells the following morning the weather cleared and a pale sun blanched the dark water. At two bells the lookout reported sighting a ship, hull down, and bearing south by west.

By four bells the ship had become four ships and the pattern hardened and took the shape of an approaching convoy of thirty ships escorted by four Flower-clad corvettes.

At noon the *Kentucky Minstrel* took up her allotted position at the rear of the starboard flank and soon they were back to the familiar drudgery of keeping station at the speed of the slowest ship as the convoy zig-zagged its way northward.

Time passed monotonously. The watches changed. Day became night, then day again. The surrounding sea sparkled with wind-whipped spray. Banks of cumulus sailed overhead, bombarding the convoy with bolts of sunlight.

On the afternoon of the third day they heard the unmistakable drone of a high-flying aircraft. It emerged from a piled thunderhead and, keeping well out of range, lazily circled the plodding ships.

Page lowered his binoculars and swore loudly. 'The bastard's just hanging around and reporting our position.'

Turner was squinting into the sun. 'Long-range, four-engine aircraft.'

'Fokker-Wolf Kondor,' said Page. 'Probably based at Bordeaux.'

'It's Christmas Eve,' said Turner. 'I wonder what surprise packets they'll have in store for tomorrow?'

'They'll be queueing up to deliver 'em,' said Page grimly.

The aircraft continued to circle for another hour then disappeared over the horizon.

At nightfall the convoy made a radical alteration of course and steamed west by south in an effort to evade the skirmish line of U-boats no doubt alerted by the prowling F-W.

At dawn on Christmas Day the sun rose above the eastern horizon, flooding the sea with light and heralding the birth of a new day. The escorts fussed about, wishing everyone a Merry Christmas and ordering laggard ships to keep closed up. A light breeze scattered tufts of golden cloud about the sky as though dispensing goodwill to all mankind and the sea sparkled azure blue, wide and empty as though hugging its secrets to itself.

The stewards had given the saloon a festive air with lines of bunting looped across the deckhead and Chippy had mocked up a Christmas tree from bits of dunnage and teased out rope-ends, and camouflaged with brown, silver and green paint. It stood in a red-lacquered paint drum decorated with cotton-wool and bearing the legend: *A Merry Xmas From All Hands.*

At breakfast they exchanged gift-wrapped presents: a mountain of cigarettes for Captain Turner: a box of cigars to share between them, and a bottle of wine apiece from Turner: an assortment of bottles, cigarettes, razor blades and identical cigarette lighters, stamped *Made in Germany*, to one another.

The crew's messroom had been decorated in similar fashion, and Turner and the officers had donated cigarettes, rum, whisky and a crate of beer. The crew formed up into the traditional band of washboard, musical combs, and upturned pan as a kettle-drum, and marched through the saloon singing: *God Send Ye Merry Gentlemen,* with Lowrie as a mendicant Santa Claus bringing up the rear, cap held out in supplication as he whined: 'Alms for the love of Allah.' The officers donated their annual tribute, Turner toasted them with their Christmas tot. The bos'n, as official spokesman, responded by thanking one and all for their generosity, assured Captain Turner of their unswerving devotion, and trusted that the unfortunate episode in Leixões could now be overlooked.

'You may return Lowrie to normal duties,' said Turner magnaminously. 'Provided, of course, that in future he takes a more charitable view of his fellow man. You might take a leaf out of my book, Lowrie.'

'Oh, yes, sir. Thank you, sir,' said Father Christmas gratefully.

Two hours later the aircraft returned, circled, waggled its wings triumphantly, and flew away.

At midday the U-boats attacked in strength. A tanker in the starboard wing column was suddenly engulfed in flames and disappeared beneath the surface in a savage hissing roar as the flanking corvettes foamed away in a fruitless search, their depth charges thudding and raising ineffective fountains of water.

A second ship in the port column fell away, slowly settling by the stern and listing heavily to port. Two lifeboats, packed with seamen, pulled away. Then the ship sank with a long-drawn-out gurgle, leaving nothing but a widening stain on the sea and the familiar trail of flotsam bobbing to the surface.

A three-island freighter, in defiance of orders, left her station, stopped her engines, and boldly picked up the survivors. Miraculously, although a sitting duck target, she remained unscathed as the crew of the stricken freighter scrambled up her nets.

By now she had dropped well astern of the convoy and from the *Kentucky Minstrel*'s bridge they watched her bow wave creaming as she set off to overtake the cluster of ships. A few hundred yards off the *Kentucky Minstrel*'s port quarter she sounded a triumphant *cock-a-doodle-do* on her whistle; then a new sound intruded: a rapid bang-bang-bang-bang from the escort's 20mm Oerlikons.

Page swung his head, narrowing his eyes against the sun's glare. He pointed: 'There he is!' Right ahead, sweeping over the convoy in a long shallow dive, came the hated F-W, this time no longer a shadower, but an attacker from a new dimension.

'Take cover!' said Turner and pressed the alarm button.

Sparkles of light winked from the diving plane and the drone of its engines became an ear-splitting roar. Bits and pieces flew from the bridge of the ship ahead, then the hail of machine-gun fire ripped across the *Kentucky Minstrel*'s foredeck, gouging holes in the deck plating, splintering hatch-boards, ricochetting from the steel drums of the winches, tearing into the fore-part of the midships housing and ringing against the armour-plating of the pill-boxes. The wheelhouse windows burst into flying fragments of razor-sharp glass. Able Seaman Parslow, mouth agape, fell across the wheel in a welter of blood as bright red buttons stitched across his chest and his skull suddenly blossomed into an obscene crimson flower.

Without a guiding hand at the helm the ship sheered off course and began to describe a wide semi-circle, ploughing toward the stern of the next ship in line.

Page, lying prone on the deck, picked himself up, dragged Parslow's body clear and grasped the wheel, finding the spokes slippery with blood as he rammed the helm hard over.

'Keep her going, son,' said Turner, lumbering to his feet.

The plane's engines were a wild howl, its guns stuttering and kicking up flecks of water as it flattened out of its dive and concentrated on its next target.

The Kentucky Minstrel, in her accustomed position in the rear rank, curved through the wake of her portside neighbour. Page spun the wheel, splattering himself with blood, and steadied the ship on a southerly heading. At the same time he clearly saw the bomb falling from the F-W's fuselage. It fell lazily, like an elongated egg, to plunge into the sea twenty yards from the bows of the rescuing freighter. The bomb exploded and threw a curtain of spray across the ship's foredeck. The whistle tootled again derisively as the plane roared away, skimming across the surface of the sea.

'Near miss,' said Turner. 'Bring her back to course, Mr Page.'

Page put the helm hard aport, holding it down against the pressure of the telemotor, his hands sticky with gore, until the convoy once more loomed ahead.

A mile to starboard a U-boat's conning tower broke the surface. It's gun crew piled on to deck and loosed off half a dozen shots at the convoy. The lead corvette turned in wrath, its 4-inch gun coughing savagely from its bucking foredeck. The U-boat, having achieved its purpose, crash-dived with fountains of water leaping about its rapidly submerging conning tower. The corvette continued on its course spilling depth charges from its stern. Its wild rush, however, left a gap in the protective screen to allow two of the lurking pack to move in and fire twin spreads of torpedoes.

They heard the hammer blows as four ships lurched, shuddered, staggered out of line, and began to settle into the sea. A fifth, evidently loaded with ammunition, disintegrated into one huge eye-searing flash; a cataclysmic explosion that drummed and reverberated across the ocean; the sea puckered with splashes from the rain of pieces torn from the ship and hurled skywards. Smoke from the burning ship drifted across the convoy and, far astern, the plane climbed, banked and turned for its second bombing run.

It was a well co-ordinated attack and boded ill for the future.

The pilot evidently took the *Kentucky Minstrel* to be a wounded straggler. The F-W dropped two bombs; one fell wide, raising a pluming spout of water glittering in the sun; the other dropped with an iron clang on the *Kentucky Minstrel*'s foredeck. There was a sickening delay, then – like a slow-motion film – the plates buckled and opened into a jagged crater. A gush of flame followed immediately; the tarpaulins covering number one hold bulged then burst as the force of the explosion pulverised the wooden hatchboards into splinters and spouted the remains high into the air. Fire roared from the hold; a searing incandescent heat that swept across the deck, licked around the base of the foremast, set alight the tarpaulins of number two hatch, smothered the forward housing in fire and raged along both outboard alleyways, consuming everything in its path like some voracious, angry beast.

'Bring her round out of the wind!' shouted Turner.

Page spun the wheel and the ship once more circled to bring the wind astern, the flames now turning in wild yellow sheets to envelop the forecastle head.

Turner rang the engines to STOP as Furlong and Dean arrived on the bridge.

'Mr Furlong, take charge of the fire party. Mr Dean, a man to the wheel and a stretcher party to remove – this.'

Dean's gorge rose as he looked down at what had once been Able Seaman Parslow, but was now nothing but a ragged tatter of blood and bone. 'Aye, sir,' he replied and hurried away, quelling a rebellious stomach.

Page shifted a foot and queasily discovered that he had been standing on Parslow's hand.

High in the crow's nest Able Seaman Chambers crouched and whimpered. When the bomb struck he had been peering out through the wide eye-slits, afraid but fascinated by the U-boat attack. As a precautionary measure he had opened the trapdoor in readiness for a hasty escape. The attack, coming from astern, had taken him unawares. One moment he had been looking out at the badly mauled convoy, and privately thanking his lucky stars that he was not in among them, the next moment he had been staring into a blazing inferno. The heat had scorched his face so fiercely that the skin had erupted, puffing up around the eyes until he had imagined that he was blind. Then flames, coiling up the mast like fiery serpents, had poured through the open trap, melting his oilskins and feeding greedily upon the oil-based canvas. Trapped in his tiny cubicle, suspended between sky and water, he had turned into a human torch. Instinctively he had kicked the trapdoor shut before rolling about his minute steel cell in an effort to beat out flames that licked at his face and frizzled his legs like frying bacon. He had screamed; but his screams had gone unheard; he had yelled into the phone, but the shock of the explosion had ripped out the wiring. Now, having quenched the flames, he lay cowering and whimpering in his private hell.

The pilot of the F-W was pleased with his work. He flew low over the stricken ship while his observer took photographs and the gunners rattled off another burst. To his inexperienced eye the British ship, engines stopped, engulfed in flame and smoke, was finished. *Kaput*. He banked and returned his attention to the battered convoy limping northward. He could see the sickle pattern of white wakes as the ships zig-zagged, turning and twisting this way and that, like a flock of helpless sheep running from a pack of wolves, their only protection four small, ineffectual terriers snapping at their heels.

The pilot waggled his wings to give himself a better view and caught a glimpse of a dark cylindrical shape gliding beneath the surface as it manoeuvred for position ahead of the convoy.

The F-W carried a bomb load of four 200Kg bombs. Only one remained. The pilot looked for a fresh target and singled out the lead ship in the centre column. He put the nose down, throttled back and then firmly held to his course as the bomb-aimer squinted through his sights and lined up the ship until it loomed as big as a barrel. The corvettes spat fire and hurled long arcs of tracer shells into the air. The pilot contemptuously ignored the erratic streams of flak and kept the plane steadily on target. The plane shuddered once or twice as 20mm cannon shells exploded against the armour-plating. The bomb-aimer squeezed the button, then cursed luridly as the mechanism jammed.

The pilot put up the nose, gained altitude and circled patiently while the front gunner and bomb-aimer busied themselves with the damaged release gear. Comfortably out of reach of enemy flak he gazed contentedly at the drama below.

The U-boat he had seen gliding below the surface had found its prey and another ship had fallen out of line, heeling over, its lifeboats dangling from the davits, smoke and steam pouring from its shattered engineroom, a wide stain darkening the surrounding sea.

The pilot smiled and took a wide sweep. The U-boats of the Kriegsmarine were evidently having a field day. Soon the enemy convoy would be obliterated, but before the culmination of that happy circumstance it fell to him to uphold the honour of the Luftwaffe. He curtly ordered the two sweating crew members to hurry before the Kriegsmarine gained all the credit, and at that moment his eye lighted upon the disabled ship, lagging far behind the convoy, vast clouds of smoke pouring from its forward hatches. He took the plane down for a closer look.

The cargo of cork – long layers of bark stacked in the tween decks and against the shipside in the lower holds – had muffled and contained the initial explosion. But the drums of olive oil and thousands of cases of sardines had spilled their contents until number one hold was awash with burning oil and pouring out choking black clouds of thick oily smoke.

Mr Furlong and his fire party had rigged hoses and quickly extinguished the fiercest of the flames. Clothed in asbestos suits and breathing apparatus they did not hear the accelerating drone of the plane's engines until it roared overhead at mast height. Then the backwash from its four propellers almost bowled them over and sent the clouds of smoke into frantic eddies and swirls.

The rear gunner sprayed the ship with a five-second burst as the plane zoomed away and had the satisfaction of seeing the ant-like creatures running and tumbling and diving for cover.

One short burst tore into the dyspeptic Mr Furlong's stomach, smashed through his chest and hurled him over the hatch coaming into the simmering cauldron below. Ordinary Seaman Mason collapsed with a shattered leg, and a richochetting bullet tore through the calf of Able Seaman Parker's leg leaving him with a limp for the rest of his life.

From the bridge Turner watched the plane wheeling as it prepared to make a second pass.

'Kick her ahead, Mr Dean,' he ordered. 'Hard astarboard and bring her up into the wind,' he told Conroy at the helm. He kept his gaze fixed upon the antics of the plane. 'He's making a tour of inspection. Probably, being an uneducated Nazi, he imagines we are foundering and not worth the waste of a bomb. We'll keep up the illusion.' He gave his orders sharply and crisply as the *Kentucky Minstrel* turned her head to the wind and the smoke from number one hold enveloped the ship in a pall of black fumes.

The F-W's pilot decided upon a figure-of-eight course which would cover the lone ship and take them in a wide circle around the convoy. Once the fouled trigger of the release mechanism had been repaired he would decide upon his target.

He made a long lazy turn and swooped toward the ship. Looking down he saw lifeboats pulling away from a vessel which seemed to be on fire fore and aft. Smoke billowed from the fore part to swallow the ship in a dense cloud of thick black fog, hiding bridge and upperworks from view. The ship seemed to be drifting helplessly with only small sections of bows and stern showing.

The gunner experimentally strafed the vessel, raking it from stem to stern. There was no reply; no sign of life; only the lifeboats crawling across the face of the sea like wounded insects.

The bomb-aimer gave a thumbs-up signal. The pilot considered carefully: it was a difficult target, aiming through the covering smoke; on the other hand, if he expended the bomb on one of the convoy, no doubt one of those swaggering U-boat commanders would claim the credit. He made up his mind. It was his prize and, if they could manage a direct hit, would make a most satisfying photograph. It might even be published. Such splendid evidence would make excellent propaganda. Medals had been given for less. And promotion. Heady with rosy dreams he alerted the crew and put the nose down until they were just skimming over the sea. One last tour of inspection to choose the precise target area, then an undisturbed bombing run – yes, it should make a most satisfying photograph.

The drifting smoke gave him a clear indication of wind direction. Throttling back he lowered the flaps and lumbered slowly past the ship's stern.

'Got you, you bastard,' said Corporal Jackson and squeezed the trigger.

The shell screamed from the gun and a quarter of a second later blew the plane into whirling fragments. Sheets of flame from its exploding petrol tanks spiralled in cascades of golden rain. One engine, its blades still whirring, plunged skittering into the sea. The tail plane with its black and white swastika fluttered down last of all, bobbed for a few moments on the scum of the waves, then disappeared for ever.

'Good riddance,' said Turner emerging from the wheel-house, a handkerchief clutched to his nostrils.

Dean, coughing and choking, eyes smarting, left the refuge of his steel pill-box and grinned happily. 'A sitting duck,' he crowed. 'A sitting duck.'

'So are we, son,' said Turner laconically and jerking the whistle lanyard, sounded the recall signal. 'Hard astarboard, Conroy. Slow ahead, Mr Dean. Let's get out of this smoke, it's enough to choke a pig.'

The *Kentucky Minstrel* swung until long trailing banners of smoke waved over the sea. Page, standing in the stern-sheets of number one lifeboat, guided his small flotilla around to the weather side and, leaving the boat crews to hook on to the davit falls, clambered over the side, grinning hugely from ear to ear. 'Our Sloppy is as cute as a cartload of monkeys,' he told the bos'n.

'It's Sloppy's way,' said the bos'n. 'Tempt the other feller into an error, then hit him hard. He'll never change.'

'Amen to that,' said Page piously.

They extinguished the fire, buried their dead and attended to the wounded.

The forgotten Able Seaman Chambers had died curled at

the bottom of the crow's nest. Mr Furlong's body had been fished out of the bubbling mess in number one hold, decently enshrouded in canvas, and reverently consigned to the deep.

In the saloon Page queasily helped Turner to patch up Able Seaman Parker and Ordinary Seaman Mason.

'Easy as pie,' said Turner, strapping up Parker's leg. 'He'll probably yell a bit when he comes round, but I reckon that's as neat a job as you'd find in many a major hospital. I always fancied meself as a sawbones.' He wiped bloodied hands down the front of his apron. 'Next,' he called with the aplomb of a surgeon in a front line dressing station.

The attendant stewards, who acted as stretcher bearers and were becoming battle-hardened after handling their grisly cargoes, lifted the drugged Parker down from the saloon table and deposited him gently on a stretcher. Then they picked up Ordinary Seaman Mason, moaning in spite of a massive dose of morphine, and laid him on the table.

'Now this one's something of a challenge to me skill,' said Turner.

Page averted his gaze from the mass of flesh and shattered bone that had once been Mason's leg.

'In the old days,' continued Turner reflectively, 'they used to saw 'em off.' He scratched an armpit. 'Of course, in those times they weren't too particular. Half the Navy was stumping around on wooden legs.' He cast a professional eye over the splinters and protruding ends of bone. 'But I daresay between us we can sort out the bits and pieces, eh, Hubert?'

Page gagged at the thought of touching that raw flesh and quivering nerves. 'Aye, sir,' he replied as Mason rolled his eyes and moaned again.

'Squeamish, are you, son?' asked Turner affably. 'Understandable. Takes a strong stomach does this kind of work.' He rinsed his hands in a basin of water and wiped them on a towel. 'Well, the sooner we get started, the sooner we get finished.'

From time to time Turner refreshed his memory from an open book, mouthing and mumbling instructions as he worked, while Page passed him scalpels, scissors, needle and thread.

Eventually Turner straightened his back. 'Right, Mr Page,' he announced. 'He's all yours.'

'Mine?' He stared down at the blood-soaked bandages.

'I've given it a dusting with sulphanilomide. All it needs now is a nice case of plaster and, as long as we haven't put his leg on back to front, in a day or two he'll be hopping around like a new-born chick.' Turner gazed proudly at his pudgy spatulate fingers. 'Got the hands of a surgeon,' he announced. 'Everyone remarks on it. I expect you've noticed?'

'Well,' said Page, mixing plaster-of-Paris. 'You've certainly got stronger nerves than me.'

'Nothing to it, son – he did all the moaning – I never felt a thing.' Turner stretched blood-caked arms. 'I'm off to swill this muck off. I'm bumping you up to Mate and young Dean to Second. The bos'n can stand the eight-to-twelve as a watch-keeper. Think you can handle it?'

'Aye, sir.'

'Good. You can put your three stripes up and I'll make it official by signing you off as Chief Officer and recommend that the office confirms your promotion.'

'Thank you, sir.'

'Parcel him up, Hubert, and report to the bridge when you've finished. We're not out of the wood, yet.'

'Aye, aye, sir.'

Turner lumbered away and Page bent to his task reflecting that promotion came swiftly in war-time and lent a new and grisly meaning to the old phrase 'waiting for dead men's shoes.'

With the convoy out of sight below the horizon the *Kentucky Minstrel* swung west and made a wide sweep out into the Atlantic.

'The convoy will be keeping the subs busy and I see no point in sticking our head into a hornets' nest,' Turner told his new Second Mate.

'Aye, sir,' said Dean. His new responsibilities were already weighing heavily on his shoulders. Chart work was not his forte, and although Sloppy Joe dressed like a superannuated tramp he had a well-deserved reputation as a meticulous navigator, so he cleared his throat nervously. 'I have laid off a Great Circle course to bring us to a departure point at around 50 north, 20 west.'

Turner eyed him mournfully. '*Around* 50 north? Not good enough, young man. I like to know precisely where I'm going, and exactly where I've been.'

'I have worked it out accurately,' Dean assured him. 'I only meant . . .'

'A rough estimate. I understand.' Turner was evidently in one of his avuncular moods. He laid a hand on Dean's shoulder as though patting a stray dog. 'Just remember that all a good navigator requires is a plumb line and a time piece, and you can't go far wrong.'

'Thank you, sir,' said Dean, mystified. 'I'll try to remember.'

He repeated the conversation to Page when that worthy arrived to relieve him. Page wore an extra gold band on each sleeve. 'I took 'em off my old uniform, and I advise you to do the same. Sloppy don't like his hints to go unheeded.' He ruminated a moment. 'A plumb line? One of Sloppy's more subtle interpretations of the obvious.'

'Obvious? I'm damned if I can see the connection.'

'If you are ever adrift in an open boat and in your haste you've left your sextant behind, how would you take a sight?'

Dean shrugged. 'By guess and by God?'

'No doubt. But you could improve on it with a plumb line and a couple of crossed sticks.'

'A sextant . . .'

'Rough and ready. But it would work. You know, it might not be a bad notion to stow a spirit level and a couple of pieces of looking glass in every boat. I think I'll mention it to Sloppy.'

'You're the Mate,' said Dean.

At dinner, with Matt Honest patrolling the bridge, smart in reefer jacket and peaked cap, Page broached the subject.

Turner helped himself to roast turkey, onion stuffing and half a dozen chipolata sausages. 'I'm glad to hear that you fellers have been applying your wits to me little conundrum. Does you credit, Hubert, does you credit.' He raised his glass. 'A merry Christmas, gentlemen.'

'Merry Christmas,' they responded.

They swallowed their wine and applied themselves to their Christmas dinner. Only it did not feel in the least like Christmas. Just another day in a war that seemed to be growing bloodier every minute.

CHAPTER NINE

THE *Kentucky Minstrel,* scarred and smoke-blackened, entered port beneath a lowering sky and a biting wind that funnelled up the Mersey and roared through rubble-strewn streets deep in icy slush.

Turner's tram deposited him at the doors of the Royal Infirmary then trundled away toward the marble-fronted Rialto cinema.

He pushed open the main doors, spied a white-coated figure flitting along the corridor and gave a stentorian hail. The figure stopped, turned a forbidding face toward the source and stalked purposefully toward the intruder.

'This is a hospital,' he began waspishly.

'So I noticed,' said Turner affably. 'Not a bad little place.'

'Kind of ye to say so,' replied the man acidly. 'We like it. Now if ye'll state your business to the receptionist . . .'

'A doctor, aren't you?'

'I am.'

'Then you are just the feller I'm looking for.' Turner cocked his head. 'You are not English, I'll be bound?'

'My name is McMorran. Doctor McMorran. And I'm no' quite a Sassenach yet.'

'From north of the border, eh? Glasgow for a penny.'

'Aberdeen.'

'No mistaking that accent. I'm Turner. Captain Turner. We put one of our crew ashore with a busted leg. I gather you have him tucked up in bed somewhere in this rabbit warren? Name of Mason.'

The doctor reflected a moment. 'Ah – Mason? Yes, indeed, we have him. Ward 4. Second floor.'

'How is he?'

'As well as can be expected. Who actually set the leg?'

'I did. He didn't half yell. Good job I got a strong stomach. Always fancied meself as one of you sawbones. Some folks reckon that I missed me vocation.'

'Really? If you take the flight of stairs at the end of the corridor . . .'

'Leg set all right, did it?'

'The plaster held it quite firmly in place until we could X-ray it. Then we re-set it.'

'Well, of course you got all the facilities here,' conceded Turner. 'End of the corridor and two flights up, eh? You carry on with whatever you were doing, Doctor, I'll find me own way. Soon make meself at home.' He wallowed away cheerfully, leaving McMorran to gaze murderously at his departing back.

Ordinary Seaman Mason, his leg encased in its new plaster cast, his back propped against a mound of pillows, puffed contentedly at one of Dean's cigarettes and beamed at his visitors.

Page and Dean stood beside the bed, stifling yawns and desperately seeking fresh topics of conversation. Aboard ship Mason had always appeared to be a quiet, self-contained young man. It was only now that they had come to realise that Mason was quiet because he had nothing to say.

'How's the leg?' asked Dean brightly for the third time.

'All right,' said Mason. He puffed at his cigarette, then seemed to think that the statement needed amplifying. 'Gives me gyp sometimes. Usually when I cough.'

'Do you sleep all right?' asked Page.

Mason nodded. 'I think they put something in the tea.'

Dean looked around the ward. 'You seem to have plenty of company.'

'Bombed-out civvies. The feller in the end bed lost a foot. He doesn't half go on. Moan, moan, moan.' Mason lapsed into silence again.

'I saw a smashing little nurse just going off duty,' said Page. 'Cute little number. She'd raise anyone's spirits.'

'Battle-axes on this ward,' said Mason.

The blankets on the next bed heaved and Able Seaman Parker's head emerged like a tortoise after a long hibernation.

'Hullo, Parker!' said Page enthusiastically. 'How are you feeling, old man?'

Parker's eyes rolled in his head and he fell back asleep.

'They took him off this morning and sewed him up again.'

'Oh?'

Mason evidently considered that he had exhausted that topic, for he stretched his arms and yawned. 'Lovely places, hospitals. Nothing to do, and all day to do it in. I could lie here forever.'

'What happens if there is an air-raid?' asked Dean searching for a fresh subject.

'I dunno,' said Mason. 'I never asked.'

Page looked at his watch. 'Take care of yourself, cobber. We've got to be going.'

'Yes,' Dean agreed with false bonhomie. 'We mustn't keep the ladies waiting, eh, Bert?'

'We'll look in again,' said Page, edging away.

'Hullo – I see you fellers got here before me,' boomed a familiar voice.

'Just leaving, sir,' said Dean hastily.

Turner picked up a chair from the bedside of a distant sufferer and plonked it down beside Mason. His eyes lighted upon the ash tray littered with cigarette stubs. 'Well,' he announced, settling himself comfortably, 'if I'd known smoking was allowed in hospitals I'd have brought some fags. These yours, Mason?'

'Mr Page and Mr Dean brung some, sir,' said Mason.

'Ship's fags, eh?' said Turner, lighting up. 'Plenty more where those come from. We'll see you don't go short, eh, Mr Page?'

Page and Dean smiled non-committally and eased themselves out through the door. They paused to listen.

'How's the leg?'

'All right. 'Cept when I cough.'

'Sleep soundly?'

'I think they put something in the tea.'

'Come on,' whispered Page. 'The boozer's open.'

'It's getting to be sheer bloody murder,' said Matt Honest.

His father sucked at his pipe. 'That's true. They fly over, knock down a street of houses, then fly off again. I don't know what good they think it'll do 'em. All it does, is get your monkey up.'

'I mean convoys,' said Matt. 'No protection beyond a

couple of corvettes. And they're nothing but glorified fishing boats.' He leaned over and spat disgustedly into the fire. 'And we're supposed to have a Navy.'

'Tha can't blame 'em, I suppose,' said Albert Hodge philosophically. 'There's a power o' water to cover.'

They were seated comfortably in Matt's front parlour. A small room reserved for special occasions, its atmosphere redolent of mothballs and a faint mouldering dampness which was being rapidly dispelled by the heat from a glowing coke fire. The overmantle was a clutter of ornaments and framed photographs. A heavily patterned wallpaper enclosed the room in a motif of autumn leaves broken by pictures brought home by Matt from as far afield as Rio and Tokyo. Against one wall stood a bulbous-legged sideboard with echelons of family photographs in silver-gilt frames. Benares-ware ashtrays, a bridge of elephants carved in bone, and small figurines from Africa and Madagascar. The spoils of a lifetime spent roaming the oceans of the world.

All in all it was a small, overcrowded, comfortable room, cherished and polished and filled with memories.

Matt and Albert had struck up a quiet and undemanding friendship and Albert, a widower living with a married sister in Leeds, had readily accepted an invitation to spend the first few days of the new year with Matt's family.

Matt's father sat in a fireside chair, mulling over a rag-bag of memories. He was an old man, lean, grey and grizzled, his hands knobbled with arthritis after half a century of sea-faring.

'It were the same in the last lot,' he said. 'Of course, Kaiser Bill, he had a Navy as well as us. Jutland. Ah, there was a battle. Now they got airyplanes and bomb the poor bloody civvies. It inn't right. Bloody 'itler.'

'That's more than enough swearing for one day, Father,' announced Matt's wife. She cast a warning glance toward their daughter, a golden-haired child perched on a leather pouffe and staring wide-eyed at the strange man who erupted periodically into her life, crowing and hugging, and bearing parcels of exciting presents. This time he had brought her a box of sticky sweetmeats and a doll in Portuguese national costume which she had already christened Thelma after her best friend.

Her mother smiled encouragement. 'She's very shy at first,'

she told Albert. 'But once she finds her tongue there's no stopping her. A born chatterbox.' She clicked away industriously at her knitting needles, content to relax within the nucleus of her family. She was a motherly, placid woman with a dumpling face and a few strands of grey in her hair. The house was one of a row of brick terraces separated from the street by a girdle of iron railings. During her husband's enforced absences she kept it spick and span, scrubbing, polishing and cleaning from top to bottom until the very house itself seemed to croon with the loving care lavished upon it.

Matt glanced at the clock softly tocking to itself on the mantlepiece. He rose and stretched. 'Time I took Albert round for a pint. You coming, Dad?'

The old man creaked from his chair. 'I fancy a pint o' mixed. Although nowadays it's either one or t'other and more often than not, neither.'

In the hallway they collected caps, coats and mufflers and stepped out into the street. Grandfather Honest sniffed the air, eyed roofs frogged with snow and the glitter of ice from puddles in the roadway. 'It's a brisk night,' he said, rubbing mittened hands together. 'But too much cloud for they devils to discommode us. Step out lively, you two, afore they run short of ale.'

It was but a short walk from Eversley Grove to the Grapes. They pushed open the door, made their way to the tiny snug and settled themselves comfortably in a corner.

'Hullo?' said Albert, peering over the top of his second pint. 'Look what the cat's dragged in.'

Page entered first, standing aside to usher in Marjorie, Olwyn and Dean. He selected a table at the adjacent corner and escorted the ladies to their places. The front snug was small, selective, with latticed windows, chintz curtains and half a dozen circular tables with surfaces of beaten copper. Leather-upholstered settees with dark oak arms carved into gargoyle heads ran around the room giving the maximum of intimacy and the minimum of privacy. The landlord had an ascetic face and the manners of an old English gentleman. He greeted Page as an old and valued customer, and waited politely to be introduced.

'Peter Cavanagh,' Page told them. 'He owns the place and picks and chooses his customers like family guests.' He patted Marjorie's knee. 'So watch your p's and q's, love, and no swearing.'

'Get stuffed, lover,' said Marjorie inelegantly. 'He'll never throw us out as long as he can get a free view. The old boy was peering down my dress with his eyes sticking out like organ stops.'

'Really?' asked Olwyn. 'He seems such a nice old gentleman.'

'He is, and I wouldn't change him for a sack of coal,' said Marjorie. 'But he had you stripped the moment you walked through the door.'

'You mean he's a lech?'

'You bet. God bless his cotton socks.'

'Good evening,' said Dean.

'How d'ye do?' replied Albert.

'What are you having?' asked Page.

'Same again, if it's alright with thee,' said Albert.

'Pint o' bitter, thank you, sir,' said Matt.

'Boat's out and on a free passage,' said Page.

Protocol satisfied, both groups returned to their private affairs as though they were but distant acquaintances.

The landlord returned with their drinks, squinted down Marjorie's blouse, winked at Olwyn and took the order for the other table.

Dean raised his glass. 'Cheers, Bert.' He sipped his drink and furtively eyed Page's girl friend. She was a stunner, he thought, and mentally comparing her with Olwyn, came to the conclusion that Page had the better of the bargain. After leaving the hospital they had had a couple of rounds at the Philharmonic and Page had suggested that they make a foursome. 'A couple of scoops, then take 'em to the Rialto ballroom,' he had suggested, adding diffidently, 'It's by way of being a sort of celebration. We are thinking of getting married.'

Dean had pumped him by the hand. 'Congratulations! When is the happy day?'

'Well, not yet awhile. Marge has to wait for the divorce to go through. One more trip, I reckon, then we'll be looking for a best man. If you fancy the role?'

Dean had accepted with alacrity and a burgeoning friendship had been cemented with two or three more drinks and by the time the pub had closed its doors, and they had reeled out in search of a taxi, they had become comrades-in-arms, exchanging confidences and swearing eternal fidelity.

Olwyn had listened to Dean's exposition with rounded eyes. 'A divorcee!' she had breathed. 'Oh, David, you do know some funny people.'

'You'll like Bert Page,' he had answered, somewhat shiftly.

'Oh, I am sure I shall. And I am looking forward to meeting his – lady friend. She must be terribly sophisticated. What should I call her? Mrs? Or –?'

'Marjorie, I imagine. And she is not divorced yet.'

'But she is living with him, quite openly, as his mistress? Mmmm, I bet she's a tigress, a real man-eater. I must keep an eye on you, darling, you are such a ninny when it comes to dealing with the opposite sex.'

Dean took another pull at his beer with a sense of relief. In truth he had been rather afraid of Olwyn's insouciant prattle which, although falling upon his ear like the tinkle of music could, he realised, be a source of irritation to others. However, Olwyn was evidently on her best behaviour and had shown a chameleon-like ability to instantly adapt to her surroundings.

She wore a dress of green and white patterned crepe with a full skirt and had carelessly slung her squirrel coat on the seat beside her. She had eschewed all personal jewellery with the exception of his engagement ring sparkling on her finger, and a silver chain with a horse-shoe pendant about her neck.

Dean felt quite proud of her and stole a glance toward Marjorie. There was no question about it, she was a stunner, an absolute stunner. She wore a simple, close-fitting, black wool dress scalloped around neck and throat, and a ponyskin cape draped about her shoulders. Her red hair gleamed like burnished copper and her skin glowed honey-coloured in the soft radiance of the pear-shaped clusters of overhead lights. Bert Page, he concluded once again, was a lucky, lucky dog.

The pub filled with a motley crowd of the well-heeled; from spivs in razor-sharp suits to fresh-faced Wavy-Navy sub-lieutenants, self-conscious in brand-new uniforms; from portly ladies smothered in furs, to slender maidens with enamelled fingernails and hopeful mascaraed eyes. The landlord and his son, Percy, moved easily through the crowded room, expertly sorting the sheep from the wolves, and bearing glasses of unobtainaable Scotch and gin for favoured customers. Page was evidently held in high esteem for their table was kept liberally supplied with short drinks of mellowing influence.

Dean, having finished his initial glass of beer, was now sipping contentedly at his fourth whisky. Olwyn, he noticed, was keeping pace and holding an animated conversation with Marjorie. Pleased that the girls had taken to each other he raised his glass and beamed across at Page. Page beamed back and added a knowing wink.

'That's the one,' called Albert across the hubbub.

Page cupped an ear. 'What?'

'Ah said, that's the one,' repeated Albert at the top of his voice. 'The red-haired lass ah saw thee with afore we sailed. She's a gradely lass.'

'Thank you,' said Page.

'Who's a what?' asked Marjorie.

'Ah said,' shouted Albert, 'that tha's a gradely lass.'

'Thank you,' smiled Marjorie.

'And Third Mate's on to a lovely touch, too. It's the uniform that attracts 'em. Like moths to a candle.'

Marjorie popped out a ring of smoke. 'It's the candle that attracts me,' she said, linking arms with Page. 'Isn't that so, Bert?'

Page grinned. 'The one you burn at both ends?'

'My candle burns at both its ends,' declaimed his lady-love. 'It will not last the night. But, ah, my foes, and oh, my friends, it gives a lovely light.'

Dean glanced at his watch. Time seemed to be racing past. 'If we are to eat first?' he ventured.

They made their way across to the Rialto where the display board announced that the second house performance of *Alexander's Ragtime Band* would commence at 8.15. A queue snaked around the corner, patiently stamping their feet and beating their arms against the cold.

Page recognised a familiar face and raised an arm in greeting. 'Hi, Chippy.'

Angus MacPherson, the ship's carpenter, shoulders hunched, hands deep in pockets, creased his morose features into the semblance of a smile and shuffled forward a few more paces toward the enchantments of Alice Fay, Don Ameche and the foghorn-voiced Miss Ethel Merman. The cinema was Angus MacPherson's overriding passion. It was said that after forty years of journeying over the face of the earth Angus had seen nothing beyond the inside of a picture-house. He was a solitary man who stayed at the Sailors' Home when ashore, but much preferred to make his home aboard ship where, in the monastic seclusion of his spartan cabin, he could browse through his enormous collection of movie magazines and lose himself in the fantasy worlds of his idols. Angus listed his favourite ports of call by the number of feature films he could see in one day. New York, where the movie houses opened early and closed late, headed the list, but Liverpool was not far behind. Today he had whetted his appetite with *Algiers* featuring Miss Hedy Lamarr and Mr Charles Boyer, followed by the more solid fare of *Night Must Fall* with Dame May Whitty and Mr Robert Montgomery and now, like a gourmet rounding off a well-chosen meal, Angus had chosen a light but satisfying soufflé.

A flurry of snow gathered the wind in white arms and danced down the street to speckle the queue with flakes of white confetti. Angus moved forward another pace or two. Tomorrow he would see *Gone with the Wind*. He had booked for two separate performances. An aisle seat in the circle. Unimpeded view and room to stretch his legs. Two hundred and twenty minutes of unalloyed pleasure followed by an interval for refreshment, then back again for a leisurely savouring of the plot accompanied by the spice of anticipation. He consulted his large turnip of a watch, and counted the number of people queueing ahead. With luck he would be in time for the Laurel and Hardy two-reeler.

The quartet made their way up to the first floor restaurant where they ate with the ravenous appetites of the young. Then, replete with food and slightly fuzzy with drink, they climbed another flight of carpeted stairs to the ballroom above.

They danced until eleven, gliding around the floor in waltz-time, exchanging partners for a fox-trot, linking arms for the grand parade of the Marche Militaire. Then, all too soon, it was over and they emerged into a white world and a crystal night.

Dean and Olwyn piled into a taxi and Page and Marjorie crossed the road and set off on the short walk to their flat.

'What do you think of her?' asked Page.

'She's a doll,' answered Marjorie.

'Certainly a cute little number,' he agreed guardedly.

'She's a doll. With a doll head, doll eyes and a doll brain. Immature and emotionally unstable. Your friend David would be better out of it.'

He shrugged. 'There's nothing I can do. He's besotted with her.'

'She's nineteen years of age. After two years of marriage she'll be fat and forty.'

They walked on in silence for a while, their feet crunching the fresh snow, their breath forming white clouds in the crisp, clear air. Besotted, he mused. That was a fair description of how he felt about Marjorie. Besotted and deeply and inescapably in love for the first time in his life. He remembered her greeting as he stepped over the threshold the day they docked. She had wrapped her arms about his neck, leaned back and looked at him, half-mockingly. 'How do you fancy being a co-respondent, lover?'

It seemed that her brother-in-law, the ape-man, had written a long and scurrilous account of their liaison to her husband. He, for his part, had taken the obvious step.

'His solicitors served the papers while you were away,' she had told him. 'So what are you going to do, lover? Make an honest woman of me?'

Page could imagine nothing more desirable than spending the rest of his life with her and had said so. 'How long must we wait?' he had asked.

'Not long. He's applied for an Army divorce. It's quick and cheap.'

'We'll be married by special licence,' he had promised. 'I wouldn't mind meeting him. I reckon I owe him a debt of gratitude.'

She had shaken her head. 'I wouldn't recommend it. Arthur's a bad-tempered devil.'

Arm linked in arm, fingers intertwined, they made their way along the short, deserted street. As they reached the front steps of the house a figure detached itself from the shadows and planted itself solidly in their path.

Marjorie released his arm and gave a gasp of shocked surprise. 'Arthur!'

It was an awkward and embarrassing moment. 'Arthur,' she said uncertainly, 'this is Bert. Bert, my husband.'

For a moment the two men eyed each other with the rigid

formality of a pair of duellists, then Arthur hawked and spat into the snow.

'You bleedin' whore,' he said.

Page had often wondered what Arthur looked like. Now he knew. Arthur bore an uncanny resemblance to the Michelin man built entirely out of rubber tyres. His shaven head looked like a stone cannon ball and his piggy eyes seemed to be buried in a mound of rubbery flesh.

'So you're her fancy man!' he snarled and launched himself forward.

'Hey! Take it easy, cobber,' said Page, holding out his arms in supplication. The air went out of him in a whoof as Arthur clouted him in the ribs and then pirouetted past on the slush of snow and ice.

'Look, feller,' began Page as Arthur, recovering his balance, came back at him like a rubber ball.

'Oh, hell,' said Page and poked out a long arm.

The rubber ball allowed the half-hearted punch to glide over his shoulder and then bounced back. A fist like a lump of concrete crashed into Page's jaw and he skidded backward, brain reeling, to lie flat in the snow. A hob-nailed army boot caught him in the ribs.

'Oh, Jesus!' he wheezed, rolled aside and clambered to his feet.

The rubber ball swung another foot. Page jumped aside and Arthur slid past to somersault on his back.

Page had had enough. As Arthur heaved himself to his feet he dipped his shoulder and smashed his fist into Arthur's face. The shock ran along his arm like a red-hot wire. For a moment he thought he had broken his knuckles. The punch had no other discernible effect whatsoever. Arthur advanced like a tank, seized Page by the shoulders and butted him in the face with his cannon-ball head.

The world went black, a knee caught him in the crutch and he rolled into a ball and retched into the gutter. A scream from Marjorie brought him to painful consciousness. He struggled to his feet, bowed and griping, to see that Marjorie had hurled herself upon Arthur and was raking his face with taloned fingernails. Arthur swore obscenely, pushed her away, slapped her savagely across the face knocking her off her feet, then returned to give his full attention to his adversary.

Page spat blood and waited for the rubber ball to come bouncing back. It was painfully evident that no amount of blows about the head would slow him down. He stepped aside and Arthur flailed past blowing like a grampus. He's a beer-belly, Page thought. A beer-belly, full of piss and wind.

Arthur turned, lowered his head and charged.

Page hit him in the stomach. It was as though he had driven his fist into layers of dough. Arthur blew out his cheeks in a great whoosh of air and Page, driving his arms like pistons, pummelled his mid-riff again and again until the rubber ball collapsed into a punctured balloon and Arthur, mouth agape, fell forward on to his knees.

'You stupid bastard,' gasped Page and, sticking out a foot, shoved him over to lie twitching and groaning in the snow. Then he helped Marjorie to her feet. 'Are you all right, love?' he asked solicitously.

She put a hand to her face and nodded dazedly. 'He always was a pig. Let's go inside.'

Arthur crouched on his knees, arms folded protectively about his stomach. 'Slut! Whore! Bitch!' he wheezed to the empty street. 'Bitch, slut, whore!'

'Minstrel Shipping Company. Catering department? One moment please, I'm putting you through.' Gladys, whose lair was the switchboard just inside the portals, allowed no one to pass unchallenged. She was a motherly woman of blotched complexion, myopic eyes and a brain like a calculating machine.

'Good morning, Gladys,' said Turner, entering through the swing doors. 'Mr Barraclough is expecting me. Go right through, shall I?' He pushed open the small wicket gate.

'Good morning, Captain Turner,' Gladys replied briskly. 'I am sorry, but the Marine Superintendent is engaged at the moment.'

Turner looked affronted. 'Engaged? But I distinctly told him ten o'clock.'

'I am sorry, Captain, but Mr Barraclough left strict instructions that he was not to be disturbed.' Gladys eyed the large office clock pointedly. 'And it is already past the hour.'

Turner sniffed. 'You'd expect a feller in Barraclough's position to be a stickler for punctuality. It beats me how these bowler-hats manage to hold down a job.'

Gladys sighed. 'It is a quarter past ten, Captain.'

'Just as well,' grumbled Turner. 'Otherwise I'd have been kicking my heels here for the past fifteen minutes. What's delaying him, Gladys? Who's with him? The Lord Mayor?'

'Mr Barraclough is interviewing your new Chief Officer, Mr Samuels.'

'Soapy Samuels? Is he, indeed? I'll soon take a hand in that. He's not saddling me with that smarmy bible-puncher. I've got me Mate already picked out. Don't trouble to announce me, Gladys, I know me way.'

Turner marched purposefully forward and unceremoniously pushed open the panelled mahogany door leading to the Marine Superintendent's private office.

'Captain Turner!' squeaked Gladys. 'You can't – you mustn't . . .' She gave up as the switchboard buzzed. It was going to be one of those days.

The Minstrel Line's Marine Superintendent was a thin wisp of a man with pursed lips and a tight accountant's face. He looked up irritably as Turner marched purposefully toward his desk.

'Captain Turner! I left strict instructions . . .'

'I know you did, Barraclough,' growled Turner. 'That's exactly why I'm here. D'you imagine I'm going to sit around cooling me heels while you play ducks and drakes with my crew?'

Barraclough drew a deep breath. 'Captain Turner . . .!'

'Plotting behind me back, eh? Trying to lumber me with some lah-di-dah, hymn-singing, creeping Jesus . . .?'

The Marine Superintendent ground his teeth. The directors seemed to look upon Turner as a lovable eccentric, but they did not have to deal with the monster. If it were not for the man's uncanny knack of earning quick-turn-round bonuses, and thereby handsome profits for the company, he would have rid himself of the scruffy old rogue years ago. But in this life every man had a cross to bear, and it seemed that Turner was his.

A figure, hands clasped prayerfully together, sat slumped in a chair near the desk.

'Captain Turner,' said Barraclough icily. 'This is Mr Samuels. The *Kentucky*'s new Chief Officer.'

Turner affected a start of surprise. 'Hullo, Samuels. I

didn't see you hiding behind the door. I thought you were on the beach?'

Barraclough had crossed swords too often with Turner not to recognise the technique. He determined to hold on to his temper.

Samuels uncoiled from his chair and extended a limp cold hand. 'I count it a privilege to serve with a man of your reputation, Captain Turner,' he said unctuously.

Turner ignored the hand. 'I don't mean it unkindly, Samuels, but the *Kentucky* is not the sort of ship that would suit a man of deep religious convictions such as yourself. They're heathens, Mr Samuels. Heathens to a man.'

Samuels permitted himself a Uriah Heep smile. 'All the more reason, Captain, why they should be brought to the light.'

'That's the spirit,' said Turner. 'You leave 'em to me and Page. We'll tame 'em for you. In a couple of trips they'll be eating out of your hand. In the meantime, Barraclough, why not turn Samuels loose on a passenger boat? They could have a little sing-song every Sunday morning. Passengers go for that sort of thing. Makes 'em feel they're getting their money's worth.'

'That will do, Captain Turner,' said Barraclough coldly. 'The ship will be signing Articles at eleven tomorrow morning. You will be going aboard today, Mr Samuels?'

'Yes, indeed, Mr Barraclough. Just to see that everything is ship-shape and running smoothly. It will also give me the opportunity of finding my sea-legs again.'

'I knew it,' said Turner. 'Been on the beach, haven't you, Samuels?'

'Mr Samuels,' said Barraclough wearily, 'has been convalescing after a particularly dangerous voyage. His ship was torpedoed and he spent five days in an open boat.'

'Then you'd best keep him off the *Kentucky*, because we seem to be in the thick of it. You're a hard man, Barraclough. A hard man. I couldn't do it.'

'The choice is not yours,' said Barraclough.' It is mine, and I have made it. Thank you, Mr Samuels, that will be all.'

'Thank you, Mr Barraclough,' said Samuels oilily. 'Good morning, Captain Turner, I look forward to a safe and successful voyage.'

Turner glowered after his departing back. 'Got a hide like

an elephant, that feller.' He reached across and helped himself from the Marine Superintendent's cigarette box. 'One of these days someone will drop a shackle on his head, mark my words.'

Barraclough smiled thinly. It wasn't often he emerged victorious from a clash with Sloppy Joe and he wanted to savour the moment.

'Saddling me with a man on the edge of a nervous breakdown,' Turner was saying. 'You've no feeling, Barraclough. No sense of the fitness of things. It goes against the grain to say it, but you are losing your grip.' He shook his head dolefully. 'The Board won't like it.'

'The Board?'

'Set great store by their ships, do the directors. I doubt they'll take kindly to having one of their crack ships in the charge of a bag of nerves like Samuels.'

'Mr Samuels will not be in command, Captain Turner. You will.'

'I'm an old man,' said Turner mournfully. 'And at my age you never know the day. Now take that feller, Page, I've been talking about . . .'

'Page?' asked Barraclough, lost.

'Nerves of steel. A bright young feller. Keen, ambitious, and a chain-smoker to boot.'

'A chain-smoker?'

'Shows he don't count the cost. Not like that mealy-mouthed psalm-singer you are bent on encumbering me with.'

Barraclough breathed deeply. 'Mr Samuels . . .' he began.

'That's the one. Doesn't drink. Doesn't smoke. He'll come to a bad end, mark my words. Now you know me, Barraclough. I never interfere, but I'm always willing to lend a helping hand. Now if you want my advice . . .'

'I don't,' said Barraclough briefly. 'I have given careful consideration to your reports on Second Officer Page and Third Officer Dean, and in my judgement neither qualify for promotion at the present time.' He spread his hands. 'Another trip or two, perhaps . . .'

'Judgement? Qualify?' Turner leaned forward. 'Being a bowler-hat it's probably escaped your notice, Barraclough, but there is a war on, and we are in the middle of it. I want the best, and I intend to have the best.'

'I have made my decision,' said Barraclough. 'Good day to you, Captain Turner.'

'You'll live to regret it,' said Turner, reaching for his hat. He lumbered to his feet. 'Good day to you, Barraclough. I only hope you can sleep easy o' nights.'

The Marine Superintendent watched him go. 'I will now,' he promised himself. 'I will now.'

Page was whistling softly to himself as he tidied up the chart-room. Philosophically he had resigned himself to the fact that the hoped-for third stripe still evaded him and consoled himself with thoughts of Marjorie and marriage. *Marriage.* He hauled open one of the chart drawers and paused dreamily. He had always looked upon himself as foot-loose and free, but he could imagine a no more desirable future than a life spent with Marjorie. Even her absence somehow strengthened the bond. The soft tentacles of recollection wove silken patterns about his memory. It wasn't sex, he mused, although that certainly played its part and Marjorie was no mean performer; it was more that he actually enjoyed just being with her; just to sit silent and relaxed, content in the knowledge that she was there. It must be love, he decided, and concluded that if such were the case then love was a most desirable state of affairs and there should be more of it to go around.

The opening door broke into his meditations and he glanced up to meet the stern gaze of a waxen-faced man of balding head and gooseberry eyes.

'Mr Page?'

'Yeah,' Page acknowledged affably. 'You must be the new Mate. Settling in all right, Mr Samuels?'

'Have you had an accident?' asked Samuels solicitously.

Page raised a hand and tenderly touched his bumps and bruises. 'Sort of,' he admitted. 'I had a bit of a run-in with a swaddy.'

Samuels subjected him to a disapproving stare. 'Am I to understand, young man, that you engaged in a public brawl with a common soldier?'

'He didn't give me much choice,' said Page. 'Not that you could blame him. After all, she was his wife.'

Samuels looked as though he could not believe the

evidence of his ears. 'You are involved in an adulterous relationship with a married woman?'

'Yeah. Although I wouldn't put it quite like that.'

'I would. In my opinion you are a disgrace to the company's uniform.'

'You keep your opinions to yourself, sport,' said Page. 'We don't go for dog on this ship.' He turned away, rummaged in the chart drawer and fished out a flat fifty box of cigarettes. Quelling his rising temper he held it out and summoned up a placating grin. 'Look, cobber, we've got to work together. Maybe we'd best forget it, eh? Cigarette?'

Samuels looked down his nose. 'Thank you, no. I do not approve of the habit.'

'That so? Sloppy's just going to love you.'

'Sloppy?'

'Sloppy Joe Turner. Our chief gondolier.'

'I take it,' said Samuels coldly, 'that you are referring to *Captain* Turner?'

'The head serang himself,' replied Page easily. He lit a cigarette and replaced the box in the drawer. 'I'll just hide these fags out of his way, there's no sense in tempting Providence. I'll put 'em with the Third Mate's – under the Pacific charts. Although when Sloppy's around, nothing is sacred.'

Samuels' pop-eyes protruded even further. 'Am I to understand, Mr Page, that you are accusing the Master of this vessel of stealing cigarettes?'

'No, sport, you got it wrong. It's just that Sloppy never seems to have the makings when there are spare cough-sticks lying around. We don't hold it against the old boy – it's just one of his funny little habits.'

Samuels tightened his lips. 'I find your attitude toward authority somewhat offensive, young man.'

'You what?'

'And I would prefer it if, in future – and certainly in my presence – you would refer to the Master in less derogatory terms. Additionally, I would suggest that smoking be confined to your off-duty moments. In your quarters, or on deck, as you think fit; but not in the chartroom, nor on the bridge.' He took a pace forward. 'I might also remind you that the chart drawers are designed as containers for charts, and not as receptacles for junior officers' miscellanea.'

Page slammed the draw shut. 'Keep your fingers off, you

little pimple,' he warned dangerously. 'Or I'm liable to forget I'm an officer and bite off one of your big red ears.'

Samuels shook with rage. 'How dare you! How dare you threaten me! I shall report this conversation to the Master.'

'Good luck,' said Page and blew out an insulting cloud of smoke as the door banged shut behind Chief Officer Samuels.

Dean, lounging by the gangway, a cigarette dangling from his lips, was suddenly awakened from the dream of his taxi-ride with Olwyn by a waspish voice demanding: 'Mr Dean! Why is no gangway watch being maintained?'

Dean unhitched himself from the rail, took the cigarette from his mouth and carelessly flicked ash on the deck. 'Ah – Mr Samuels.' Already forewarned by Page, he eyed the new Chief Officer warily. 'I daresay he's in the galley, brewing up. It is smoke-O time.'

'I am aware of the time, Mr Dean, thank you. But the company pays the man to keep watch at the head of the gangway, not in the galley.'

Dean pitched his cigarette over the side. 'Not my pigeon,' he said. 'I'm only taking a breath of fresh air.'

'An officer should exercise his authority at all times,' rejoined Samuels tartly.

A burst of raucous singing announced the arrival of a happily inebriated quartet. They lurched up the gangway to be halted by the severe gaze of Mr Samuels.

Cloud grinned amiably. 'Move over, mate, and let the fast traffic through.'

'And where do you imagine you are going?' demanded Samuels.

'Going?' Lowrie hiccuped and laid a friendly hand on the Mate's shoulder. 'We're going to get oor heads down. Inn't that right?' he asked the others. 'We've had a session ashore. Lovely boozer. Barmaids wi' great big knockers. Inn't that right?'

'I'm skint,' said Cloud happily. 'Skint and skinned.'

Samuels brushed away Lowrie's hand. 'You men have no right to be aboard. The ship does not sign Articles until eleven tomorrow morning.'

'Don't give it thought,' said Cloud. 'We'll be there, books at the ready, and all willing. We wouldn't sign aboard no other ship but the *Kentucky*,' he added earnestly. 'So don't worry about a thing. You'll have the best crew sailing out of the Pool. Sloppy picked us.'

'Did he indeed? And what is your name?' asked Samuels acidly.

'Cloud, sir. And this is me mate, Jason – we allus ship together – and this is Lowrie – he's a Scotch, but don't hold that against him. And the other is Matt Honest, our bos'n.'

Samuels had fished out a small black notebook and was scribbling industriously. 'Cloud. Jason. Lowrie and Matthew Honest – bosun. I shall remember.' He pocketed the notebook.

The bosun steadied himself against the rail. 'We are the regular hands, sir. Mr Dean will vouch for us.'

'I am sure he will. But Mr Dean does not choose the crew. I exercise that privilege.'

'Oh, Sloppy won't stand for that,' said Cloud drunkenly. 'Old Sloppy allus . . .'

'Stow it, Cloudy,' ordered Matt, suddenly sober. 'Look, Mr Samuels, it has always been the custom for the regular hands to come aboard a day early and settle in . . .'

'I am aware of the practice, bosun, but that does not mean that I applaud it. I may add that I do not approve of drunkenness ashore and will not tolerate it aboard. You may present yourselves at the shipping office tomorrow morning when I will give consideration to your applications. Now, off ashore with you. This is a ship, not an hotel.'

'Applications? What's he on about?' demanded Cloud.

'Applicate your bleedin' self, Mister,' snarled Lowrie.

'What!'

'We've got privileges, too,' said Jason. 'And one of them is that we pick our own ship.'

'And we wouldn't sail with you, you pussyfooting crustacean, not if you come to us on your bended knees,' added Cloud.

'What? What did you say?'

'Crustacean,' said Cloud. 'She knows some lovely words, does my Sonia. Come on, lads. Off ashore.'

They trooped away down the gangway.

'I would sail this ship single-handed before allowing one of you to set foot aboard again!' Samuels roared after them. He clasped his hands behind his back and glared at Dean.

'Laxity, Mr Dean. Lax discipline means a lax crew.' He strutted away, shoulders squared, head high.

'Pompous bastard,' muttered Dean. 'Sloppy will nail his ears to the mast. I hope.'

Page pushed open the chartroom door to discover Turner in the act of rummaging through the chart drawers.

'Can I help, sir?' he asked.

Turner looked up and rumpled a hand through his thinning hair. 'Ah – it's you, Hubert. You don't happen to have seen my cigarettes around, by any chance?'

'Cigarettes?' Page looked puzzled. To his knowledge no one had ever seen Sloppy with a packet of cigarettes. 'No, sir. Can't say I have.'

'Funny,' ruminated Turner. 'I usually bury 'em in here. I don't see how they could walk off on their own. Do you?'

'No, sir.'

'There's something odd going on aboard this ship. Things keep disappearing. Have you noticed?'

'No, sir.'

'Ever since that Mr Samuels came aboard. What is your opinion of our new Chief Officer, Hubert?'

'I heard a nasty rumour that he had a father,' said Page.

'Don't hit it off, eh?'

'Let's say that we don't laugh at one another's jokes.'

Turner rooted around in the chart drawer. 'Ah – here we are. No – not mine. Are these yours, Hubert?'

Page inspected the box. 'No, sir. They're the Third Mate's.'

'Best put 'em back in that case. *I* don't want to be accused of snaffling. Where is Mr Samuels, by the way?'

'In the radio room, nagging the life out of Sparks.'

'Tender my compliments and ask the Chief Officer if he would be good enough to step round to the chartroom for a few minutes private conversation, Mr Page.'

'Aye, aye, sir.'

Mystified, but hopeful, Page made his way around to the radio shack, poked his head inside and delivered his message.

'What do you think of our new Mate?' he asked, settling himself comfortably on the settee as Mr Samuels departed.

Paddy Phelan poured a generous tot of whisky. 'I think the Great Potter broke the mould before He made our Mr Samuels.'

Page swallowed a mouthful of Scotch. 'I keep closing my eyes, but when I open them again he's still there. Cheers.'

'You wish to see me, sir?' asked Samuels, sidling into the chartroom.

'Yes, Mr Samuels, I did,' said Turner. He turned a severe gaze upon Samuels, dipped his hand into the open chart drawer and held out Dean's box of cigarettes. 'Are these yours, Mr Samuels?'

'Certainly not, sir!' Samuels replied indignantly. 'I do not indulge in the habit.'

'Glad to hear it, Mr Samuels. Glad to hear it. I can see you are a man after my own heart.' He thoughtfully tapped the cigarette box. 'Now I wonder who owns these?'

'Mr Page, I believe. I have already had occasion to reprimand him. I trust you do not condone smoking on watch, sir?'

'They are at it every time my back is turned. A monstrous habit and difficult to stamp out. They are addicts, you see, Mr. Samuels. Tobacco addicts.'

'I shouldn't stand for it, sir. I should put my foot down, once and for all,' advised Samuels firmly.

'You would, would you?'

'I should confiscate them, if I were you, sir.'

'Difficult in my case,' said Turner. 'It would be like a reformed alcoholic confiscating a case of booze. I used to be a tobacco addict myself once.' He raised his eyes piously towards the deckhead. 'Until I saw the light.'

'The Tempter comes in many guises, Captain.'

'He does. He does, indeed. I'm a martyr to temptation. A martyr. But with your fellow officers puffing and blowing smoke in your face and hiding boxes of fags all over the ship, what can you do but weaken, Mr Samuels?'

'You should pray for guidance, sir.'

'Oh, I do, Mr Samuels, I do. Lately I have been doing a power of praying.'

'They will be answered, sir.'

'I am sure they will. With your help, Mr Samuels, with your help.'

'I assure you, sir, that anything I can do . . .'

Turner rolled his eyes toward the open chart drawer. 'Your example, Mr Samuels, shines forth like Eddystone

Light: a warning to all of life's rocks and reefs lying ahead.'

Samuels smirked and rubbed his hands together. 'It is very good of you to say so, sir. I had not realised that you . . .'

'Of course you hadn't. I keep my own counsel on these little matters – I expect you've noticed? But you are an open book to me, Mr Samuels. An open book.'

Turner rolled away leaving the drawer wide open and Mr Samuels to fight a losing battle with the Tempter.

The Marine Superintendent leaned back in his chair and stared in disbelief at Page and Turner. 'He's a – what?'

'A kleptomaniac,' repeated Page.

'Mr Samuels? I'll not believe it!'

'It's no use hiding behind that desk, Barraclough,' said Turner. 'I have had a formal complaint from my Second and Third Officers.'

'I caught him in the act,' said Page. 'He was squirreling away a hundred and fifty cigarettes. Mine and the Third Mate's.'

Barraclough shook his head. 'To my certain knowledge Mr Samuels has never smoked a cigarette in his life. He abhors the habit.'

'It's the after-effects of that nervous breakdown you were telling me about. It takes 'em like that sometimes,' said Turner unctuously.

Barraclough gritted his teeth. 'Mr Samuels has not had a nervous breakdown. He merely . . .'

'There's something wrong with him,' interrupted Page. 'He told me that Captain Turner was a non-smoker.'

'What?'

'He's off his head,' said Turner. 'Only yesterday he booted half the crew ashore and told 'em he was going to sail the ship single-handed.'

'He – what?'

'The Third Officer witnessed the entire incident.'

Barraclough drummed his fingers on the desk top. The story seemed beyond the bounds of credibility, and yet – sanity was said to be one of the first casualties of war. He looked from Turner's bovinely innocent features to Page's earnest face. The young man, at least, believed he was telling the truth.

'I shall hear Mr Samuels' version,' he announced.

Turner looked ostentatiously at his watch. 'You'll need to put your skates on. We sign Articles at eleven.'

'It is rather short notice to find a replacement.'

'I was coming to that,' said Turner. 'There is that other little matter I mentioned. You may remember I strongly recommended . . .'

'Promotion.' Barraclough smiled thinly. 'I begin to see the light. I can promise you that Mr Samuels will be temporarily relieved of duty, pending a medical report.'

'Don't hurt his feelings,' urged Turner. 'I reckon the poor feller has suffered enough.'

'So do I,' said Barraclough. 'The other matter you may leave safely with me. Good-day, gentlemen.'

Page and Turner took their leave and made their way round to the Customs House.

'It's too easy,' said Turner. 'That Barraclough's up to something, mark my words.'

The word spread quickly and Matt Honest singled out Cloud, Jason and Lowrie. 'Step up lively, lads,' he said. 'We've got a new Mate.'

They had. Turner, trudging up the gangway last of all, was met by a perspiring Mr Potter.

'I have just been transferred from the *Troubadour*,' he said displaying the three rings on his sleeve. 'I have just been promoted, and I understand that I owe it all to you, sir.'

CHAPTER TEN

PORTRAITS of Captains and Kings looked down upon the forty Master Mariners assembled about the long conference table in the smoke-filled room. To a man they wore shore-going rig of civilian suits and fawn or navy-blue raincoats. Some clung to bowler-hats, others to soft-brimmed felt trilbies. In such nondescript company even Sloppy Joe Turner did not seem out of place. He puffed at one of his neighbour's cigarettes and owlishly eyed the Senior Officer of the Escort who was demonstrating convoy tactics with the aid of blackboard and pointer.

In contrast to the Merchant Captains the S.O.E. wore gold-braided uniform and addressed the meeting with the rounded vowels and carefully articulated accents of higher education. He was a young-old man learning the trade of war and had long come to terms with the fact that the motley collection of middle-aged men gathered about the table were battle-hardened veterans. Quirky individualists, abrupt of speech and harsh of diction, but with the ingrained habit of command, they entertained little regard for rank and were not the sort of men to suffer fools easily.

Commander Quayle, R.N., was far from being a fool. His experience, enriched by promotion from frigate to destroyer, and toughened by successions of convoy battles, had marked his face with worry-frowns and the tired lines of sleepless nights. But, an incurable optimist, he maintained a cheerful demeanour as he imparted his information.

'This will be a forty ship convoy, gentlemen, made up of ten columns, four deep, and covering about twenty square miles of ocean. For escorts we shall have seven corvettes and two destroyers. The general pattern will be for the destroyers to sweep an Asdic path ahead at a distance of eight or nine miles. Three corvettes to each flank and one bringing up the rear. Any questions?'

A man with a mournful face and a Geordie accent raised a hand. 'What's top convoy speed, lad?'

'Eight and a half knots.'

A groan rose from around the table.

Quayle grinned. 'I'm sorry, gentlemen, but at least a slow convoy will give you plenty of time to admire the scenery.' Having made his joke and received a few sour smiles in response, he became brisk and businesslike. 'The enemy have adopted new tactics. They now hunt in packs – Wolf Packs, they call themselves with typical Teutonic overstatement – and their technique is to spread across known convoy routes unil one of them makes a sighting. His mission is to shadow from a safe distance, transmit his information to U-boat Command who, in their turn, re-transmit his sighting to the rest of he pack. It is, I am forced to admit, a pretty efficient system.'

Turner lifted his head. 'Are you saying, son, that we are in for a battle?'

'Every Atlantic convoy is a battle now, sir,' replied Quayle. 'Last month we lost over three hundred thousand tons of shipping. If that rate of attrition keeps up we've lost the war. We know it, and the enemy knows it.'

He swept his pointer across a large-scale map of the Atlantic pinned to one wall. 'This is where the outcome will be decided, gentlemen. Not on land, not in the air, but at sea. Where we have always won, and will win again.'

'I wish I shared your confidence, young man,' growled Turner. 'But in my experience wars are lost the moment someone begins reminiscing over past glories.'

'I think I can set your mind at rest on that score,' said Quayle. 'We have a new C-in-C. Western Approaches. Admiral Sir Percy Noble.' He paused in the evident expectation that his announcement would bring a gobble of applause. Instead they stared back blankly.

'God love us,' said Turner disgustedly. 'Another bowler-hat come to plague us. Is that the best they can do?'

Quayle shook his head. 'This one is a live-wire. He has already reorganised our anti-submarine tactics, taken tactical control out of the hands of the shore wallahs and given the fighting escorts freedom of decision. No convoy now sails without a well-trained escort group – the days of pottering along with a couple of converted trawlers are over. Now, as to tactics ...' He tapped the blackboard with his pointer indicating a chalked diagram of the convoy and escorting vessels. 'The Wolf Packs' preferred method of attack is to come in on the surface at night. Our response will be to send up Snowflake flares to illuminate the scene and drive 'em under. A submerged U-boat is blind and slow and vulnerable to depth charges. So we hunt him with Asdic and plaster him with our dustbins.'

'Sounds like the mixture as before,' said the Geordie.

Quayle smiled. 'Oh, we have one or two tricks up our sleeves, this time. If you look closely at some of the escort vessels you might notice an affair like a minature lighthouse lantern above the bridge. It contains a secret device thought up by the boffins. I don't pretend to understand how it works, but I do know that it can see in the dark and pick out a submarine's conning tower at a few thousand yards.'

'New, is it?' asked Turner.

'Very new. Very hush-hush. It doesn't even have a name yet. We only know it by its initials: ASV.'

Turner nodded sourly. 'So that makes us the guinea-pigs.'

'There is always a first time,' said Quayle cheerfully. 'I think that will be all, gentlemen, unless you have any further questions?'

They shook their heads, stuffed their papers into battered attache cases and trooped from the room. Turner was among the last to leave.

'How many of these ASV gadgets do you have, son?' he asked.

'Three only. They are as scarce as hen's teeth.'

'And how many U-boats are you expecting?'

Quayle shrugged. 'I have no idea.'

'I thought as much,' said Turner.

'Don't worry, sir. We'll take good care of you.'

'I always worry,' said Turner heavily. 'Particularly when I find a cocky young feller like yourself putting all his faith in contraptions.'

'Not quite all my faith,' said Quayle easily. 'But I'm prepared to accept anything that might lend us an advantage. Thus far the U-boats have made all the running. It's time that we handed out a few surprises.' He smiled affably.

Perhaps you would give me the pleasure of joining me for a drink in the wardroom?'

Turner eyed him suspiciously. 'Very civil of yer.'

'There is someone I want you to meet.'

'Oh?'

'The Commodore. You will be seeing a lot of each other.' He led Turner from the room, along a corridor and pushed open a door.

The wardroom was small, comfortably furnished with leather-upholstered chairs, a scattering of tables and a couple of deferential stewards in attendance.

'Do yourselves proud,' commented Turner as Quayle guided him across to a corner table where a broad-shouldered man with blue eyes pouched beneath shaggy eyebrows sat concentrating upon a thick folder of typewritten papers.

Quayle introduced him as Commodore Sir Jethroe Croath-Jones.

'Devilish short notice, I'm afraid, Captain,' said the Commodore. 'But we will try to disrupt your routine as little as possible.'

He was about sixty years of age. Six foot three of smartly tailored uniform with a Commodore's broad gold bands glittering on each sleeve.

Turner, in his usual shore-going rig of thick tweed suit and knitted tie, eyed the apparition askance. 'You are not thinking of setting up shop on the *Kentucky*?'

The Commodore waved him to take a seat. 'The exigencies of war, Captain. The *Perseus* has developed engine trouble and your ship is the only one available which combines suitable accommodation with speed.'

Turner shook his head. 'Only a couple of cubby-holes. Nothing high-hatted. Terrible facilities.'

The Commodore smiled. 'I am not expecting a comfortable ride, but you do have six spare staterooms, I am advised. They should prove more than ample. My staff are transferring their gear at this moment.'

'Staff?'

'Only a Yeoman of Signals and a couple of Tels,' said Quayle reassuringly. 'Will you take something, sir?'

Turner shook his head. 'A bit early in the morning for me, but you fellers wet your whistles if you fancy it.'

'Tea, perhaps?'

'That's more like,' said Turner, plumping in one of the armchairs. 'I could manage a pot of tea and a smoke.' He patted his pockets. 'I seem to have come without mine.'

The Commodore proffered a gold cigarette case. 'Only Passing Cloud, I am afraid.'

Turner selected one. 'That's what I call a real cigarette. A gentleman's cigarette. Wish I could afford 'em.'

A soft-footed steward materialised as though summoned from a bottle. The Commodore ordered tea for Turner and Quayle. 'And a packet of Passing Cloud for Captain Turner. On my chit.'

'That's very handsome of you,' said Turner. He inhaled a lungful of smoke. 'Have you been a Commodore long?'

'Sir Jethroe was a Rear Admiral,' Quayle told him.

'Retired for many long years,' said the Commodore. 'Then My Lords of the Admiralty saw fit to put me back into harness with a Paddy's promotion.'

'You weren't always a Commodore, then?' asked Turner conversationally.

'It is often said that Commodores are born, not made,' interjected Quayle tactfully.

Croath-Jones' eyes crinkled. 'There is also a school of thought which holds that they are not born, but dug up on a dark night.' He sighed and indicated the mass of papers. 'Just as I was beginning to enjoy retirement they drag me back to this. I bought m'self a converted farmhouse and a couple of acres. Grow our own stuff. M'wife looks after the rose garden, and for the past five years I've been keeping bees.'

'Bees?'

'Fascinating creatures. Extraordinary social habits.'

Turner drank weak tea, sucked at his cigarette and listened to a dissertation on the social life of *apis mellifera.*

The old boy did not seem a bad sort of chap, for a bowler-hat.

He made his way aboard after enjoying several pink gins and a bottle of wine with his lunch. A hand-wringing Mr Potter met him at the head of the gangway.

'I know, I know, Mr Potter,' he said gently. 'We got a Commode with us, this trip.'

'Sir?'

'Keeps bees. It's a hell of a way to win a war.'

The *Kentucky Minstrel*, flying the Commodore's broad pennant, led the van. Half a mile astern the lead ships of the convoy rose and fell, lifting over the grey Atlantic rollers; a stately procession like the nodding horses of a giant merry-go-round.

The two destroyers scouted ahead, knifing through the seas and throwing up plumes of spray. They were of ancient vintage with four funnels, flush-decked hulls and the bridge carried far forward, but they could cruise at 14 knots and reach a maximum speed of 32 knots. Both *Whip-poor-will* and *Vulture* were part of the first consignment of superannuated First World War U.S. destroyers recently transferred to the British Navy to make up the heavy losses suffered at Dunkirk. Now modified for long-range escort duties they had been rearmed with six 3-inch guns, four 20 mm A.A. guns, a Hedgehog mortar of twenty-four depth bombs mounted forward, and two stern racks which could release a pattern of fourteen depth charges at a time. In addition each was fitted with H/F-D/F and the mysterious ASV device housed in its opaque dome.

Six Flower-class corvettes cruised on either flank at a three-mile distance. The seventh, plodding along far in the rear, had a mission entirely its own. At daybreak it would drop far astern, keeping the convoy barely in view and playing a cat-and-mouse game in its search for a shadowing U-boat. At nightfall it would close up and cover the rear.

Thus far the Atlantic had been kind to them, the sky overcast, the sea sullen, and a sharp nor'-east wind that brought occasional blankets of rain to blot them out from the view of even the keenest lookout.

In the engine room the vaulted steel walls rose high to the blacked-out skylights. The cold sea rushed and gurgled past no more than an inch from the sweltering heat of a space as large as a ballroom and packed with the driving force of the ship; a spider's web of ladders and galleries angled around the enormous twin Doxfords. Giant crossheads, yoked to smooth connecting rods, rose and fell with ponderous regularity. Rocker arms clattered their own staccato rhythm. The dynamos hummed quietly to themselves like a distant murmuration of bees. Over all hung the unmistakable, all-pervading smell of hot metal, oil and grease.

Unaffected by the clamouring roar of the engines and the pendulum roll of the ship, Mr Grogan, the Third Engineer, threaded his way between flailing metal arms and eccentrically rotating discs, checking bearings, temperatures and water salinity. He had learned to blank out the thoughts of a torpedo bursting through the thin shell of plating to turn the engine room into a horror of burning oil and flying machinery by training his mind to play a trick. While one half concentrated upon the work in hand, the other was far away in his red brick terrace house with its small back garden and his curly-headed daughter reaching out chubby arms in greeting. He played variations on the game by imagining walking through the park, going on shopping expeditions, listening to her prattle, carrying her upstairs to her cot, watching over her while she slept. He was a father, loved being a father and thought parenthood the greatest gift ever bestowed upon mankind. His wife Joyce sometimes intruded upon these dreams, but he invariably relegated her to a secondary part. It was not that he did not love her. He did. Longingly and passionately. But she was an adult and therefore capable of comprehending and accepting the finality of loss. But Brenda was only a child, a soft, plump, gurgling child who would grow and grow and never remember her father unless he concentrated upon keeping the machinery turning. And so Grogan went about his work, pushing the war into the background of his consciousness, and willing himself home.

Looking down from the gallery of the port engine he noticed Simon, the greaser, making his way to take up his regular stance beneath the engine room ventilator.

Simon always stood beneath the ventilator whenever he had a spare moment. Not to enjoy a respite from the stifling heat of the engine room, but because he had read somewhere, or someone had told him – he couldn't remember which, but he knew it to be true – of a ship receiving a direct hit in the engine room when, at that very moment the Donkeyman had been standing under the ventilator. The force of the explosion combined with the inrush of water had created a pocket of air pressure and the Donkeyman had been propelled up the shaft and straight to the surface. According to the story the Donkeyman had been the only survivor. So Simon stood shivering in the cold down-draught of air, listening to the moan and wail of the wind high above, and waiting for the explosion which would blow him to the surface and safety.

In the stokehold two firemen sat on upturned buckets, munching sandwiches and drinking cold tea while behind the furnace doors the oil-burners sheeted roaring jets of yellow flame beneath the boilers. Copper pipes, regulated by valves, controlled the in-flow from the fuel pump to the furnaces. The fuel pump drew its supplies from a thousand tons of bunker oil rolling sluggishly beneath their feet and waiting to burst into a roaring ocean of fire which would char them to calcined sticks.

The third fireman, the youngest, lounged by the straight steel ladder leading directly to the deck above. He was not of a religious turn of mind, but in the back-to-back terrace house which he shared with a brawling family of three brothers and four sisters, there was an old family bible lavishly illustrated with brightly coloured pictures representing passages from the text. As a child he had pored over the book, turning the pages and ignoring the incomprehensible archaic English, to concentrate upon the pictures as he would the cartoons of a comic. One in particular had embedded itself in his memory: Jacob's dream of a ladder reaching to heaven. This would be his Jacob's ladder leading him from the Satanic hell of the stokehold to the angelic heaven of clean fresh air and open skies above. At the end of each watch he had made a point of being first to the ladder. Racing up like a monkey, mentally timing himself and memorising each and every hand and foothold, he had convinced himself that God had placed the ladder there for his own personal salvation. So he lounged at its foot and listened to the roar of the fires and the hiss of steam and the steady beat of the engines, while the deck plates, slippery with oil, trembled beneath his feet and the cool winds of heaven blew down the shaft as the dark cold seas of the Atlantic pounded at the shipside. He was eighteen and did not want to die.

Polly Perkins, the galley boy, was sixteen years of age. A pimply-faced gangling youth with a white pork-pie hat of the type worn by U.S.N. sailors, perched on top of a scrub of yellow hair. He wore a pair of fine check trousers, a thick woollen shirt and a grubby apron. Seated on number 4 hatch outside the galley, he reached into a sack of potatoes, selected a large knobbly King Edward and removed the peel with a practised twist of the wrist. Then he dropped the potato into a ten-gallon boiler of water to join the others. Every day he peeled a hundredweight of potatoes, a sack of carrots and a mountain of greens. Later he would scour the pots, pans, skips and soup tureens; clean and polish the knives and cleavers before hanging each in its allotted place. He rose at six, finished at seven, with a little time off in between, and thought the war a great adventure. It was his first trip to sea, the work no harder than he expected, and the food a great improvement on the scant diet to which he was accustomed at home. All of which he wrote laboriously with a thick stub of pencil to his girl, Jenny; and all of which would be immediately deleted by an outraged censor.

Polly peeled another potato. Whistling tunelessly between a gap in his front teeth he eyed the restless grey waters of the Atlantic and, adaptable as a chameleon, thought it a great life.

Kapitänleutnant Hans Kroller eased the steel safety belt which, passed around his waist and clipped to the fore part of the conning tower, held him securely in place. Slitting his eyes against the driving spray he stared out across the empty wastes of the Atlantic. He was tired and every bone in his body ached from the constant, unremitting buffeting of the sea. His beard was caked with salt spray and he hadn't had a bath nor been out of his clothes for six weeks. From the open hatch below came the stench of oil, sweat and decaying food. He raised his binoculars and began to sweep the horizon, cursing as a rain cloud drifted toward him, blotting out his vision. Nevertheless, in spite of the leaden skies, the endlessly rolling sea and the acute discomfort of a long patrol, he had reason to be well satisfied. Just five days ago, in the company of four other U-boats, they had savagely mauled a heavily laden eastbound convoy, sinking eight ships and bringing U223's total up to six. They would have had more, he thought, if daylight and that damned rain had not robbed them of their prey.

The rain swept down upon them, drenching him to the skin and turning his body to ice. He raised his head and let it wash over his face and trickle down his throat in a cool stream of God-sent fresh water. After the foul, oil-flavoured stale scum sloshing around in their tanks it tasted like champagne.

Then the rain passed. He raised his binoculars and once again scanned the horizon. Then suddenly, with startling clarity, a row of toothpicks marched across his vision.

Kapitänleutnant Kroller came out of his lethargy, sounded the alarm bell, ordered full speed ahead, and kept his eyes glued upon the masts until he could just make out the shadowy bulks of the ships. Then he stopped engines, calculated the course and speed of the convoy and transmitted a short ciphered message to Admiral U-boats: *Sighted westbound convoy. Estimated speed 8 knots. Course West North West. Grid Square AL. Will shadow. Await instructions. U223.*

Then U223 submerged to periscope level and commenced its slow, stealthy crawl toward its objective.

Leading Telegraphist Ormond had been a piano-tuner in civil life, so his hearing was peculiarly adapted to the fine tuning of the H/F-D/F set. He sat in a steel and leather chair, headphones clamped to his ears, both hands fully occupied. His left hand gently spun the knob which turned the D/F aerial, his right hand delicately twisted a calibrated dial which ranged over the V.H.F. frequencies known to be used by U-boats. He listened with unbroken concentration to the squeaks, squawks and whistles filtering through the background mush; selecting, discarding, waiting for the rapid, high-pitched parp-parp-parp of morse.

His task was made more difficult by the short duration of the signals. The enemy cipher was so arranged that a short burst of no more than ten seconds could convey a great deal of information. Furthermore, to add to his difficulties, the U-boat telegraphists changed their frequencies every day.

Ormond had been listening in for an hour. His head was beginning to ache and his back and shoulder muscles were tense with cramp. His relief arrived and tapped him on the shoulder, but Ormond brusquely waved him away. Something had impinged upon his consciousness. It may have been intuition, or subconsciously his acute hearing may have detected the faint, low-pitched hum of a transmitter's warming-up signal, but his concentration increased. He closed his eyes and held his breath, straining to read through the echoing rush of static. His fingers turned the dial gently, patiently searching, closing in on the frequency.

Suddenly, with startling clearness, the signal stuttered into his earphones seeming to fill his head and the whole room with its garbled imperatives. His right hand, as though it had a life of its own, left the dial, picked up a pencil and began to scribble rapidly upon a message pad. His left hand spun the pointer of the Direction Finder. Then, as the chatter of morse stopped as abruptly as it had started, he read off the bearing, removed his headphones and rang the bridge.

'Huff-Duff signals bearing red one-O-one,' he reported. 'Loud and clear. Estimated distance ten to fifteen miles.'

He tore the top sheet from the message pad, put it in his cap and, leaving his relief to continue the watch, made his way to the bridge.

When he arrived Quayle had already detached *Vulture* and two corvettes to carry out a sweep. The destroyer was foaming along at a full thirty knots on a reverse bearing, hoping to catch a glimpse of the U-boat before it dived. Just one short glimpse, even if it were no more than a swirl of water, would be enough. Then the area could be plotted, subjected to a painstaking Asdic search and depth-charged while the U-boat was trapped like a fish in a barrel.

Kapitänleutnant Kroller was too experienced a commander to be caught napping on the surface. The moment the all-important message had been transmitted he dived to 200 metres and boldly headed toward the convoy, reasoning that attack vessels would approach at high speed when the high energy pulses of their Asdics were at their least efficient. At speeds above ten knots the reflected echoes tended to be scattered and, as an Asdic's maximum range was no more than 2,500 yards, the deeper a U-boat dived, the better its chances of escape. Unconcerned, he listened to the thrash of the destroyer's propellers pounding above. At that speed the surface vessel was as blind as the submarine.

Quayle took the message and read the jumble of letters and figures making up the cipher. They meant nothing to him but in due course the pencilled scribble would find its way to Naval Intelligence where the cryptanalysts had the thankless task of trying to crack an unbreakable cipher. Quayle didn't envy them. One of the boffins had once told him that each separate letter admitted of several million permutations.

He looked carefully at Leading Telegraphist Ormond. A lot depended upon that sharp intelligent face. 'You are quite certain that it is a lone U-boat? No others in the vicinity?'

Ormond considered carefully. 'Yes, sir.'

'Why?'

Ormond thought the answer obvious, but he was only a Leading Telegraphist and to back-chat so august a personage as a Commander would inevitably dash all hopes of promotion, so he collected his thoughts and gave his assessment.

'There is its distance off, sir, and it sounds like the report of a sighting. A first sighting – I mean it is broad daylight so he's taking a chance. Then, if there were others around ...'

Quayle smiled. 'They wouldn't be wasting their time chattering. Anything else?'

'Well – he was transmitting on full power and the cipher is about the right length for one of their H.Q. efforts.' Ormond began to understand what Quayle was driving at. 'If he was a decoy, sir, he would have used low power and made certain that we picked him up.'

'Thank you Ormond. That is exactly what I wanted to know.'

He recalled the destroyer and corvettes from their fruitless search and set up his battle dispositions. The convoy was the Commodore's pigeon. 'Chief Yeoman,' he ordered. 'Make to Commodore: Sharks expected our vicinity. Over to you. Good luck.'

Information concerning Wolf Pack tactics was regularly collected and collated by Naval Intelligence and passed on to all Commodores and Escort Commanders. The nerve centre of U-boat operations was known to be at Admiral Doenitz's Operations Room in Lorient. Here reports of convoy sightings were received, assessed and acted upon. Orders were then transmitted to all units within striking distance. It was only then that the prowling U-boats formed a pack to descend upon a convoy in overwhelming strength.

The Royal Navy, naturally, devised counter-measures, one of which was the ASV device tucked away in its secret housing. The lantern-shaped cupola protected a revolving aerial, both from the weather and prying eyes. Beneath, in a small darkened cubicle, sat the operator, his gaze fixed upon a small, eerily glowing screen about which swept an arm in synchronisation with the rotating aerial. Strange splodges representing the convoy glowed and disappeared to glow again upon the screen. The device was as yet in its infancy, its complicated and delicate electronics all too easily disturbed by the shock of gunfire.

Attack and counter-attack made for a bloody but see-saw battle, with the advantage lying with the Wolf Packs, and the prize Britain's lifeline.

Dean quartered his own half of the bridge and furtively eyed the Commodore. The man certainly seemed to have settled in and, after one or two initial blunders, was obviously in his element. His first mistake had been to appear at dinner on the first night out in full mess kit, looking, said Turner eyeing him askance, like a par-boiled lobster.

Croath-Jones had taken the hint and now contentedly roamed the ship in an outfit which would have done credit to Sloppy Joe himself. He wore golf shoes, a pair of grey flannel bags, an out-at-elbows turtle-necked sweater, and was as happy as a sand-boy in his new-found freedom from protocol. True, it had taken him a few days to accustom himself to the easy-going indiscipline of the Merchant Service, and discover that far from being in awe of his rank the crew had apparently adopted him as a lucky mascot and tended to treat him and his staff with the friendly good-nature reserved for the dim-witted. The problem of his rank had been resolved by the officers politely addressing him as 'Sir'; the hands as 'Chief'. 'Give us a free passage, Chief, afore you get your feet wet,' a villainous-looking individual had once demanded in a ferocious Scottish accent as he had splashed water from a hose one morning. And the appellation had stuck, to the fury of his affronted Chief Yeoman of Signals, a turkey-wattled disciplinarian who had first seen action at the battle of Coronel and had never forgotten the insult of defeat.

The Commodore's staff consisted of his Chief Yeoman and two Signallers, plus three Telegraphists who had set up their V.H.F. equipment in the radio shack and an R/T set in the wheelhouse.

Being Commodore ship brought mixed blessings. On the one hand they bore the burden of responsibility of being out in front and, therefore, the cynosure of hundreds of critical eyes; on the other they were relieved of the irksome duty of trying to maintain station amid a crowd of surging ships.

They also enoyed the doubtful privilege of being first with the news, so that Quayle's signal, read off by Cherry Blossom idly leaning against the midships rail, was rapidly passed from mouth to mouth until all hands were aware of the situation almost as soon as the Commodore himself.

The bosun poked his head into the messroom. 'Subs in the offing,' he told them. 'So keep your panic-bags handy.'

Cloud spoke through a mouthful of Albert's steak-and-kidney pie. 'No bother. The Jerries'll be stuffing themselves with sauerkraut and sausages; it's only the Army that marches on an empty stummick.'

While the escorting corvettes increased the vigilance of their Asdic search and their wakes traced random arabesques across the surface of the sea, Kapitänleutnant Kroller quelled the pangs of hunger with mouldy bread and a spoonful of jam and listened to the thunderous roar of propellers and ships' engines a few fathoms above his head. Submerged, U223's top speed was eight knots and therefore could barely keep pace with the convoy, but here, with twenty square miles of ships pounding the ocean, it was safe and secure from enemy Asdics. At nightfall, Kroller decided, he would drop astern and come up for a breath of fresh air. In the meantime there was nothing to do but wait and listen for any alteration of course made by the convoy.

A hoist of flags fluttered from the *Kentucky Minstrel*'s starboard yardarm. Benson, the Chief Yeoman of Signals, scanned the convoy through his binoculars, lips moving silently as he counted them off. Eventually satisfied he breathed heavily: 'Acknowledged, sir.'

The Commodore nodded briefly and the Signaller promptly hauled down the horizontal-striped blue-and-red flag and its accompanying numeral pennants. Benson continued to stare at the following ships. 'You'd think they was 'anging out lines o' bleedin' washing,' he muttered disgustedly as flag succeeded flag in tumbling to deck or bridge and the convoy lumbered about in a ninety degree turn to starboard.

'Not our fault,' said Turner softly in Benson's ear. '*We've* moved on since the pretty pocket handkerchiefs of Nelson's time.' He snuffled up his nose and gazed morosely at the Commodore. 'You'd never credit that Marconi had invented the wireless.'

The Commodore smiled affably. 'We don't want to advertise our presence more than necessary, Captain.'

Turner hawked and spat over the side. 'A bit late in the day. They know we are here, Mister Croath-Jones. They know we are here.'

The convoy drew first blood.

The corvette *Wildwood*, code-named Guard Dog, was patrolling well astern, and at sunset began to close up on the rear ranks of the convoy.

As darkness fell the dim shapes of the receding ships disappeared into a night as black as pitch and the only reminders of their presence were the flickering images on the *Wildwood's* oscilloscope.

The bored ASV operator yawned, counted off the blips, rubbed tired eyes, waited for the sweep of the arm and counted again. Suddenly he became alert and concentrated all his attention upon a tiny luminous pin-point of light, flickering and fading in a position where it had no right to be. It had appeared suddenly from nowhere and, from its unvarying and undeviating position, was evidently keeping pace with the convoy. He picked up the phone and rang the bridge. 'I have a contact, sir. A small echo astern of the convoy. Bearing right ahead. Distance five miles.'

'Can you identify it?' asked a disembodied voice.

The operator looked again at the screen. It *might* be a ship's lifeboat adrift in an ocean of water; it *might* be a small ice floe wandering aimlessly from wave crest to wave crest; but the echo remained persistent, unchanging; and it had appeared suddenly as though out of the depths. 'It's a conning tower, sir,' he said decisively, and offered a silent prayer that it was more than just wishful thinking.

Kapitänleutnant Kroller never knew what hit him. He had dropped U223 astern of the convoy and surfaced into a night of secretive darkness with nothing to give away their position but the faint, barely discernible, wash of the sea against the base of the conning tower. Around them sky and sea merged into an impenetrable darkness that covered their low silhouette with a cloak of invisibility.

Two lookouts shared the bridge deck with him and occasionally one would turn to glance astern. But confident that they were safe as fledglings in a nest from the sharpest-eyed of predators, they concentrated their attention upon holding fast to the faint outline of the convoy ahead. From the darkened interior beneath their feet came the steady muted throb of the diesels which, together with the gentle lapping of the sea against the hull, acted as a lullaby to their senses.

A new sound intruded itself and one of the lookouts jerked his head around. He opened his mouth to yell a warning. Then a wall of steel bore down upon them, smashed the conning tower and its occupants into pulp, rolled U223 over on to its back and then ripped it open from bilge to keel. A pattern of depth charges turned the sea into a boiling cauldron and the watchers on *Wildwood* saw a deep red glow slowly pulsing beneath the surface. Then there was nothing but the stench of oil and a spreading moil of water to mark the U-boat's grave.

At dawn a weak sun painted the horizon an ochrous yellow before disappearing behind a swollen bank of rain cloud. The *Kentucky Minstrel*, like a bell-wether leading sheep to the slaughter, plodded ahead, rising and falling to the lift of a surface broken only by the columns of ships and their attendant escorts.

Since the sinking of U223 they had passed a peaceful, if anxious, night, and daybreak brought a sense of false security, as though the killing of a sentry had destroyed an army.

They were soon disillusioned. The first skirmish, a probing attack to test the defences, came from the starboard hand, the track of a single torpedo leaving a long streak of bubbling wake aimed plump at the centre of the convoy.

Far out on the flank one of the escorting corvettes squawked a warning, the Commodore yanked down twice on the whistle lanyard and the entire convoy, wheeling sharply in a ninety degree turn to port, bore away from the lurking U-boat like a well-trained squadron of cavalry. The torpedo ran away, clearing the sterns of the retreating formation, to disappear into the distance in a trail of white bubbles.

The manoeuvre had brought the *Kentucky Minstrel* from her station ahead to a new position far out on the starboard side with the convoy now steaming in four columns ten abreast on their new course. Even bunched together at two cable lengths apart they presented a front 4,000 yards wide, which meant that the furthermost ship now lay more than two and a half miles from the Commodore and was forced to read her signals through a forest of masts and heaving superstructures. The result was inevitable. The next alteration of course, designed to bring them back into line, brought the newly formed rear ranks into a confusion of laggards straggling far astern as they struggled to keep station with their fellows.

Given time, as in their often rehearsed practice manoeuvres, they would have caught up and straightened the line. This, however, was not a practice. Three conning towers broke the surface and a calculated spread of fifteen torpedoes eliminated the stragglers in cataclysmic eruptions of flame and smoke.

It had been a well co-ordinated attack by a disciplined force trained to a hair, and boded ill for the future. The whale-backs of the U-boats were visible to all eyes as they turned tail, fanned out and raced away at their top speed of eighteen knots, far in excess of the lumbering corvettes' twelve knots, while the two destroyers with their superior speed had been isolated far ahead of the targets.

From the bridge of the *Kentucky Minstrel* they watched the slaughter and the covering corvettes foaming after the enemy, their forward guns barking in fury, the shells thrumming through the air to throw up fountains of water around the fleeing submarines.

Fore-shortened in the lens of Turner's binoculars one of the U-boats suddenly reeled; her conning tower turned into a pepper-pot of gaping black holes, and tiny, gesticulating figures jerked convulsively before slumping across the bridgework like so many sawdust dolls. Then the sea closed in a smother of water as the U-boat crash-dived leaving the mannikins to bob restlessly in its wake.

'Heartless bastards,' he commented, lowering his glasses. 'Fair-weather friends, the Boche. Always have been. Noted for it.' He gazed resentfully at the Commodore. 'On the other hand we don't have much to sing about, do we? There'll be some of our lads floundering around back there, with the nearest land a mile beneath their feet. Isn't someone going to pick 'em up?'

The Commodore, perched on his high chair, turned tired eyes upon Turner and shook his head. 'The risk is too great,' he said. He was by no means a callous man, but a lifetime's training had disciplined him to accept casualties as a necessary consequence of warfare. The goal was all that mattered and, to that end, ships and men were expendable. It was an attitude of mind which brought the Royal Navy into conflict with the Merchantmen, whose nature was to respond to distress at whatever the risk to themselves.

Turner stuffed his hands into his pockets and wobbled his chins. 'I'm not leaving 'em,' he announced. 'If you don't fancy your chances, then shift your dunnage to another ship. I'm going after them.'

Croath-Jones looked at the scowling features set in obstinate lines, and considered carefully. The division of responsibility was finely drawn. In theory the Commodore was in overall command. In practice the Senior Officer Escorts decided upon battle tactics and reported his activities to the flagship, always with the proviso that the Commodore bore the ultimate responsibility and could overrule him. The Commodore's guiding principle was the safety, and safe arrival, of the convoy. Had his pennant flown from one of His Majesty's ships there would have been no problem but aboard a merchant vessel it behoved even those of the most exalted rank to tread carefully, for a ship's Master was a law unto himself and well used to exercising the prerogative of command without regard for friend or foe.

He reflected a moment longer, his eyes watching two corvettes seeking out the first attacker like dogs sniffing out a bone, his ears picking out the thump of the starboard escorts' guns as they harried the remaining U-boats.

'Full ahead both,' said Turner decisively.

As the pale-faced Mr Potter moved nervously toward the telegraph handles Croath-Jones held up a hand, levered himself from his chair and spoke briefly into the hand microphone: 'Father Bear to Guard Dog. Stand by to pick up survivors. Over and out.'

He returned to his perch as plumes of water soared into the air and the dull boom of depth charges rolled across the sea.

'We've found one of 'em,' said the Commodore laconically, and gave his undivided attention to manoeuvring the mass of ships out of immediate danger.

The signaller ran up a hoist of coloured flags and the convoy turned its collective stern to the rocketing plumes of water and bore away south and west. The V.H.F. loudspeaker, hooked to the wheelhouse bulkhead, crackled into life and a calm voice announced in matter-of-fact tones: 'Guard Dog to Father Bear. No survivors. Request permission to resume station. Over.'

'Acknowledge, Yeoman,' said the Commodore. He nodded heavily to Turner. 'Depth charges. I am sorry, Captain. It is the price of war.'

Turner expelled a breath. 'I wouldn't have your job for a gold clock,' he pronounced and trudged away to his quarters.

Throughout the hours of daylight the convoy zig-zagged westward with the escorts once again frolicking about their business. The sky slowly cleared to show a pale wash of stars, and the rim of a bright quarter-moon began to bathe the sea in a cold glow.

Turner returned to the bridge bearing a peace-offering in the shape of a flask of whisky. Croath-Jones drank gratefully and proffered his cigarette case in a return gesture of goodwill.

Turner eased himself into his own high chair and the two men sat side by side, smoking peacefully and quietly, while the escorts' sonar beams probed the depths and the convoy darkened ship and plunged through a lambent sea toward the gathering Wolf Packs.

The Commodore regretfully stubbed out his cigarette. 'No more until daylight. I must say that I do miss the occasional cigarette.'

'It must be a terrible deprivation for an addict,' agreed

Turner. 'But you can always nip into the chartroom for a quick drag. I'll keep an eye on things.'

The Commodore grinned into the darkness. The pair had long established a professional working relationship and, because even Commodores must sleep from time to time, had adopted the practice of sharing watch and watch about throughout the long monotonous days and nights. The result had seen the genesis of a casual friendship based upon a grudging respect for each other's abilities.

'You could get your head down for an hour,' Turner added solicitously. 'I reckon it's going to be a long night.'

The Commodore understood Turner's ploy. Ship's Captains had a natural aversion to sharing command, and therefore sought every opportunity to oust the interloper, even if it were only for a God-given hour or so. Sometimes Croath-Jones had the feeling of being accepted only on sufferance, rather as though he were a lodger temporarily occupying furnished accomodation.

'I have a feeling in my bones that it will be a short night for some, and a busy one for the rest,' he answered grimly. 'So, under the circumstances, I think I'll stay put.'

'Suit yourself,' grumbled Turner. 'I'm off for a thinks.' He scowled at one of the signallers posted as a lookout on the port wing, grunted at Mr Potter quartering the other half, muttered that the bridge was becoming as cluttered as a barrelful of fish, and stumped away to his quarters.

The attack came at midnight, timed to create the maximum confusion as the watches were changing over. The only warning was a dull boom and an ugly roseate glare of light as a ship in the outer port column, once a creeping shadow, suddenly stood out etched sharply against the darkness, her stern settling as she struggled to lurch forward like a wounded animal dragging its hindquarters.

Seconds later came a second explosion, then a third; the bunched ships as helpless as ducks in a shooting gallery.

Quayle, however, had reorganised his defences. Under cover of darkness he had withdrawn the two destroyers from their stations far ahead to lie between two columns of the convoy. It was a risk, but warfare consisted of risks, their justification depending upon success or failure.

On the *Kentucky Minstrel*'s bridge the VHF set crackled

into life: 'Mother Bear to Father Bear. Port ninety, if you please, sir,' said an urgent voice.

The darkened lights were already swinging in position from the *Kentucky Minstrel*'s signal yard. Two red for port, one green for starboard. The Chief Yeoman depressed the tumbler switch and the pair of vertical red lamps flicked on, seeming to bathe the ship in a halo of ruby-red light that, in their exposed position at the forefront of the convoy, gave every man aboard the sense of becoming an illuminated target.

Cloud, coming off watch, gaped at the blood-red glow. 'Christ Almighty!' he swore. 'What the 'ell's he trying to do? Make bleedin' heroes out of us?'

'He's after a medal,' said the sanguine Lowrie. 'All that Navy brass ever thinks about is medals.'

'I'm not sharing no boat with no medal-hunter,' said Cloud. 'I'll drown the bastard first.'

In broad daylight altering course ninety degrees in unison was a tricky manoeuvre; during the hours of darkness it was a nightmare and called for seamanship of the highest degree from Masters and Mates alike as they peered at the lumbering shadows ahead and on either beam, each intent on jostling for position and avoiding collision with his fellows. Some vessels were quick to the helm, others slow on the turn. Some were deep-laden, others in ballast and riding high out of the water. Some grossed ten thousand tons, others but three and a half thousand. All represented as motley a collection of vessels as were likely to sail out of any one port.

The fact that all turned in accord was due in no small measure to the Commodore's daily ritual of constant practice. In fair weather and foul the ships had jostled and bumped and bored like a herd of ill-mannered cattle while the officers-of-the-watch had heaped invective upon the head of their tormentor.

But now all that sweating and cursing paid dividends. As the twin rubescent points winked out and the *Kentucky Minstrel*'s siren bellowed two short imperative blasts, the entire convoy wheeled, opened its ranks and headed in a solid phalanx toward the direction of attack. At the same time a dozen Snowflake flares rocketed into the air. Night turned into ghastly day, illuminating the stricken ships, men floundering in the heaving sea, clinging to rafts and upturned boats, the tiny red lights of their life-jackets flickering on and off like myriads of fireflies as they rose and fell in the troughs of the waves and tossed and turned in the wash of passing ships.

The *Kentucky Minstrel*, now far out on the starboard flank, increased speed to take up her new position ahead of the advancing convoy.

Page, shielding his eyes from the sudden eye-aching glare of the starshells slowly parachuting toward the sea, saw four conning towers riding high and clear above the surface. They were standing off at a distance of about three miles and a further mile or two away he could see the superstructure of two corvettes, their bows shouldering aside the sea as they converged upon the U-boats. Page raised a pair of night-binoculars to his eyes, adjusted the focus and concentrated his vision upon a group of figures clustered in one of the conning towers. One seemed to be staring straight at him until he realised that it was no more than an illusion caused by fore-shortened distance and high magnification. The figure pointed, waved an arm that obviously encompassed the lead ships of the steadily approaching convoy. The man bared his teeth in a grin, turned his head and began to shout orders.

If the U-boat commanders had at first been startled at the spectacle of the mass of ships bearing down upon them, they were by no means alarmed. In their eyes the convoy was, in fact, obligingly decreasing the range and, at a plodding eight knots, was no match for a U-boat's surface speed of eighteen knots. The advancing corvettes they viewed with contempt, confident that on the surface a Pack could out-gun, out-fight and out-run any pair of modified fishing boats.

They formed into line ahead and, with their screws churning the sea into frothing wakes, sped forward to take up new attack positions off the convoy's starboard point.

Page lowered his binoculars and turned his head. Against an apocalyptic sky a host of black shapes surged across a velvet sea. The flares from exploding starshells rained down from the heavens and the dull thudding of depth charges shook the air. Far away on the port quarter an empty tanker, riding high out of the water, suddenly erupted into a sheet of searing, incandescent flame and blew itself to pieces. Searchlights from distant escorts wavered across the convoy lending to the faces of the watchers the pallor of corpses.

As the *Kentucky Minstrel* ploughed ahead, outstripping the lead ships, Page returned his gaze to the line of U-boats. With the sea foaming against their conning towers they broke formation, turned to face the leading corvette driving down upon them, and opened like the jaws of a trap. The corvette's lone forward gun was coughing and spitting flame, and splashes from its shells rose in miniature fountains about the dark whale-back shapes. Then the U-boats' gun-crews, standing thigh-deep in the swirling seas, opened a concentrated cross-fire. Page saw red splotches running along the corvette's hull like scarlet claws; one wing of the bridge shattered and tumbled drunkenly; tracer shells curved through the air; then a shell found the row of depth charges racked at the stern. There was a cataclysmic explosion and the corvette disintegrated into a roaring pillar of fire.

The U-boats, ignoring the advancing convoy which still had a mile-and-a-half of sea to cover, turned to concentrate their fire upon the second corvette lunging vengefully toward them.

Page, entranced and horrified at the swift, almost clinical destruction, found time to be irritated at the Commodore's inaction. The man sat stolidly on his high chair, chin cupped in hands, simply staring fixedly ahead. *What the hell is the matter with with the fool?*, he wondered. *He's going to get us massacred.*

At that instant two long, lean shapes raced from between the columns of lumbering ships. Knife-like bows slicing the sea into sharp arrowheads, the two destroyers leaped across the open stretch of water, then swung left and right, heeling hard over, decks awash as they brought their broadsides to bear.

Sheets of flame poured from their guns and even as the first torrent of steel fell upon the hapless U-boats the second broadsides shrieked on their way. The guns bellowed again and again and on the bridge of the *Kentucky Minstrel* they could feel the hot breath of their flames as the shock waves rolled across the sea and concussion after concussion rocked the ship and numbed their senses.

One U-boat was obliterated with the first salvo. Seconds

later another, its conning tower glowing red, geysers of black oil spouting from a dozen gaping holes, spun crazily about its axis before raising its tail high in the air and plunging into the depths below. The third turned into a ball of orange fire, rolled over and sank leaving nothing behind but a cloud of hissing steam. The fourth was already racing away, twisting and turning with the desperation of a hare trapped between two greyhounds. Around it the sea was thrown into convulsions from the steady rain of shells. Its foredeck and after deck became awash and its conning tower sank lower.

Turner, standing beside Page, eyed the drama with a speculative eye. 'Trying to crash-dive. He'll never make it.'

As the sea closed over the conning tower the destroyers ceased firing. They had already altered course and were now bearing down upon their target at a speed of thirty knots. Crossing each other's sterns they dropped a string of depth charges and, even as the sea erupted into a boiling cauldron, swung away into a tight, enclosing circle, penning the U-boat within a wall of high-explosive.

The sea went mad, became a gigantic whirlpool, spouting and erupting in a frenzy of tormented water, out of which slowly rose a monstrous black shape, slimy with weed and leprous with barnacles. It fell upon the seething water like a broaching whale, the hatch of the conning tower opened and a couple of figures clambered up, arms upraised.

At point-blank range the destroyers reopened fire and smashed the U-boat back into the purgatory from which it had emerged.

'They were surrending!' Page protested angrily.

'Unrestricted warfare, they call it,' said Turner. 'Don't let your conscience bother you, son. They brought it on themselves.'

CHAPTER ELEVEN

THERE WERE no further incidents that night, nor the following day. The remaining U-boats seemed to have retired to lick their wounds.

The convoy closed up, filled the gaps left by the torpedoed ships, and marched steadily westward. The wind backed and brought sudden squalls and a mounting cross-sea that tried to push the *Kentucky Minstrel*'s head northwards. They stood on and on for hour after hour of low driving cloud, sweeping showers of rain, with the seas breaking over their bows and sluicing along their foredecks.

At seven bells with the moon breaking through riven cloud the wind blew fiercely, flaying the tops of the waves into sheets of white spray. Then, just as suddenly, it dropped to a near calm with veils of rain masking the horizon and offering concealment to the prowling Wolf Packs.

At eight bells Cloud, Jason and Lowrie turned-to. Jason to the wheel, Cloud to the first lookout and Lowrie as farmer.

'Lucky sod,' said Cloud, buttoning into his oilskins. 'A whole hour to yourself, then two more snoozing in the nest, and then another hour to get your head down with nothing to do but call the watch.'

'And make sure the coffee's hot,' Jason reminded him, hauling a thick Guernsey over his head. 'And make it strong. The last time you was farmer it could hardly crawl out of the spout.'

Lowrie was stand-by man and, as such, had the privilege of being an idle hand for the first hour of the watch, his only commitment to listen for the summoning whistle of the officer of the watch, in the unlikely event that that individual should require his services when the watch below were getting their heads down and the ship was wrapped in peace. But it did happen from time to time.

Lowrie grinned evilly at Cloud. 'Turn and turn about. It was your farmer last night.'

'A dead loss,' grumbled Cloud. 'Dixie Dean rousted me out and had me turning ventilators back to wind for the whole flamin' hour. It inn't right, the four-to-eight should've seen to it.'

Jason's tousled head emerged from his jersey. 'You can hardly blame them for that, Cloudy. The wind shifted.'

Cloud, grunting at the injustice of it all, picked up his gloves from the top of the steam radiator, and drew them over his fingers. 'I wonder if there'll be any more fireworks tonight? Last night was bloody marvellous. I had a grand-stand view from up in the nest. We didn't half give them U-boats a pasting. And the sky lit up like Guy Fawkes night. Bloody marvellous. It's a bit of all right being Commodore ship. Way out in front you can see everything.'

'Aye,' said Lowrie sourly. 'And it's the feller out in front that gets potted at, don't forget that, Cloudy.'

'Don't you believe it,' answered Cloud. 'Whoever heard of a Commodore being drowned? Those fellers have a gentlemen's agreement – you don't bump me, and I won't bump you. Like Army generals.'

Jason shrugged into a heavy pea-jacket, pulled two pairs of worn socks over his hands as double insulation against the cold, and glanced at the brass chronometer screwed to the forward bulkhead. 'Two minutes,' he announced. 'Don't forget, Lowrie – lashings of hot coffee.'

'No bother,' replied Lowrie, stretching himself comfortably along the length of one of the messroom's long wooden benches. 'Polly Perkins will be looking after us. I promised him thrippence a head for supper.' Suppers were recognised as the galley boy's perks. A private trade to which authority turned a blind eye. It was a long-established practice that certain clearly defined individuals had a right to trade. The bosun, for example, traded articles of used ship's stores – the dregs of paint from the ten-gallon paint drums, poured into paint pots, thinned with turps and sold to gullible longshoremen, added to Matt Honest's finances. Albert Hodge rendered down pork and beef dripping and invariably took a couple of hams ashore at the completion of each voyage. The pantryman claimed his trade of tea and coffee, the engineers' steward supplied the black watch with oceans of tea and cold collations.

Polly Perkins' trade was supper for the quartermasters coming off watch. For these favours the galley boy charged a standard rate of threepence a head, the amount being meticulously entered in a grubby notebook and claimed at the end of the voyage, when all debts were honoured as a matter of principle.

'Ham, fried bread and two eggs,' Cloud ordered. 'And plenty of dip, tell him.'

'Hoping for your money's worth, aren't you?' asked Lowrie.

'Got to keep me strength up for Sonia,' said Cloud. 'Come on, Jase. Eight bells coming up.'

The pair departed leaving Lowrie to doze peacefully, undisturbed by the pitch and roll of the ship and the occasional clanking of the steering quadrant housed a few yards from his head.

He awoke to the sound of a tremendous, reverberating *boom* as though someone had struck a gigantic gong within an inch of his ear. Tumbling off the bench he scrambled upright to feel the ship shaking and shuddering and the dim blue pilot-light flickering crazily on and off. His heart seemed to wing its way into his throat and expand until he was choking. With the fear of God at his heels Lowrie raced up the companionway and out on to the open deck above.

He was just in time to meet a vast eruption of water and catch a glimpse of a squat grey shape rushing past in the darkness.

'Christ Almighty!' he demanded. 'What the 'ell's going on?'

Corrigan, one of the four-to-eight watch, was standing by the rail, placidly munching a bacon sandwich. 'They think there might be a sub underneath, so they're trying to bomb him out. There y'are – there goes another.'

The fast disappearing corvette spilled another depth charge. In a few seconds a dull booming sounded from deep below, then a cascade of water rose high in the air to sweep across the foredeck of the following ship.

'Jesus!' said Lowrie. 'I near had a heart attack. I thought me last day had come!'

Corrigan munched, swallowed, and picked a piece of gristle from between his teeth. 'I bet the engine room gang have been shitting themselves. It must be like sitting inside a drum down there.' He selected another sandwich from his greasy parcel. 'I'm not risking turning in. I got Polly Perkins to make me some bacon sarnies. If I'm bound for an open boat I'm going wid a full stummick.'

'What time is it?' asked Lowrie, in the grip of a new panic.

Corrigan shrugged. 'Dunno. Around two bells, I reckon.'

'Oh, Gawd,' moaned Lowrie. 'I'm going to be late. Cloudy will do his nut!' He rushed back to the messroom, spared a glance for the chronometer implacably ticking and showing the time to be two minutes after one, cursed vilely, gathered gloves and oilskins and clattered noisily up the companionway to the fury of the watch below.

Puffing and blowing he scrambled up the foremast ladder, banged on the trapdoor and piled into the crow's nest, apologies rising to his lips.

Cloud greeted him cheerfully. 'Hullo, Lowrie. It's bloody marvellous up here. You get a bird's-eye view of everything.' He kicked the trapdoor shut and held out a helping hand. 'Two bells already, is it? Time don't half pass quickly when you got something to take your interest.'

Lowrie had always loathed the isolation of the crow's nest, the more so after Able Seaman Chambers' grisly end. Once left to his own devices, his imagination played ghoulish tricks, tormenting him with visions of the trapdoor jamming to drown him like a rat in a trap.

'But you don't half miss the bells,' Cloud continued. 'And what's more, I went and left me watch in me locker.'

Lowrie breathed a sigh of relief. Cloud had evidently lost all track of time and he could, therefore, hope to escape the expected recriminations, for aboard ship there were few crimes more heinous than that of a late relief.

'The thing is,' Cloud mused, 'you can't keep track of time these days, what with no bells sounding on account of the subs might hear, and the clocks going back twenty minutes because we're heading west.'

Lowrie had forgotten. 'Oh, Jesus,' he wailed. 'I'm bloody early.'

At eleven-thirty the U-boats attacked in strength and with renewed ferocity. A group of three surfaced between escorts and convoy and raked the port column with a spread of nine torpedoes. The leading ship was struck simultaneously by three torpedoes which blew out the entire port side of the ship, converted the engine room into an inferno of burning oil and scalding steam, and turned her into a wreck of molten metal and flying debris.

The third ship in line was luckier. The torpedo hit the rudder, blew off the propeller and wrecked her steering gear. Her engineers succeeded in closing the watertight door leading to the shaft tunnel and she simply wandered off course to drift slowly astern of the convoy, with the crew taking safely to the boats as she rolled sluggishly in the swell. One torpedo careered erratically across three columns to find a target in the last ship in the fourth line. It exploded in the chain locker, ripping open most of the bows and tearing a gaping hole in the forecastle deck plating. The port bower anchor fell from the hawse pipe dragging a tangle of cable with it, the weight momentarily hauling the bows around until the senhouse slip at the bottom of the locker tore loose and the rest of the massive steel links, lashing in fury, tumbled into the sea. The collision bulkheads evidently held, for the ship dropped back to straggle behind the convoy at reduced speed. A corvette hurried to her assistance and stood off, her loud hailer squawking words of encouragement, while starshells burst above and slowly drifting flares turned night into sickly day.

The second attack, following hard on the heels of the first, came from the opposite direction. A small three thousand ton freighter suddenly buckled and broke in two, with men slithering down the tilting decks to plunge into the boiling chasm between.

The escorts responded fiercely, driving the attackers below the surface and plastering the sea with depth charges. Flashes of gunfire from the dark horizon beyond the loom of the flares indicated that one of the escorts and a U-boat were fighting it out on the surface.

The continual harassing and depth-charging by the escorts began to have their effect. The U-boats, twisting and turning, driven ever deeper, plates springing, pipes ruptured, air foul, crews half-poisoned from battery fumes, finally broke off the action to retire and re-group, leaving a long slick of oil to mark the destruction of one of their number.

The Commodore crossed off two more ships from his convoy plan. He scribbled question marks beside the names of the two damaged vessels and rubbed at the stubble on his chin. 'The *Windrover* can't be expected to keep up with us. Her Master has reported that the collision bulkheads have been shored up and seem to be holding, but with half her bows shot away he can't make more than five knots. I'm afraid there is nothing for it but to detach her and send her north to Iceland.'

'Best pack her off now,' advised Turner. 'While there's a lull. The more distance she can put between us before day-break, the better.'

The two men were leaning against the chart table with one of the 38 x 25 inch sections of a north Atlantic chart un-rolled before them. The *Kentucky Minstrel*'s course was laid off in a series of staggered zig-zags. Turner stared at it dis-gustedly. 'We are crawling around like flies in a barrel of treacle. I bet that *Windrover*'s Master don't appreciate his good fortune. Superficial damage and a free agent, to boot.' He shook his head mournfully. 'Probably not. I met him at the conference. A gloomy feller with nothing to say. Mean as ditchwater – never had the courtesy to offer his cigarettes around.'

The Commodore sighed and took the hint. Turner blew out a satisfying lungful of smoke. 'And what about the Dutchman? You can't just leave her adrift in mid-Atlantic. She'd be a menace to shipping.'

'My thoughts entirely,' agreed the Commodore. 'With no rudder, no propeller and her tunnel filled with water, I'm afraid we'll have to sink her.'

'My first introduction to this war,' said Turner moodily, 'was to watch our lot shooting up the Frog navy. Now it seems we've taken to sinking Dutchmen as well.'

'She's a derelict in any language. But her crew are safe. She never lost a man.'

'Well,' said Turner with heavy humour, 'no doubt with a

name like the *Pierspoort* they'll not be sorry to hear the last of her.'

While the convoy crept slowly through the darkness the Commodore gave the necessary orders and Cloud, lounging in the galley doorway, polished his plate with a hunk of fresh bread. He burped contentedly and returned the plate to the galley boy. 'Worth every penny. We'll make a chef out of you yet, Polly.'

Polly finished scouring the frying pan, plopped in a piece of dripping, added a dozen rashers of bacon and laid the pan to one side. He put half a dozen eggs in a bowl, placed a new loaf of bread on the chopping board, fished out a string of sausages and decorated them neatly around the edge of the frying pan.

Lowrie picked his teeth. 'The twelve-to-four do their-selves proud.'

'Ah, well,' said Polly. 'They got to do their own cooking. I'm not heaving out of me bunk at four o'clock in the morning, not even if they offered me a tanner a time.'

'You must be making a fortune, Polly,' said Jason. 'What are you going to do with all that money? Buy a row of houses?'

Polly, the entrepreneur, picked up the coffee pot and inspected the contents. 'More coffee? Before I make some fresh?'

Lowrie shook his head and followed Jason out on to deck. 'Not for me. I'm as full as a boot.'

There was a thrumming sound followed by a rush of air. Cloud looked up. 'What the 'ell was that?'

A second later a distant bang echoed across the sea.

'Jesus!' swore Jason. 'One of them sods is taking pot shots at us!' They threw themselves flat as a second shell shrieked overhead.

The U-boat had surfaced, picked out the lead ship, and opened fire. It poured out a stammering hail of shells and then dived again before one of the escorts could pin-point its position.

The third shell passed miraculously through the open galley door, tore through the opposite bulkhead and exploded outside. Polly felt the hot wind of its passing then, as fragments of shrapnel whirled and rang against pots and pans, and a lick of flame scorched its way into the galley, he dropped the coffee pot and screamed as the contents emptied over his chest and legs.

Simon, the greaser, was not so fortunate. He had taken his customary stance beneath the ventilator when the fourth shell plunged through the closed skylight to burst inside the engine room. It inflicted little in the way of damage. There was a flash of flame, a deafening explosion, and the air was filled with red-hot pieces of shell-casing that whined and ricochetted about the clattering machinery like a swarm of angry bees. Grogan, the Third Engineer, dropped flat on the grating as a pressure gauge shattered behind his head. One of the bilge pumps wheezed to a stop, and an oil feed pipe suddenly fractured to spout a steadily pulsating stream of black fluid across the churning crankshaft. Score-marks ran across the top of the dynamo casing ,and one of the overhead lights burst to shower the engine room with shards of glass. A tiny, jagged fragment, no larger than a pea, sang past Simon's ear and punctured the main steam pipe. He turned his head and a whistling gout of superheated steam hit him full in the face. It tore the flesh from his skull, melted his eyeballs in their sockets and, as his mouth gaped open in a scream of mortal terror, tore down his throat and ruptured his lungs. Simon died with a bubbling sound deep in his chest, while above his body the ventilator sighed and moaned a wind-borne elegy.

The fifth shell was a dud. It went straight through the funnel-casing, leaving a modest entrance hole at one side and a wide ragged exit hole at the other.

In the stokehold the firemen stood for a few moments in shocked surprise, then Morgan, the young fireman, jumped for the rungs of the vertical ladder and raced up hand over hand with all the fears of hell at his feet. Heart hammering, blood roaring in his head, he stumbled from the stokehold entrance into the darkness of the night. He tripped over a ring bolt, pitched forward barking his knees, then staggered to the shipside rails.

The sixth shell plunged through the top strake of plating just beneath his feet to explode with an echoing boom in the empty tween deck. The sudden bright yellow glare combined with the shock of the explosion gripped him in a blind unreasoning panic. Without a moment's hesitation he put a foot on the rail and launched himself over the side.

The icy waters of the Atlantic closed over his head and drew him down and down, tumbled him over and over, then threw him to the surface again. He had time to see the enormous bulk of the ship lumbering past and the moon lowering a golden ladder of light across the sea then, as he reached toward the rungs, the sea seized him in its cold grip and held him close forever.

That had been the last shell. The U-boat disappeared and the convoy plodded on, a funereal procession of ships crawling over the face of the ocean, their wakes trailing behind like mourning veils.

They were subjected to further sporadic attacks, but the U-boats seemed dispirited by their losses and no longer pressed forward with their earlier determination but contented themselves with a policy of harassment, launching their remaining torpedoes from periscope level and at near-maximum range.

'Typical of the Nazis,' commented Turner. 'Give 'em a basinful of their own medicine and they fall to pieces. Of course it's only to be expected of foreigners; and square-headed ones at that.'

The Commodore was jotting notes for his day-to-day report of the progress of the engagement. 'My assessment is – One: They have probably lost their leadership and, for the time being, are at sixes and sevens. Two: They have never come up against an ASV device before and their losses from night surface attacks are making them wary.' He transferred his gaze to the heaving grey waters of the Atlantic. 'Fortunately they will be unaware that our ASVs are no longer operative.' He smiled at Turner. 'Teething troubles. The first salvo knocked two of 'em out of kilter. The other seems to have developed an attack of hiccups. It's back to the drawing board, I am afraid.'

'Gadgets,' said Turner sourly. 'The world's growing top-heavy with gadgets. One fine day we are going to wake up and find the world run by gadgets.'

'It might make it a better place to live in.'

'Not with the kind of gadgets you fellers have in mind.'

They lost no more ships. Polly Perkins basked in reflected glory. Fussed over by the crew, chest and legs painted yellow and swathed in bandages, a blanket tucked beneath his chin, he lazed contentedly on a deckchair in the lee of the funnel, handy for the lifeboats and within sight and sound of the bridge. Simon's body was consigned to the deep and Morgan's disappearance logged as, *Lost at sea. Believed drowned.* Two more names to add to the ever-lengthening list of merchant seamen who had found a common grave beneath the restless sea.

Six days later they were off the Newfoundland Banks and exchanged one danger for another. Here the warm Gulf Stream, flowing north from the Caribbean, met and was deflected eastward by the icy waters of the Labrador Current, producing a vast area of dense, rolling fog clouds.

The U-boats finally abandoned their attacks and returned to their regular hunting grounds, leaving their prey to grope its way through banks of rolling fog.

With visibility down to ten yards, each vessel streamed a buoy a cable length astern and station-keeping became a never-ending nightmare. Daytime was, if anything, worse than night. At night the nearest ships were dark silhouettes momentarily pushing aside the fog. But in daylight the ships were monstrous spectral shapes, looming like enormous shadows projected on an ever-changing screen. High above their heads the sun hung in a cerulean blue sky, its rays, reflected with dazzling brightness from the myriads of tiny white particles, creating a constant eye-aching glare that blurred the nearest objects with haloes of light. The fog seemed to find its way everywhere: condensing in little droplets that dripped from the deckheads and ran in rivulets down the bulkheads, soaking bedding and clothing: it curled like a white beard over the face of the sea: wound in ghostly fingers about masts and stays: and the wind blew constantly, making ever-changing hallucinatory patterns of light and shade that stretched the watch-keepers' nerves to screaming point.

Eight hours from Halifax the fog turned to softly falling snow.

In line ahead they entered a harbour surrounded by snow-clad hills and packed with shipping. The town sprawled in a clutter of wood-framed buildings bunched between folds of rising ground that leaned away from the waterfront as though cowering from the fierce northerly winds that blew steadily from the Arctic to pile the snow waist-high in the narrow streets.

The *Kentucky Minstrel*, rust-stained and battle-scarred, lay panting alongside her berth, derricks rigged, hatchboards off and the first cases of ammunition stowed in her holds. Turner, leaning over the bridge rail, watched the departure of the Commodore and his staff.

'There goes a feller who can thank his lucky stars that he ain't paid by results,' he commented sourly and turned his accusing gaze upon Mr Potter, shivering in the icy northern blasts. 'I'll say one thing in his favour. He understood the value of tobacco in moments of stress. You should take a leaf from his book, son. It would put colour into your cheeks. Strengthen the juices. Put you into fine fettle. Just think of that handsome wife waiting for you with open arms. Take the advice of an older and wiser head – start with one a day and work your way up.'

Mr Potter, thinking of Madeleine's lean, twitching shanks, watched the ammunition coming aboard, sighed, and prayed for a merciful release.

CHAPTER TWELVE

'IT'S A shanty town,' said Cloud.

By no stretch of the imagination could Halifax be described as a sailor's paradise. Narrow streets knee-deep in snow. Frame buildings. Seedy restaurants. The ripe stench of fish from canning factories and the wharfs where the heaving, slithering, silver catches were landed, gutted and packed. A charmless town whose sole virtue lay in possessing a fine natural harbour, land-lockea and ice-free the year round. Its Calvinistic inhabitants, imbued with the belief that mankind should shun luxury and be thrifty, had carried their doctrine to the extreme of banning the public sale of spirituous liquors. Not unnaturally this led to a conflict between their free-wheeling visitors and the forces of law and order, a conflict which, however, was resolved by certain backsliders who catered for swarms of demanding customers by opening 'blind pigs'.

'Shebeens,' said Cloud. 'There's no pleasure in it. I mean, sitting in a back room of a two-up-two-down, supping bottled ale that tastes like boiled onion water and paying through the bleeding nose for it, just inn't worth it.'

'Bug-roosts,' agreed Lowrie. 'Halifax is the devil's arsehole.'

'A miserable town stuffed with misery-gutted sods who wouldn't give you the time of day, even if you offered 'em a dollar a minute.' Cloud stood on the forecastle head, muffled and gloved, his long, lanky frame encrusted in drifting snow. He stamped his feet and beat his arms. 'Roll on home. Christ, what a bleedin' town!'

The *Kentucky Minstrel*, deep-laden with cases of ammunition, rifles and machine-guns stowed below, and tanks and armoured cars as deck cargo, cleared the quay and moved out into the bay to join the straggling lanes of ships jostling for position as they formed into two lines and pushed their way through a blizzard of finely falling snow, out beyond the buoyed channel, to stretch for the open sea beyond.

They cleared the shrouded hills of Indian Harbour to the south and butted their way out into the heavy rollers of the waiting Atlantic.

Here they re-formed into four columns, nine deep and, escorted by a frigate and an ancient flush-deck destroyer accompanied by four corvettes of the R.C.N., headed east toward the deeps beyond the Flemish Gap.

As the northern headland of Imperoyal disappeared behind a curtain of snow, watches were set and the shivering deck crowd made their way below to the overheated steamy comfort of the messroom and three-bunk cabins, with the sea sluicing past the shipside and rivulets of condensation trickling down the studded metal plating.

Cloud divested himself of all but shirt and shorts and threw himself thankfully upon his narrow cot.

'Jesus!' he gasped. 'I don't know where Sloppy found that bastard, Potter, but he ought to throw him back. I'm frozen to the marrow. He could have knocked us off an hour ago.'

Jason dragged off his seaboots. 'Ah, well, it's only Potty Potter's first trip as Mate. The bosun'll soon tame him.'

'He's taking his time about it,' grumbled Lowrie. He perched on the upper shipside bunk, his stockinged feet dangling over Jason's head. 'The trip's half over and that fish-faced article hasn't changed a bit.'

'I think he's got a secret sorrow,' said Cloud. 'Have you seen that wife of his? Like a great hairy spider out of a horror film. Looks like something that's just crawled out from under a stone. Gawd, I bet she eats him alive.' He clasped his hands behind his head and closed his eyes. 'Don't disturb me for an hour or two, I'm getting back to Sonia.'

The snow turned to rain and the rain to a blustery wind that blew the tops of the waves into a marching white army. The skies remained dull and leaden, with barely the sight of a weak sun. The horizon closed in to a murky haze and sea and sky merged into an indistinguishable greyness.

It was a fast twelve-knot convoy with the more vulnerable ships placed in the centre and protected by the outer columns which consisted of mixed-cargo vessels loaded with machine-tools and foodstuffs. The *Kentucky Minstrel,* fourth ship in the second rank, steamed a couple of cable lengths abeam of a 12,000-ton tanker loaded with aviation spirit. Immediately ahead was another ammunition ship and, plodding astern, a small Norwegian freighter loaded with case oil.

Turner stood on the bridge casting a critical eye over the station-keeping of the surrounding vessels. At length he permitted himself a grunt of satisfaction as the ships kept steadily to their appointed places with the practised discipline of seasoned veterans. Grey and weather-stained, many, like the *Kentucky Minstrel,* showing the scars of hard-fought battles, they plunged through the long, serrated Atlantic rollers, tossing spumes of spray over their foredecks and rolling sluggishly from the deadweight of their cargoes.

He transferred his gaze to the escorting corvettes snuffling around their charges like puppies over-eager for a romp and, remembering the sight of their crews straggling aboard in Halifax, entertained serious doubts as to their capabilities.

Three of the four corvettes were obviously brand-new, straight from the shipyards and gleaming from recently applied coats of war-paint. The fourth had a short, salt-encrusted funnel, and rust stains showed beneath her counter. But all were officered by fresh-faced young men, self-conscious in smart new uniforms with wriggly gold bands about their sleeves, and yet to be blooded in battle.

On the other hand, the destroyer and frigate were commanded by hard-nosed R.C.N. Lieutenant-Commanders and manned by tough-looking professional crews. But even they were of limited battle experience, their activities restricted to the first leg of the convoy shuttle service.

Iceland, dominating the north Atlantic convoy routes, acted as a refitting and refulling base for the ocean escorts and, a few miles south, in an area designated as Mid-Ocean Meeting point, the Canadian escorts would hand over to their British counterparts for the second, and most dangerous, stage of the passage.

As more and more U-boats were launched the Wolf Packs grew in strength, extending their operations further and further westward. The U-boats now patrolled a battle-line that stretched from the North Western Approaches to Greenland. They grouped and regrouped and attacked with renewed ferocity. It was a never-ending battle, fought without quarter. There were no prisoners and few survivors. Ships and crews died floundering in the savage seas. U-boats sank to the bottomless depths, men and machinery crushed like sardines in a can.

Each convoy fought its battle in isolation from the others. They were small villages, moving through space and time, their inhabitants conscious only of the surrounding sea and sky while they waited for the sudden devastating attack from an unseen enemy. They watched their neighbours die and lived in ignorance of the fate of other distant villages.

The first attack came at dawn on the fourth day when they were 500 miles south of Cape Farewell, the southernmost tip of Greenland.

A U-boat of the *Marodeur* Group operating out of the Denmark Strait, sighted the formation of ships. It reported to the other five members of the flotilla spread out thirty miles apart in a wide-pronged rake that combed 150 miles of ocean, then submerged, took up an attack position, rose to periscope depth and launched three torpedoes.

The convoy fortuitiously zig-zagged even as the U-boat lowered its periscope and her commander counted off the seconds as he waited for the tell-tale explosions. Two torpedoes ran wild, missing the convoy completely. The third found a gap in the flanking ships' ranks, crossed the *Kentucky Minstrel*'s bows, and buried itself into the midships section of the tanker. Miraculously it failed to explode but hung, exactly on the waterline, wagging its tail in the ship's wash like a great sleek gleaming fish.

Turner, his face sagging with tiredness, heard the resounding clang as the head struck home, and stared in disbelief across the narrow gap of surging water.

The pale-faced Mr Potter, now paler than ever, joined him and together they gaped at the miracle.

'My God,' whispered Potter. 'She'll go up at any moment.'

The bosun was making his way along the boat deck to receive his morning orders from the Mate. He, too, heard the echoing boom of the striking torpedo, turned his head and stood transfixed, waiting for the inevitable explosion.

Turner hastily stamped out his cigarette, cupped his hands, and bawled: 'Clear the decks! Take cover! All hands take cover!'

The bosun turned and set off at a shambling, bow-legged run.

Albert Hodge took one horrified look, grabbed the now fully recovered Polly Perkins by the scruff of the neck, bundled him inside the galley and slammed the heavy iron doors shut.

Old Conroy, the lookout man, yanked open the trap-door in the crow's nest, grabbed the side rails of the steel ladder and slid down like a monkey.

Angus McPherson, yawningly making his rounds, the brass links of the sounding rod looped over one arm, was galvanised into action. Colliding with the steward emerging into the midships alley with the officers' tea, he bundled him unceremoniously back into the pantry, yelling: 'Lie flat! Get your heid doon!'

Turner and Potter took cover in the wheelhouse, closing the iron-shod doors and dropping the bullet-proof shutters over the forward windows.

The tanker rolled, and the torpedo tore loose, lifted its head to the top of a wave as though seeking a new victim, then disappeared into the depths. It left a wide round hole through which spouted a torrent of petrol. Then the tanker rolled sluggishly, burying the opening beneath the racing waves. It drew in the sea like an open mouth then, as the ship heaved its side clear, spewed out a mixture of petrol and sea-water.

A film of high-octane spirit spread across the grey Atlantic rollers, lending them iridescent hues as they flowed astern to push their way between the columns of advancing ships.

The tanker dipped and rolled, dipped and rolled. Vapour rose above the surface of the sea, condensed into tiny droplets, creating a visible cloud of inflammable gas, drifting with the wind.

At the same time, one of the corvettes eager to come to grips with the enemy, raced around in circles, depth charges cascading in its wake.

It may have been the effect of the depth charges, it may have been a spark from the exhausts of one of the following ships, it may have been a combination of a hundred tiny accidents, but suddenly the sea took fire. The cloud of vapour ignited with one tremendous searing flash. The tanker rolled, opened its gaping mouth, then blew up. A sheet of brilliant yellow flame roared into the sky. The *Kentucky Minstrel* heeled almost to her beam ends from the impact of the shock wave. The deck cargo of tanks groaned and strained against their chain lashings, and in the engine room steam pipes, valves and oil lines were fractured. The heat from the fireball scorched the starboard-side paintwork down to the metal. The lifeboats, hanging from the davit heads, burst into flames and were then extinguished as the rope falls burned like cotton and tumbled them hissing into the sea. The seams in the oak-planked boat deck melted and ran in long rivers of fire the length of the deck. The very air burned and the sea boiled like a cauldron.

On the tanker, heat from that titanic explosion melted metal, turned everything forward of the bridge into a raging inferno, pulverising heavy-duty pipes and deck plating into flying white-hot splinters.

It seemed that nothing could live through such a maelstrom of fire and heat and yet, as the fireball hurtled into the sky to turn into a whirling pillar of smoke, the cooler air rushed in and the sea closed over the heaving chasm of water that had once been occupied by 12,000 tons of cargo, and the after end of the ship floated away. Smoke-blackened, twisted and charred, the bridge a tangled mess of wreckage, it slowly turned and gyrated, lifting over the slope of each wave, sliding down into the trough of the next, swaying from side to side in the wash of passing ships. As it drifted astern of the convoy a few dazed figures could be seen emerging from below to stagger about the stern-walk. Blood running from ears and noses, deafened and half-blinded, they pawed helplessly at the air in shocked incomprehension.

Turner picked himself up from the chartroom deck as the *Kentucky Minstrel* righted herself with a slow pendulum swing. Mr Potter also hauled himself to his feet, gingerly massaging a lump at the back of his head. He summoned up a weak smile. 'It's good to be alive.'

'It's always good to be alive, young man,' said Turner. 'Let's take a look-see at the damage.'

They walked through to the wheelhouse where Corrigan still clung to the helm, his glassy stare concentrated upon the small rectangle of armoured glass set into the steel shutters.

Turner raised the shutters. 'Are you all right, Corrigan?' he asked.

'Jesus, Mother of God,' whispered Corrigan and lapsed into silence.

Mr Potter opened the sliding door and stepped out on to the wing of the bridge. The planking of the boat deck smouldered, sending up curling wisps of wood-smoke. The acrid smell of burning paint assailed his nostrils, his head ached abominably, his eyes smarted, and his lungs seemed about to burst with the intake of fresh air.

Turner reached his side, swayed and reached for support against the housing. He drew his hand away quickly and blew on his fingers. 'It's hot,' he said and slowly crumpled at the knees.

Potter held him, looped an arm about his shoulders, and stretching out a foot, dragged the fallen pilot's chair forward. He heaved the chair upright and gently lowered Turner into it. 'Are you all right, sir?' he asked anxiously.

Turner sighed. 'I'm tired. I'm getting too old for this game. War's a young man's business.' He settled his back against the chair-rest and closed his eyes. 'I'm just going to have a thinks for a minute.'

'I shan't be a moment,' said Potter. He hurried away into the chartroom and returned in a few moments to hold out a cigarette and a box of matches. 'The Second Mate's, sir. He keeps them in the chart drawer. I don't smoke, but . . .'

Turner opened his eyes, took the cigarette and accepted a light. 'I don't think Hubert Page would object. He never has in the past. You'd best roust him out, Hector. Him and his fire party.

Potter looked aft. 'He's coming now, sir.'

'Carry on, Mr Potter,' said Turner. He turned his head and watched the smoke and steam rising from the fire party's hoses as they sluiced down the boat deck. He could hear Cloud's voice raised above the chatter of the others: 'I thought me last day had come. When she heeled over I fell out of me bunk an' I thought – Oh, Jesus – all that ammo! I expected to be blown right out of me seaboots. I don't understand it,' he added as though complaining of the non-appearance of a long-expected treat. 'She should have gone up. I mean, it was hot enough to fry the balls off a brass monkey.'

'The other ammo boat didna go up, neither,' said Lowrie.

'Ah, but we was closer,' said Cloud argumentatively. 'I mean, we got the lot.'

Jason spoke with the voice of a reasonable man settling the finer points of a debate. 'It's stowed below the waterline where the 'ot 'eat can't get at it. In any case it won't go off without detonators. Like them shells for the gun. They're safe as 'ouses until they're armed.'

Turner closed his ears to a discussion which would no doubt continue until the end of the voyage. He stretched his arms, yawned prodigiously, remembering that he hadn't had more than three consecutive hours of sleep since leaving port. I'm an old fool, he thought, trying to take the entire burden of responsibility on my own shoulders. I'm like a feller driven crazy by an itch he can't reach, when all he has to do is get someone else to scratch it. Potter for example. A cold fish but his heart is in the right place. He yawned again, longing for the comfort of a bed and cool sheets, then shrugged the temptation aside. A man with a Captain's four stripes could not hand over responsibility to a man with three. It was as simple as that. His place was here, with his bones aching, eyes stinging and mouth furred like the bottom of a parrot's cage, because this is where he was expected to be.

The Second Steward appeared at his elbow with a mug of tea and a plate of hot buttered toast. 'Thought you might be peckish, sir,' he announced solicitously, adding in an aggrieved whine: 'I'd have been up earlier, only that tanker went and blew itself to pieces.'

Flint was the Captain's 'Tiger', or personal steward. A stoop-shouldered man of thinning sandy hair, rheumatic joints and watery eyes, he fussed over his charge like a mother hen.

Turner cupped the mug in his hands, took a long draught and blew out his cheeks as the hot fiery liquid burned down his throat.

'I gave it a lacing of Irish,' said Flint. 'It'll warm up your bones.'

'Thank you, Flint,' said Turner. He munched a piece of toast and felt a renewed sense of well-being coursing through his veins.

Flint cocked his head to one side and eyed Turner like a

malevolent sparrow. 'You need a shave. Them whiskers put years on your age. I'll lay out your gear and draw a bath.'

Turner shook his head. 'Not now, Flint. I can't leave the bridge yet.'

'Of course you can,' said Flint with some asperity. 'Whatcher think you got officers for? I'll give you a shout when it's ready.' He sniffed, wiped his nose on the sleeve of his patrol jacket, and rolled away on bunioned feet.

Turner smiled. The ship's routine was evidently returning to normal. The bosun had appeared and was engaged in attentive conversation with Mr Potter. The lookout man was climbing back to the crow's nest. Chippy ambled along the foredeck, sounding tanks. From the galley came the familiar clatter of pots and pans and the unmelodious voice of Polly Perkins raised in song.

Turner settled himself more comfortably, popped triangles of buttered toast into his mouth, savoured the hot, sweet, whiskey-laden tea, and reflected dreamily on the remaining two thousand miles of the voyage.

The U-boats of the *Marodeur* Pack attacked in strength that same afternoon. They kept it up for three days and three nights and only broke off when the relieving escorts hove over the horizon. The convoy lost four ships and a corvette for no apparent damage to the enemy.

Their accompanying escorts turned away and headed north. The fresh-faced young men now looked old, their faces haggard and drawn, grey with strain and fatigue.

Their replacements were weather-stained and smoke-grimed and had the lean look of experienced hunters. They were led by a Tribal class destroyer wearing, like a cockade at the head of its tripod mast, a diamond-shaped R.D.F. aerial. She was followed by a sloop tossing plumes of white water over her head as she swung in a wide arc to take up station ahead. The remainder of the escort consisted of four corvettes bobbing like corks in the deep Atlantic swell.

Dean turned up his collar and hunched deeply into his bridge coat. A pale sun peered wearily through stratified layers of cloud, and the blustery wind, which had been whipping the sea into saw-toothed edges of spume for the past week, had at last died away to a light fitful breeze. Great plains of smooth water rolled away endlessly, broken only by the curling bow waves of the ships and the creaming wakes of the escorts. Now and again, however, a cat's-paw of wind would kick up a heart-stopping flurry of spindrift from the top of a distant wave, when all heads would turn seeking the tell-tale track of a periscope.

Dean resumed his slow pacing of the bridge, struggling to stifle yet another yawn, with little to occupy his mind but a haunting, phantasmagoric memory of the last attack. It was night and the convoy had been moving like ghosts through veils of sea mist. There had been the sudden roar of an explosion. A lurid orange light had painted the drifting mist with wavering streaks of scarlet and gold, shimmering like a vast curtain of shot silk illuminated by distant fires. Then he had heard the unseen ship rolling and groaning in its death agony, the tearing shrieks of twisted metal, the roar of bulkheads giving way, the inrush of water and the howl of escaping steam. Then the veil of mist had blown away and he had seen the stern of the freighter rising almost vertically in the air, her single screw still churning crazily, men floundering in the water and screaming as the propeller churned and lashed the sea into a frenzy. He saw – or thought he saw – a man cut in half as though by a gigantic scythe. He tried to tell himself that it was a trick of the imagination, but the memory remained imprinted on his mind as though etched by acid.

Since then Dean's few short hours of sleep had been punctuated by nightmares from which he would wake sweating and trembling, a scream of fear dying in his throat as he fought his way up through layers of unconsciousness like a drowning man reaching for the surface of a bottomless sea.

He yawned again and again until his jaws cracked, and tried to direct his thoughts toward Olwyn and marriage. Marriage. That was the fulcrum upon which his desires see-sawed from the heights of exultation to the depths of gloomy misgivings. One moment she was a succubus invading his private dreams with chimerical promises of orgiastic delights, the next she was nothing more than an infantile chatterbox with the brain of a hen. He had long since deciphered the childish code buried in the letter she had squeezed into his hand at their last parting. A task made the easier by her habit of heavily underlining the relevant passages and then following up with a row of exclamation marks.

The message written in purple ink on deckled blue note-paper, far from having its desired effect, had simply filled him with a sense of queasy embarrassment.

Dean sighed disconsolately and thought of Bert Page's Marjorie. Now there was a woman worth treasuring. Bert, he concluded for the hundredth time, was a lucky dog.

He eased the ache in his shoulders and continued his perambulation of the bridge, while thirty miles astern the leader of the *Marodeur* Group surfaced to transmit a brief message, passing the convoy on to the *Faust* Group lying ahead.

The convoy fought its way through for the loss of one ship against the destruction of two U-boats.

Faust Group then signalled *Beil* Group and, after a day's respite, the savage war of attrition continued under bright blue skies and long clear nights. *Beil* Group harassed the convoy for two days and two nights but without being able to pierce the screen of experienced escorts. On the morning of the third day, a couple of hundred miles west of Malin Head, a Western Approaches escort hurried out in support, while a Lockheed Hudson of Coastal Command, circling overhead, sent the wolves racing away for safety.

They had run the gauntlet, lost seven ships from a total of thirty-six, but the weather held fine and clear and the May sun warm, bringing the promise of an English spring. The sea was a pellucid green and ran sweetly, chuckling alongside the salt-stained hulls. Gulls skirled overhead, swooped and dived for scraps, following the ships' wakes like white familiars vented by the wind. On either side of the North Channel the hills rolled back in cloud-shadowed folds, and the blue smoke from white-washed cottages curled and eddied in a soft, gentle breeze.

All in all, it was good to be alive.

The sun turned to a sullen fiery glow as they entered the Mersey. At first they put it down to no more than the usual murk of haze and smoke which invariably overhung Liverpool when there was a drop in the wind. They only became aware that something was wrong when the ship began to weave its way between the wreckage of sunken ships. Here and there masts and funnels stuck out of the water, the tide rip bubbling around them and creating fresh eddies in which bobbed odd bits and pieces of flotsam.

Cloud, standing on the forecastle head, narrowed his eyes and stared at the skyline. It no longer held its familiar pattern. Something was missing. He blinked and looked again. The distant Liver Buildings emerged from the drifting mist, the Liver birds with their outstretched wings glinted in the sun. But all around were empty spaces where there had once been buildings. A few hundred yards away the spire of St Nicholas church still pointed at the sky but the body of the church had a vaguely shattered look as though a wayward child, having finished with a toy, had poked its fingers through the doors and orifices.

Mr Potter, standing far forward at the stem, raised his head and experimentally sniffed the air. Then they all smelled it – the sharp, sour-sweet, acrid tang of charred timber, of smoke and soot, of dust and ash, and another foetid odour they could not at first define.

The river narrowed and they turned questing heads to stare in disbelief at appalling areas of destruction spreading from bank to bank. The river flowed glutinous with oil and soot. The once-familiar docks were a shambles of smashed buildings and warehouses riven from top to bottom. Transit sheds were heaps of twisted metal and smouldering rubble. Lanes of small houses which once crawled up the slopes of low-lying hills now seemed to have been stamped into the ground. On the Birkenhead side of the river gap-toothed rows of houses still glowed with interior fires amid circles and overlapping semi-circles of utter devastation.

A heavy pall of smoke drifted down river. Dead birds floated past, wings helplessly outstretched. Shoals of fish, silver bellies upturned, swirled and eddied in the tide. A bell buoy, set adrift, wandered aimlessly about the river clanging mournfully to itself.

'Holy Jesus Christ Almighty,' ejaculated the bosun. 'They haven't half copped a tidy packet!'

It was all so unfair. They had fought their way across the U-boat-infested Atlantic only to be faced with the destruction of their city.

Dean, seated comfortably at the back of his father's Wolseley, clutched Olwyn's hand and mused upon the inequalities of war, while Mr Dean took them on a tour of rubble-strewn streets and enlarged upon the iniquities of the enemy.

'They blitzed us for eight nights,' he said. 'Eight nights in a row. Hundreds of bombers dropping H.E. and incendiaries. My office was one of the first to go, so I'm carrying on at home.'

Dean only half-listened, his gaze rivetted upon burnt-out buildings. Skeletal frames that looked like the blueprints of a mad draughtsman. A signboard hung askew outside the Forum cinema. *All This and Heaven Too*, it proclaimed to the world at large. Lime Street was strewn with bricks and mounds of broken slates. Burst water-mains bubbled across the road. Telegraph poles lay in festoons of twisted wire. Lewis's Retail Store, which once stood four-square upon the corner, was no more The bombs must have fallen in a random pattern, for opposite Lewis's the facade of the Adelphi Hotel remained untouched and aloof from the surrounding destruction. Central Station was a heap of concrete slabs, from which emerged the tendrils of iron rails. Blackler's Store was a gaunt framework, seared by fire. The entire shopping centre seemed to have been blasted into oblivion. A gas main roared yellow flames into the air. People wandered about, dazed and stricken, faces blank and eyes glazed, stepping over bulging hose-pipes that snaked and looped in wild arabesques across roads strewn with the rubble of collapsed buildings. Firemen, stunned with weariness, poured streams of water into the smoking shells of blackened stonework. Impassable streets were roped off with dangling signs warning of unexploded bombs.

As they left the city centre the devastation became less severe. Charred stumps were all that remained of a tree-lined avenue. Scorched hedgerows surrounded houses with windows shattered by fire. There were oases of greenery amid rows of houses gutted like herrings. A burned out tram-car lay with its front bogie wheels half-buried in a bomb crater.

They passed between rows of surburban houses and bungalows untouched and unharmed. Splashes of colour from green privet hedges and the bright, dripping yellow candles of laburnum trees. Cherry blossom. Birds singing. A leafy arcade of dappled sunlight. They were almost home.

Dean became aware that his father was speaking. 'Well, David. What is your opinion?'

'Ah?'

Olwyn snuggled closer. 'I can hardly wait.'

'We are agreed upon a church wedding,' said his father. 'No divergence of views upon that score, eh?'

Dean looked at Olwyn. Wide brown eyes flecked with gold. Slightly pouting lips. Skin clear and unblemished. Eyebrows fashionably plucked. Mouth rouged. The fragrance of expensive perfume. Her face untroubled, unresponsive, unconcerned and empty of all feeling except those of her own immediate desires. She was selfish, greedy and infantile, but infinitely desirable. He remembered blazing ships and drowning men. The screams of the injured. The thunder of depth charges. The sea boiling beneath a mad sky lit by flares. The wild hiss of escaping steam and the scalding roar of exploding boilers. The nightmare of endurance as one nerve-wracking day merged into the next. This time he had survived. But for how long? The ship would discharge, then they would set off again to face the waiting wolf packs and the hungry Atlantic. The future was a blank. Tomorrow would never come. There was only today.

He looked again at Olwyn's upturned face and parted lips. A lifetime spent with such a creature would be an unmitigated disaster. But to ravish that warm seductive flesh for a few carnal nights before returning to the lunacy of war would bring fulfilment and reward beyond imagining.

He squeezed her hand. 'Whatever you decide,' he said.

Matt Honest and Albert Hodge picked their way over the rubble of collapsed houses and torn-up roads. They hastened their steps, turned the corner and found Eversley Grove miraculously intact, the small houses huddling together as though for comfort. They stepped over a rope strung across the street and hurried to Number 9.

'Not even cracked a pane o' glass,' said Matt. He fished out his key and inserted it into the lock. 'We'll give 'em a surprise.'

They entered the tiny hallway and stood uncertainly for a moment in the creaking silence of an unnaturally empty house. Matt halloed and his voice seemed to echo from room to room. They poked their heads into the parlour, then the kitchen. Matt ran his fingers over the polished mantelshelf and came away with a layer of dust. There seemed to be dust everywhere. It had collected over picture frames and ornaments, table tops and fire-irons. Soot had fallen from the chimney and piled in a black heap in the hearth.

'Beats all,' said Albert, scratching his head. 'No damage, as far as I can see, so they must be . . .' He was interrupted by a thunderous knocking at the front door. Matt yanked it open to be confronted by the furious face of a Warden.

'What the 'ell are you doing here?' demanded the man.

'I live here,' said Matt truculently. 'What's it to you?'

'Can't you bloody read?'

'What?'

The man beckoned. 'Come out here.'

They trailed after him into the street and the Warden spelt it out, 'Unexploded bomb. Unexploded bomb!' he shouted. 'Are you out of your bleedin' minds!'

'I'm looking for my family. Wife, kid, grandpa.'

The Warden fished out a grubby notebook, licked his forefinger and turned over the pages. 'Name of Honest?'

Matt nodded.

'Funny name, Honest. Honest as the day is long, eh?' The man wheezed asthmatically at his joke. 'Evacuated on the first night. You got an Aunt Ada?'

Matt nodded again. 'Lives in Dingle.'

'Ada Fisher, Mrs,' read out the Warden. 'That's the one. The Dingle, eh? They've had a right pasting.'

Matt clenched his enormous fists and took a pace forward. 'My family,' he demanded thickly. 'Are they safe?'

'Keep your hair on,' said the Warden nervously. 'Come round to the Post and I'll find out for you.'

Matt locked the front door, carefully pocketed the key and then followed the Warden past a small crater at the end of the road. 'That's it,' said the Warden jerking a thumb. 'Unexploded bomb. I mean, why else do you think we roped off the street? Where are you from, anyway?'

'Just back from the sea,' said Albert.

'Been at sea, eh?' said the Warden. 'Lucky sods. You missed the lot.' He led them around the corner into a street littered with broken glass and smashed slates, then disappeared into a sand-bagged A.R.P. Post.

They hung around listening to the indistinct mumble of the Warden's voice, while Matt's stomach churned into knots of tension and his mouth filled with saliva and bile.

Albert stared woodenly at a tattered poster exhorting all gardeners to Dig For Victory.

Eventually the Warden reappeared, puffing from exertion as though he had run all the way.

'Well,' he began, evidently under the impression that he was breaking the news gently. 'The street they'd been evacuated to was flattened two nights ago . . .'

Matt leaned forward and made a gagging sound in his throat.

'But your fambly was in a shelter at the time,' continued the Warden, 'and they are now at the Evacuation Centre at Lawrence Road School. You know where it is?'

'We'll find it,' said Albert.

'By the barracks,' said the Warden helpfully. 'You can't miss it. Don't worry, Mr Honest, your fambly is as safe as 'ouses.' He chuckled wetly at his second joke of the day and watched the pair trudging away. 'Lucky sods,' he told himself. 'At sea, right through the blitz. Lucky sods.'

Page entered a street of drunken houses. Some leaned precariously forward, others teetered back as though caught off balance. There were houses with bulging walls, houses split and fissured, riven with vertical chasms. Blackened rafters clawed at the air from roofs open to the skies. Windows like eyeless sockets stared blindly across mounds of bricks and mortar. Doors gaped open like the mouths of the demented.

At the corner, alongside a narrow brick-strewn passage, stood their own block of flats. The windows had been blown out and roughly boarded over, but the building itself seemed untouched. The closed front door at the head of the short flight of stone steps helped to relieve Page's fears. He took the steps two at a time, inserted his key in the lock and tried to turn it. The lock remained immovably fast. He put his finger on the bell push and rang the bell. There was no answering peal. He looked up, but the platform and wrought-iron rails of the small balcony outside their room blocked his view.

He trotted down the steps again and, stumbling over the debris part-blocking the passageway, made his way to the rear. There, where their tiny square of garden had once been, lay a veritable mountain of bricks and plaster, shattered glass, whole window frames, a tangle of pipes, and a steam radiator. The entire rear wall had been sheared off as though by a giant cleaver, exposing all three storeys. It was like looking into the wreckage of a giant's doll's house. A bed balanced precariously at the edge of the upper floor. A picture hung rakishly on half a wall. A bath was suspended by its plumbing over a splintered hole. A patterned carpet fluttered like a flag in the breeze. The cellar was choked with rubble.

Sick at heart he turned away and went in search of the nearest A.R.P. Post.

The Warden was sympathetic. ''unter,' he said, thumbing through his notes. 'Mrs M.' He brightened suddenly. 'In 'ospital. The only survivor outer the lot. The whole street went. Every mother's son of 'em. But Mrs 'unter, she survived. On'y just, mind. Buried alive for eighteen hours. We 'ad the devil's own job fishin' her out. She was brave, though. Never a whimper. A very brave person.'

Page gulped. 'Is she – Is she injured?'

'O' course she's injured,' said the Warden with some asperity. 'You couldn't expect other, could you?'

Page's heart began to thump painfully. 'How badly?'

'I couldn't tell you,' said the Warden. 'She'd broke a leg, that I do know. But for the rest . . .' He shrugged. 'I dunno. That's for the doctors to say after they've cleaned her up. I mean, when I reached her she was smothering. Covered in plaster. We 'ad to tunnel in. Took us nine hours.'

Page, remembering the shattered walls and groaning timbers, looked at the man with new respect. 'You tunnelled in? Under that?'

The Warden picked his nose. He seemed almost embarrassed by the implication of the question. 'Well, that's what I'm here for, inn't it? Better'n going to sea. I got a horror of drowning.'

'Where is she now?'

'Broadgreen 'ospital.' The Warden's finger explored the other nostril. 'It's a 'ell of a long way, and the Jerries have knocked shit out of the transport. Tell you what I'll do. I'm not supposed to, mind, but under the circumstances . . .' He trailed off as though communing with himself. 'That's what I'll do. Ring for an ambulance. If anyone asks – you're suffering from shock – all right?'

'That's very kind of you,' said Page. 'I'm more than grateful.'

'Ah, well,' said the Warden. 'She was a very brave person.'

The ambulance dropped him at the emergency entrance and he hurried inside only to be passed from hand to hand by a harassed staff. Eventually a grey-haired, grandmotherly old lady seated at a makeshift table, combed through a list of new arrivals and directed him to the women's ward on the first floor. He was about to push his way through the swing doors when a beefy Matron, starched from head to toe, barred his way with a massive forearm.

'And where do you think you are going, young man?'

Wearily he explained his mission all over again. The starched face softened. 'I have two sons in the Navy,' she told him, 'so perhaps I can make an exception.' She became efficient and businesslike once again. 'Are you aware of the extent of her injuries?'

He shook his head.

'It is always better for the visitor to be prepared. And, understand me, young man, I will not have my patients upset.'

'Yes, Matron,' said Page humbly, wishing to God the woman would come to the point.

'Dislocated hip. Right leg broken in three places. Severe lacerations of the back and torso. She has lost an eye and the left side of her face will be scarred for life.'

'Oh, Jesus!' said Page.

'She has no hair, but it will grow again. Now listen to me, young man, and listen carefully. *She* will learn to live with it. And so must you. If you feel that you cannot, then you must leave now. I want no false sentiment. Do you understand?'

Page nodded dumbly. 'Does – does she know?'

The Matron drew herself up. 'There are no secrets in a casualty ward. Very well – you may have ten minutes. No longer. The sixth bed on the right.'

She stepped aside and he entered the ward.

With the exception of his one unremarkable visit to the bedside of Ordinary Seaman Mason, Page had never set foot in a hospital before. He had always imagined hospitals to be quiet antiseptic places, with pretty nurses fluttering from bed to bed, cooling brows, popping thermometers in mouths, and offering words of encouragement.

This was different. It was as though he had stepped into one of the anterooms to hell. There seemed to be blood everywhere. Blood-stained bedding. Blood-stained bandages. And the sickly stench of blood. The beds were pushed together until the ward was packed with a writhing mass of tormented humanity. It echoed with moans and soft blubberings, babbled prayers and sudden wild shrieks that prickled the hair on the back of his head. The nurses were gaunt skeletons barely clothed in flesh. Hollow-eyed and drunk from lack of sleep, they stumbled from one bed to another, picking their way around stretcher cases lying on the floor and covered in blood-red blankets. Two white-coated doctors stared at him with dull, lack-lustre eyes, then continued at their never-ending tasks. He counted six beds along then, just to be sure, counted again. She lay, swathed in bandages between a mountainous woman who seemed to have no face and a wizened creature, all skin and bones, who seemed to have no legs.

There was, in fact, a short space about a foot wide between the cots. He squeezed his way alongside her bed and stood awkwardly looking down at her. All that was visible through her head bandages was her mouth, the tip of her nose, and one roving eye. The fingers of her right hand were spread on the metal framework of a splint and the bedclothes rose in a hump over a protective leg-cage.

'Hullo,' was all he could find to say.

She twisted her mouth into a semblance of her wolf's grin. 'I'm in a hell of a mess,' she said.

'You are alive,' he said. 'That's all that matters.' He took her free hand and clung to it as though it were a life-line.

Her single eye swivelled to meet his gaze. It glistened and a solitary tear trickled down her cheek. 'I wish they'd left me where I was. I'm in a mess.'

He dredged up a smile and squeezed her hand affectionately. 'I know all about it,' he said. 'Matron told me. Spared no details, so you can't frighten me off. We're going to fit you up with a glass eye and a wooden leg and then we're going to be married.'

'No,' she said.

He kissed her fingertips. 'Oh, yes, we are.' He leaned over

and gently kissed her mouth. 'Yes, we are,' he repeated. 'And I'm not in the habit of taking "no" for an answer. Not from ladies lying on their backs.'

She turned her head to one side and began to weep convulsively. He raised her hand and put her fingertips to his mouth once again. 'I love you,' he said simply. 'I love you. Don't go. Don't leave me. I love you.'

Suddenly he began to cry. Tears scalded his cheeks. He cried and cried and could not stop crying.

'There, there, lover,' she said trying to comfort his anguish. 'There, there. It will be all right. Don't cry, lover, don't cry.'

Try as he would he could not stop crying. Racking sobs welled up in his throat, drowning him in tears. He continued to sob and wail even though he saw the misted figure of the Matron marching purposefully toward him. He clutched Marjorie's hand the tighter and wept until he thought his heart would break.

To his surprise Matron patted him on the shoulder. 'That's the spirit,' she said. 'Cry your heart out. Men should do so more often. If the Almighty had meant to endow you with a stiff upper lip, He would have supplied buttons to go with it.'

He hauled out his handkerchief, snuffled, blew his nose and wiped his face. 'We are going to be married,' he said.

'Congratulations,' said the Matron dryly. 'I never doubted it for a moment.'

'No,' said Marjorie.

The Matron fixed her with a basilisk stare. 'Be quiet, my girl. You are a patient and in my hospital patients do as they are told.'

'Yes, Matron,' said Marjorie humbly. 'Yes, Matron.'

The *Kentucky Minstrel* swung out into the river and skittishly threw a plume of water over her head.

'She's in fine fettle,' said Page. He winked at Dean. 'How is Olwyn?'

Dean had the grace to blush. 'Likewise.' He hesitated. 'Marjorie . . .'

Page thought of the gaunt scarecrow with a fuzz of new hair sprouting from the scalp, a piratical black shade hiding the empty socket of one eye, the left side of that once beautiful face puckered and scarred. They had been married by special licence with a beaming Matron in attendance and the groans of the injured rising like a Gregorian chant. To his surprise Captain Turner had arrived, smelling of moth-balls and dressed in full uniform, to substitute as surrogate best man. 'That other young feller will be wallowing on his honeymoon,' he had said. 'So I thought I'd look in and lend me support.'

'She's fine,' said Page. 'Hobbling around on sticks, but she's doing just fine.'

'It's a bloody shame,' said Dean angrily. 'I mean, it's so bloody unfair.'

'It doesn't matter,' said Page. 'Not when you are spending your lives together.'

'It's the war,' said Dean. 'There's so little time.'

Page looked across at the pudgy, pugnacious figure standing straggle-legged on the bridge. 'Sloppy hasn't lost a ship yet, and I reckon he isn't going to start now.'

The *Kentucky Minstrel* tailed on to the long line of slowly moving ships, some deep-laden, some – like the *Kentucky Minstrel* – in ballast, all heading north for the Atlantic passage and the snarling Wolf Packs. Liverpool's jagged outline began to drop astern.

'He'll bring us back,' said Page confidently. 'That old bastard will bring us back.'

PQ 17 CONVOY TO HELL
by Paul Lund and Harry Ludlam

In June 1942 Convoy P.Q. 17 consisting of 35 merchant ships set out for Russia with an escort of cruisers and destroyers. They had a reasonable chance of success until the order came to 'Scatter!'

What followed represents one of the most terrible and tragic blunders of the Second World War.

Authors Ludlam and Lund give a first hand account of the horror and despair that faced the men left to the mercy of a cruel enemy.

NEW ENGLISH LIBRARY

THE WAR OF THE LANDING CRAFT

by Paul Lund and Harry Ludlam

At the outbreak of World War II, Britain had a mere 40 landing craft. They were a weird assortment of craft coming in all shapes and sizes; they were unnamed and known only by numbers; they were scorned as 'tin cans', 'Noah's arks' and 'those bloody kipper boxes'. Yet they were probably the most remarkable fleet that ever put to sea.

By 1944, over 100,000 officers and men were operating a vast fleet of flat-bottomed craft that varied from boats carrying 25 troops to those carrying 250, from ammunition carriers to floating hospitals to tank carriers capable of firing over 1000 rockets at a time.

NEW ENGLISH LIBRARY

THREE MEN WENT TO WAR
by David Newman

The siege and surrender of the British garrison at Kut in World War I heralded one of the most hushed-up and terrible events of that war.

Twelve thousand men began what was to be one of the hardest and most crippling forced marches in military history. Ill-fed, diseased and brutally treated, many thousands died as they were endlessly herded towards Mesopotamia to work on the German railways.

Three Men Went To War is the story of one small group of soldiers and the three men who fought for their survival led by a young American pilot, Lieutenant Holt. Amidst marauding bands of Turks, torture and starvation, their chances were small. But if they could wait until the time was ripe and be prepared to fight to the death, their risky plans might just work . . .

NEW ENGLISH LIBRARY

STORMTIDE
by Bill Knox

The boat was a wreck, her skipper dead. His death had not been a merciful one, but it had been an accident. Or had it?

A girl had died, too; drowned when she fell off the jetty. An accident?

The feud between the shark-catchers and the island fishermen was building up to a ferocious climax of arson and murder. Once again, a routine patrol by the fishery cruiser *Marlin* had plunged her crew into a tangle of lawlessness and death which would be resolved in the stormy seas and rocky islands of the North Atlantic.

NEW ENGLISH LIBRARY